I Can Do Better All By Myself:

New Day Divas Series Book Five

I Can Do Better All By Myself:

New Day Divas Series Book Five

E.N. Joy

www.urbanchristianonline.com

Urban Books, LLC
78 East Industry Court
Deer Park, NY 11729

I Can Do Better All By Myself: New Day Divas Series
Book Five Copyright © 2011 E.N. Joy

ISBN 13: 978-1-60162-806-0
ISBN 10: 1-60162-806-4

First Printing November 2011
Printed in the United States of America

10 9 8 7 6 5 4 3 2

This is a work of fiction. Any references or similarities to actual events, real people, living, or dead, or to real locales are intended to give the novel a sense of reality. Any similarity in other names, characters, places, and incidents is entirely coincidental.

Distributed by Kensington Corp.
Submit Wholesale Orders to:
Kensington Publishing Corp.
C/O Penguin Group (USA) Inc.
Attention: Order Processing
405 Murray Hill Parkway
East Rutherford, NJ 07073-2316
Phone: 1-800-526-0275
Fax: 1-800-227-9604

I Can Do Better All By Myself:

New Day Divas Series Book Five

By

E.N. Joy

Other Books by E.N. Joy

Me, Myself and Him

She Who Finds A Husband

Been There, Prayed That

Love, Honor or Stray

Trying To Stay Saved

Even Sinners Have Souls
(Edited by E.N. Joy)

Even Sinners Have Souls Too
(Edited by E.N. Joy)

Even Sinners Still Have Souls
(Edited by E.N. Joy)

The Secret Olivia Told Me
(children's book written under the name N. Joy)

Dedication

This book, this entire series, almost everything I've ever written since my first published title, is made possible because of Earth Jallow with Down to Earth Public Relations. Mother Earth, you were there when I self-published my very first title back in 1998. You have done everything with and for me besides write the books yourself (although you treated them as if you'd written them yourself). You set up my book signings for me. You went to my book signings with me. You even drove me state to state to and from the book signings.

You were with me when there were lines of people wanting to get a book signed by me. You were there when there were only a handful of people wanting to get a book signed by me. You were there when nobody wanted to get a book signed by me. I could not have asked for nor been blessed with a more fitting PR person than yourself. But most importantly, I could not have asked for nor been blessed with a more fitting sista-girl-friend such as yourself. Your support is truly priceless. We're like Jazzy Jeff and the Fresh Prince back in the day. I'm the rapper; you're the DJ.

I know God has called you to do so much more than PR for authors such as myself, but I pray He'll still allow you to be a viable part of my literary career as you move forth mightily in your own destiny.

Stay blessed, because you already are!

Acknowledgements

I'd like to acknowledge my mother-in-law, Gwen Marsh (Ross), who just loves me to no end. She drives back and forth from Toledo to Columbus, Ohio, to keep the kids for me while I go on book events. Gas round trip—fifty dollars. McDonald's for all the kids on the way—fifteen dollars. The support for going through such extremes just so that your daughter-in-law makes the *New York Times* Bestseller's list—Priceless. You are priceless indeed.

I can't leave out my sisters-in-law who hold it down when granny has to go to work and the kids are in Toledo: Nicole Ross Byrd, NyGale, and Nichelle. I love you all!!!

And for the new hair braider, Cousin Kee-Kee. Love ya!

I love you too T-Town nieces and nephews. The kids would be bored without you there.

Last, but not least, I have to give a shout out to the artist who brings each and every diva to life with the wonderful covers he has designed for the entire series, Charlton "CP the Artist" Palmer. Charlton even took some photos of me and created portraits of the photos to appear on the book covers. He is truly an artistic genius, and anyone who wants to experience his work should visit him at www.cptheartist.com.

Stupid!!!

I'm a stupid, stupid girl. I live in La-La Land, that secluded place where the wife is madly in love with her husband and vice versa. Where she wants to shout it out from the mountaintop for the entire population of 10,001 to hear. Where she hopes the echo will be him shouting the same back in return.

In the real world, though, I'm the only one starring in this stupid act. It's a one-woman show. He always forgets his lines because he never shows up for rehearsal. I always have to ad-lib; fill in for him. There's even been a time or two where I've had to feed him his lines. "This is what you're supposed to think. This is what you're supposed to say. This is how you're supposed to feel."

He still couldn't deliver them properly though. Sometimes I wonder if he even read the script before agreeing to take on the part. If he even knows his role, the character I made him up in my mind to be.

Come to think of it, did he even audition? Or did I just give him the part, hoping, praying, wishing he would eventually get into character?

Nonetheless, when it's all over, when the curtain drops, when we take our final bow, there won't be a standing ovation and the reviews won't be that great.

Instead of marriage counseling, perhaps we should have signed up for acting lessons, because that's what this entire thing has been—an act. A comedy. One big joke. But if that's the case, why am I crying instead of laughing?

Stupid!!!

Stupid tears. Stupid, stupid tears. But what else did you expect out of a stupid, stupid girl . . . like me?

—Written by E.N. Joy
For New Day Diva, Paige Dickenson

Chapter One

Paige had no idea how long she had been sitting in her car outside of her best friend's house. She had no idea until Tamarra told her. That wasn't until after Tamarra scared the living daylights out of her when she wrapped on the driver-side window.

"Jesus!" Paige yelled out. She was calling on the name of Jesus all right, but not just because her best friend had frightened her. "Jesus!" Paige said again; this time as if she were summoning Him down from heaven for help. "Jesus!"

"Paige, girl, are you okay in there?" Tamarra asked through the window.

Without replying, Paige stared straight ahead.

"Paige, do you hear me?" Tamarra cupped her hands around her oval-shaped face and pressed against the window.

Still, Tamarra heard no reply from Paige, but she did hear the clicking of the locks. Tamarra went to open the driver's door, but that's when she realized the car doors were locked. "Paige, unlock the doors," Tamarra said as she wiggled the handle. "You locked the doors instead of unlocked them."

Tamarra wasn't telling Paige anything she didn't already know. She knew she'd just locked the doors. She meant to do that. As a matter of fact, she wished she'd locked them sooner—like as soon as she had pulled up. She couldn't believe she'd been sitting there in the late-night hours with the doors unlocked, especially after what had just happened to her. But still staring straight ahead, Paige realized that it was better late than never.

"Paige. Paige," Tamarra continued to call out, but now there was a hint of worry behind her tone. "Unlock the door," she ordered. "Unlock the door, sweetheart." Realizing her voice was getting a little loud, Tamarra thought she might sweeten up her request a bit by adding a term of endearment at the end of it.

"Sweetheart," Paige mumbled under her lips. She then turned her head to face Tamarra. "He called me that too."

Tamarra's hand immediately flew over her mouth in shock once she saw Paige's face. "Paige, oh my God. Wha . . . what happened?" Now Tamarra frantically began trying to open the car door.

Paige just turned her head and stared straight ahead. Tears began to fall from her eyes, one drop at a time. The hot tears glided over the deep dimples in her dark chocolate skin.

Her eyes weren't the only ones leaking the salty liquid. Tears now made their way down Tamarra's oak with a gloss finish complexion. After seeing her best friend's face, she was beside herself. In a panicked style, she ran her hands down her shoulder-length hair that she wore natural. She didn't know if she was really doing it out of panic and nervousness, or if she just wasn't used to the length yet since having let it grow out.

"Paige, let me in this car right now," Tamarra demanded. Tears continued to flow from her eyes as she still made attempts at opening the door. She had to get her best friend out of the car. Something wasn't right. Something was very, very wrong. It was as if Paige had just driven her car into a lake, and slowly but surely, the car was filling up with water. Paige was drowning inside. Tamarra had to save her.

"Come on, please unlock the door," Tamarra begged. "It's one-thirty in the morning. I know something's going on. You've been sitting out here over an hour." Tamarra knew this because one of her neighbors had told her so. It was her neighbor's phone call informing her that a car had been parked outside of her house since around midnight that had awakened her out of a good sleep. Her neighbor also informed her that someone was sitting in the car. Tamarra was a little frightened by this news at first. She didn't know if she had a stalker or what. Once she got out of bed, inched over to her window, and peeked through the curtains, she realized it was Paige's car. She breathed a sigh of relief, then told her neighbor that she recognized the car, the person in it, and everything was okay.

Putting on nothing but a housecoat to protect her from the evening air of the last days of spring, Tamarra quickly walked outside. She stopped and put on the pair of flip-flops she kept by the side door that she always threw on if she had to go do some lawn watering or whatnot. But right now, the fact that she was standing outside in a robe and flip-flops was the last thing on her mind. Getting Paige out of that car was the first—the only thought.

"Paige, honey, you've got to get out of that car and come inside the house. We've got to get your face taken care of," Tamarra said.

Paige, as if having an epiphany, raised her hand and touched her face. It was swollen; her cheek. It was swollen; her eye. It was swollen; her lip. Even when it came to her hand; it was swollen too. Paige began to cry at the touch. She'd never felt this way before; in so much pain. She'd never felt this way before; either internally or externally.

"Paige, you're hurt. We have to get you inside. I can't just let you sit out here. So if you don't unlock the door, I'm going to have to call the police because I'm scared, Paige. I'm scared," Tamarra confessed as her voice cracked and more tears spilled from her eyes.

Paige shook her head, signaling that she didn't want the police called. Then lowering her hand from her face, Paige turned to look at Tamarra. The expression on her face was questioning. It was questioning Tamarra. "Can you believe this? Is this really me?" Paige's eyes asked her best friend.

"Who did this to you, Paige? Did somebody hurt you?" Tamarra inquired.

Paige turned her face away in shame.

"It's okay; just tell me. Did someone hurt you?"

Paige nodded.

Tamarra swallowed her cries. She already knew the answer before asking. She'd seen the answer by the look in Paige's eyes. Tamarra, once upon a time as a young girl, had worn that same expression many times. Usually it was after she'd bathed and looked at herself in the mirror each time after her brother raped her.

"Paige, did someone . . . did someone rape you . . . sexually assault you?"

Once again, Paige nodded.

"Then, Paige, honey, please let me call the police. Or at least let me call Blake," Tamarra offered, thinking that maybe her husband could talk her out of the car.

"No!" Paige yelled.

Although her harsh response had made Tamarra jump, at least Paige had finally shot off a verbal response. Before Tamarra could part her lips to say anything else, swirling red and blue lights grabbed her mind's attention.

"Paige, the police are here," Tamarra said through the window. "One of my neighbors must have called them. I know you didn't want me to call them, but they're here now. Please, Paige, talk to them. Tell them what happened to you."

Tamarra felt as though she had some nerve. She never told the police what had happened to her. Maybe if she had reported the rapes to the police, she could have prevented other girls from being assaulted by her brother. Although she'd made a mistake, she didn't want to sit by and watch her friend make the same one.

"Is everything okay?" an officer walked up and asked after parking his vehicle. "We got a couple complaints about a suspicious vehicle and possible disturbance," he informed Tamarra.

"No, everything is not okay," Tamarra was quick to say. "My friend's been assaulted. She's hurt, and she's scared." Tamarra began to break down.

"It's okay, Miss . . ." the officer stated as he waited for Tamarra to fill in the blank.

"It's Miss Davis," Tamarra informed him, gathering her composure. "I live here." Tamarra pointed to her house. "I got a call from one of my neighbors not too long ago telling me that a car had been parked outside of my house for a while. When I realized it was my best friend's, Paige, I came out. I've been trying to get her to come out of the car, but she won't." Tamarra began to break down again.

"It's okay. It's okay," the officer told Tamarra. "Let me see what I can do."

Tamarra moved out of the officer's way as he approached the driver-side door. "Hello . . . Paige." He looked at Tamarra to make sure he'd gotten the name correct. Tamarra confirmed with a nod. "I'm Officer Lavene. Your friend here is very worried about you. She says someone hurt you. Is that true?"

Without looking in the officer's direction, Paige nodded.

"What did they do to you, Paige?" the officer asked.

This time she didn't nod, she just looked in the officer's direction. That's when he saw how battered her face was.

"Did this person or persons hit you?" he asked.

Staring in the officer's eyes, Paige nodded.

"Did they . . . did they sexually assault you in any way?" he continued questioning.

Once again, Paige nodded.

"Can you tell me what happened, Paige?"

Paige nodded, but she didn't say anything.

"It's okay. You can go ahead and tell me. I'm the police. I'm going to help you."

Paige's lips never moved for what seemed like forever. Tamarra just wanted her to hurry up and tell the officer what was going on so that they could help her and get a start on catching the bad guy who'd done this to her. So many things ran through Tamarra's mind about what could have possibly happened to Paige. Had she been on that late-night Walmart run women were known to take? Had some stranger been watching her? Followed her to her car and attacked her? What had happened?

Although Tamarra thought she was going to have one of her anxiety attacks that she hadn't had in quite some time, the officer was calm and patient. He didn't push. He asked Paige if she could tell him what happened. She'd said she could. He waited, as if he knew eventually, when the time was right, when Paige was truly ready, she would tell him.

Tamarra could tell the officer was experienced at this kind of thing by his etiquette and relaxed demeanor in the situation. She wasn't, though, as she stood at the back door on the driver's side.

"Paige, please tell the officer—"

The officer held up his hand to cut Tamarra off, halting her words. He wasn't pushing, and he didn't want Tamarra to push either. Now they both waited.

The wait wasn't long, just a few seconds, but with dead silence, it felt like an eternity to Tamarra. But finally, Paige spoke.

"He . . . he hit me." Paige's lips trembled. "And . . . and he raped me," Paige cried out. "He raped me! He raped me!" She shouted over and over as she began to lose control, locked in the front seat of her car.

"It's okay, calm down, Paige," the officer said. "It's okay. We're going to take care of you." In that instant, the officer got on his walkie-talkie and called for backup. He told the dispatch officer that he had a possible rape victim and needed female backup. Once he was assured assistance was on the way, he turned his attention back to Paige.

"Oh my God. Oh my God," Paige cried. Then all of a sudden it was as if she had been having a bad nightmare and woke up back to reality. "Where's Tamarra? Where's Tamarra? Where's my friend who lives here?" she badgered the officer.

"I'm right here, honey. I'm right here," Tamarra assured her as she put herself within Paige's view. "Unlock the car, Paige. Please."

Paige fumbled to unlock the doors. Finally, Tamarra heard the clicking of the locks; the sound she'd been longing to hear for the past twenty minutes.

Immediately, Tamarra bent down and threw her arms around Paige's trembling body. "It's going to be okay. I'm here. The police are here. We're going to take care of you."

"The police?" Paige questioned.

"Yeah, remember? The nice officer here has been talking to you." Tamarra released Paige and moved to the side so that Paige could get a view of the officer who had been so helpful.

"Nooo! Get away from me! Get away from me! Get him out of here!" Paige began to kick, scream, and holler. "It's him! It's him. He's the one," Paige cried. "I was naked. I just wanted to cover up. I just wanted to cover up."

Tamarra stood and stared at the officer in shock. Was *he* the one who'd attacked Paige? Had a neighbor really called the police, or had he just been lurking around?

Noticing the look Tamarra was giving him, the officer felt the need to clear things up. "I . . . I'm just here to help. I even have backup on the way."

The officer looked innocent enough. He looked like a good cop, but then again, what did a bad cop look like? Turning her attention back to Paige, Tamarra asked her friend, "Are you saying a cop did this to you, Paige?"

"No," Paige shook her head. "When I was arrested . . . it was *him*." Paige pointed an accusing finger at the officer. "He drug me out of the house naked for the entire world to see."

Just then a light bulb went off in both the officer's and Tamarra's head.

"Mrs. Dickenson?" the officer asked. He then looked at Tamarra. "Is this Mrs. Blake Dickenson?" Paige's face was lightweight deformed, and her hair was down versus the ponytail that she usually wore.

"Yes," Tamarra replied, "and you must be the overzealous rookie cop that arrested Paige a couple months ago."

"For that assault charge against her husband's sister or something like that," the officer confirmed to Tamarra, then looked at Paige. "I'm so sorry, Mrs. Dickenson. Trust me, when my superior suspended me for a week with no pay, I didn't complain. I deserved it. I was new to all this. I'm still new, but for the last month I've had sensitivity training. Really, I'm sorry." The officer couldn't seem to apologize enough, but Paige wasn't having it.

"No, get him away from me," she told Tamarra. "Get him away from me!"

Just then, more flashing lights appeared, and within seconds, a female officer got out of the passenger side of a second cop car. The driver, another male officer, got out of the car and walked midway to Paige's vehicle. The male officer who'd already been on the scene met the driver of the second cop car while the female officer made her way over to Paige.

"Hi, I'm Officer Moten," the woman smiled.

"I'm Tamarra," Tamarra greeted her, "and this is my best friend Paige."

Paige still sat in the car crying.

Tamarra moved out of the way so that the officer could talk to Paige.

"Hi, Paige." The officer leaned down into the car. "My partner tells me that someone hurt you. Is that true?"

"Yes," Paige said.

"That someone raped you?" The officer got more specific.

"Yes," Paige confirmed.

"We'd like to help you, Paige. We'd also like to get the person who did this to you as well. Do you know who did this to you, Paige?"

Paige's eyes closed, but that didn't keep the tears from spilling out. Her shoulders began to heave as she nodded to the officer, and then followed it up with a, "Yes. I know the person who did this to me."

"So it was just one person?" the officer asked.

"Yes," Paige sniffed.

"Paige, can you tell me who this person was?"

Taking a deep breath in an attempt to control her breathing, Paige opened her eyes and said, "Yes. I can tell you who did this to me."

"Good," the officer said, taking out a notepad and a pen. "What is the name of the person who raped you, Paige?"

"Blake Dickenson," Paige answered as the officer began to write. "My husband, Blake Dickenson; he's the one who raped me."

Chapter Two

"Why are you always the one who's gotta take that girl to her doctor's appointments?" Eleanor asked Lorain as the two finished up breakfast at Family Café. "Can't her baby's daddy take her? After all, it's his baby she's toting around." Eleanor then mumbled under her breath before taking in a spoonful of grits with cheese, "Like she needs another child to be toting around. She needs another baby like she needs a hole in her head. Matter of fact, somebody should have put a hole in her head for getting knocked up with no husband . . . again." Eleanor chewed and swallowed before concluding with, "What's this, baby number six?"

Lorain rolled her eyes in her head. "No, Mom. This is only going to be Unique's fourth baby. And I take her to her appointments because she's my friend. I've told you before she's like a daughter to me."

"Well, you're more than just *like* a daughter to me. You *are* my daughter, which means if you're supposed to meet me somewhere, I don't want to hear nothing about you being late because you had to take Octomom to the doctors."

"Mother, now that's enough," Lorain said, trying her best to hold in her laughter.

"Well, you know it's the truth." Eleanor shook her head. "I just don't see how or why that girl ended up pregnant again." She thought for a moment. "Well, I know how . . . but you know what I mean."

"Yes, Mom, I know what you mean. And that's none of our business."

"It is too our business, especially when it's our tax dollars that's gotta pay for it." Eleanor leaned in closer and now decided to whisper. "Or even our tithes and offerings. Because you know that girl ain't gonna be able to take care of that baby with no husband. She gonna be running to Pastor every month for help. Heck, forget about a Benevolent Fund. Pastor might as well start a Child Support Fund, because that's what we're about to do—pay that girl's child support every month."

"Mom, she is our sister in Christ. Are we not our sister's and brother's keeper?" Lorain shook her head with disappointment. She was disappointed in the way her mother was acting regarding Unique, but she understood why. Eleanor was exhibiting something that she'd once accused Lorain of being, which was good old-fashioned jealousy.

For the past three months, Lorain had been spending a great amount of time with Unique. That meant less time she had to spend with her mother. For the first couple months after Broady's death, Lorain had been pretty much glued to her mother's hip. She had to be there to support her; not just because her mother had lost a husband, but because after the fact, while still mourning, her mother learned that Broady had been Lorain's childhood sex abuser.

At first, that load being piled on top of Eleanor seemed like almost too much for the then fragile older woman to bear. But thank God Eleanor knew Jesus and had the support of her daughter, who also knows Jesus. Because without Him, she never would have made it through. Lorain was there to praise God and pray to God with and for her mother. She was there to intercede in a mighty way. When all was said and done, the devastation seemed to bring the mother and daughter closer. But now, in Eleanor's eyes, it appeared as though that fresh bond was being threatened by Unique. Eleanor wasn't having it. But even though Eleanor knew Jesus, right about now, she wasn't acting like it.

"Young lady, are you questioning my Christianity?" Eleanor snapped after feeling convicted. "I know we are supposed to love our neighbors. I know I'm supposed to take care of the poor. I know as a Christian I'm supposed to be concerned about that girl. But what I'm not supposed to be is that girl's baby daddy, and neither are you. That baby she's carrying ain't none of yours; yet you're running around here like you the daddy. Making late-night runs to get her pickles and ice cream. Taking her to the doctors. Watching her kids for her while she gets some rest. And I don't even know why she's so tired. It ain't like she's working anymore. Didn't she lose her job working for Sister Tamarra? And you're going to lose your job as well, going in late to work all the time so that you can take her to the doctors."

"Yes, Mom, she lost her job, but not because she was lazy or anything. It's because she was going through some things. She'd just found out she was pregnant. Not to mention her finding out about some other things as well." Lorain took a bite of her sandwich, silently praying that her mother wouldn't ask her about the "other things." Lorain hated that she was keeping the fact that she was Unique's biological mother from Eleanor. It was enough that Eleanor had learned that the man she was married to had molested her daughter as a child. Lorain felt her mother would have lost her mind had her mother realized that she'd given birth to a daughter as a result of the rapes. Not only that, but that Unique was, in fact, that daughter—that Unique was the offspring of Eleanor's daughter and Eleanor's deceased husband. It was way too much information. Eleanor had been on the verge of suicide once before. Lorain feared knowing all of this might push her mother completely over the edge.

Although Lorain sometimes felt convicted, she also felt justified. Sometimes even God deals with His children on a need to know basis only. God is known for dishing out what a person needs to know, at the appointed time in which they need to know it. Imagine what might happen if God gave a person too much information, too soon. Heck, some folks wouldn't be able to handle it. That's why the Word says that God will put on His children no more than they can bear. Well, Lorain wasn't going to put on her mother more than she could bear. She was going to spoon-feed her, dishing it out one scoop at a time.

As a matter of fact, that's why Lorain had invited her mother out to breakfast in the first place. She felt with Unique well into her second trimester that it was time to let her mother in on some things. Not everything, just some things. One spoonful at a time.

Lorain was nervous going into this. After hearing the way her mother was ranting on about Unique, she became even more nervous. She pushed away her plate that had the remains of her BLT and home fries on it, and then swallowed. Eleanor followed suit by pushing her empty bowl of grits off to the side. Lorain watched as her mother leaned back and sighed while she rubbed her stomach, indicating she was full.

Lorain observed her mother and couldn't help but hope that Eleanor still had room left, but not for the toast that sat in front of her oozing with apple jelly. Oh, no, what Lorain was about to serve up was anything but sweet. It was going to be a bitter pill for Eleanor to swallow indeed.

Chapter Three

"Dear Lord, thank you for this food that we are about to receive to nourish our bodies. Allow it to give us strength and energy to make it through the day. We ask you to bless it, Lord. Bless the hands that prepared it. In Jesus' name we pray. Amen."

After saying the prayer, Pastor's eyes opened to a smorgasbord of breakfast delicacies prepared by Mother Doreen. Pastor's kitchen table looked like a buffet at a restaurant. "Mother Doreen, I'm telling you, I know I've gained at least five pounds in the last couple of months since you've been here," Pastor smiled before digging into the country potatoes with onions. "I'm going to have to do what Marie Osmond did and join that weight loss program."

"Then don't plan on losing any weight for another month or so," Mother Doreen warned her pastor, "because that's about how much longer you're going to be stuck with me. My tenant still has about that much more time left at my house."

With Mother Doreen returning back to Malvonia on a whim, she hadn't been able to give the tenant she was renting her house out to any type of notice. This thought had never even crossed her mind until she was halfway home. So instead of pulling up to the home she'd left over a year ago, she pulled up to the only other place she knew: the church, New Day Temple of Faith.

Pastor, who had just finished up a counseling session with a married couple, was overjoyed to see Mother Doreen. And once Mother Doreen shared her dilemma of her house being occupied, it was Pastor's idea that the two temporarily become housemates until Mother Doreen was able to give her tenant enough notice to vacate.

At first Mother Doreen was a little hesitant. Not only didn't she want to invade Pastor's space, but she couldn't help but wonder what people would think. Not many pastors actually invited members of their congregation to stay with them if they needed a place to live. Sure, they'd put them up at a hotel or something, or even find another church member who had available space or housing, but to find a pastor who would actually open their own home—now that was rare.

This shouldn't have surprised Mother Doreen though. Their pastor was rare. One of a kind. One in a million, making Mother Doreen that much happier about her decision to return to Ohio.

"Does your tenant have a place to go?" Pastor asked before taking a sip of freshly squeezed orange juice.

"As a matter of fact, she does," Mother Doreen replied. She took a bite of toast, and then continued. "It just so happens that the job she was working at part-time had a full-time position become available in Houston. So she was going to have to turn in her notice to me to move anyway. The timing of everything was just confirmation in both our lives, I suppose."

Pastor stared at Mother Doreen for a minute.

"What?" Mother Doreen asked upon noticing the look Pastor was giving her.

Taking a break from the delicacies, Pastor put down the fork containing the speared potatoes. "Since you've been back, that's all you've been searching for."

Mother Doreen sat with a puzzled look on her face.

"Confirmation," Pastor stated. "You've been seeking confirmation. Did God not give you confirmation before you left Kentucky?"

Mother Doreen tried to keep that indignant look from spreading any further across her face. After all, this was her pastor sitting in front of her. But something about her pastor's tone seemed to be questioning Mother Doreen's level of obedience . . . or disobedience, for that matter. "So what are you trying to say, Pastor? That it was my flesh that brought me back here, and not a word from God?"

"Whoa, slow down." Pastor's hands were now raised. "I'm not trying to say anything. I was just asking." Pastor continued eating. But after a few moments of silence, Pastor's spirit was pushed to keep pressing Mother Doreen. "You know, in all my years of pastoring, I've found that usually when someone is constantly looking for confirmation, they tend to be walking in doubt. Are you doubtful about your decision to leave Kentucky? Did you have some type of unfinished business there?"

Mother Doreen sighed, then dropped her fork. "I wouldn't say that I'm doubtful. I mean, I know I did everything that I could for my sister and her family. . . ." Mother Doreen's words trailed off as she thought for a minute. "There's just a part of me that feels like my work is not completely done."

"Well, there's nothing strange about that," Pastor assured Mother Doreen. "You're an earthen vessel created by God so that He can use you mightily. Your work is never going to be done."

"I know that," Mother Doreen agreed. "I'm talking about my work on that particular assignment. Speaking of work, and finished works at that, I wanted to talk to you about the New Day Singles' Ministry."

Pastor tried not to frown, but this day—this moment—was inevitable. It was only a matter of time before Mother Doreen would make mention of the now-defunct ministry. Before Mother Doreen could even pitch the idea of starting up the ministry again, Pastor's feelings about the ministry were made known.

"Mother Doreen, I know the Singles' Ministry was a vision God placed in your heart," Pastor started. "And I know both you and I were operating in obedience when I gave you the okay to create it. You began to run it as its leader, and you did a wonderful job. So don't let the fact that the ministry didn't live up to the vision make you feel as though you didn't do something right. Sometimes the disobedience of others can delay or hinder a vision. When God says something will be, then it will be. He is not one to lie. So it's just a matter of when we'll bring forth the Singles' Ministry. I'm just not sure it will be any time soon."

"I know things got a little off-kilter with the ministry," Mother Doreen said, "but now that I'm back, I believe things will be different. I just feel as though I can get things back on track so that when it comes to the ministry, everything will be decent and in order. It was my vision and—"

"Let me stop you right there," Pastor said. "It was God's vision. He just gave it to you to get it done."

"And I know I can get it done this time, Pastor," Mother Doreen replied in almost a pleading manner.

Pastor noticed what appeared to be a look of desperation on Mother Doreen's face. Pastor couldn't help but wonder if Mother Doreen realized just how transparent she was sitting there at the table. "Mother Doreen, and I hope you don't mind me being honest with you, but right now my spirit tells me that although you have a true passion for the Singles' Ministry, what you really want to do is have something to keep you occupied."

Mother Doreen felt cold busted. Shocked. Stunned. Not because of what her pastor was insinuating, but because it was true. When Mother Doreen left Kentucky, she knew deep down inside she was leaving behind some unfinished business. And it had nothing to do with her sister and her family. Perhaps if she started up some new business here in Ohio—at the church— that unfinished business would take care of itself.

"Just pray about it, Pastor," Mother Doreen said to avoid either confirming or rejecting Pastor's reasoning for her wanting to reinstate the Singles' Ministry.

"I always do," Pastor smiled. "And while I'm doing that, you pray on it as well. When God does decide to bring the Singles' Ministry back into operation, what are some changes that can be made that will allow the ministry to be more effective? And what can be done in order to get members to not only join, but to take the ministry seriously?"

Mother Doreen nodded. "Yes, Pastor. I'll certainly begin seeking God."

"Good," Pastor said, scooting away from the table and standing. "Now if you'll excuse me, I'm going to head over to the church."

"All right, Pastor. You have a blessed day."

"You too. And Mother Doreen, while we're roomies, you can call me Margie; Pastor Margie at least." Pastor got all giddy, rubbing her hands together. "Makes me feel like I'm back in my college dorm days with my girlfriends." Then a serious look crossed Margie's face. "But then again, when I think back to who I was in my past, I'm not too sure I want to go back there, if you know what I mean." Margie winked at Mother Doreen, and then walked away.

"I know exactly what you mean, Pastor—Pastor Margie," Doreen said to herself. "There are some places and times I don't want to go back to either." And Mother Doreen meant that, which is why she had to get out of Kentucky. The last thing she needed right now was for her past to catch up with her.

Chapter Four

They'd questioned her. They'd poked and prodded at her. Now Paige was completely jaded of the entire ordeal and just wanted to go home. She wanted to go home, or what she once knew as home anyway. But after what Blake had done to her, she knew that was no longer an option in her life—ever.

"What is Pastor going to say? What are people going to say?" Paige worried out loud as she sat on the hospital examination table dressed in hospital scrubs. The police had collected, with Paige's permission, the clothing she'd worn to the hospital. It had evidence of her assault. The police felt that any forensics the clothing might contain might make her case stronger.

"Case?" Paige had questioned.

"Yes, Mrs. Dickenson. The—"

"Can you just call me Paige?" she had requested. She didn't want any part of that man right now, not even his last name. Ultimately, the Word said she'd have to forgive Blake for what he'd done to her, but it didn't say anything about her having to remain connected to him. She wanted to be disconnected. And that went for her body, her mind, and her spirit, and soon enough, her last name.

"Sure," the officer agreed. "Paige, the state prosecutor is going to need you to help make a case. From what you've told us, you are the only witness to the crime against you. Therefore, you are the state's only witness," the officer explained. "Do you understand that?"

Paige nodded. She understood. She'd watched *Law and Order SVU* enough times to know the legality of it all. She just never thought her true life story would ever make for an episode itself. But would it have been a believable episode? Paige could hardly believe herself that this had happened to her. When she'd parted her lips to say the words, "My husband raped me," it didn't sound real. Was that even possible? Did women really get raped by their spouses? In the real world, not on television, was it really considered rape if a man took from his wife what she hadn't been willing to give? Sooner or later, Paige was about to get the answer to all of her questions. But could she deal with the answers was what worried her most. Thank God she had her best friend by her side to help her through it all.

"Thanks for being here for me," Paige said to Tamarra, who sat in a chair next to the examination table.

"Oh, Paige, you don't have to thank me." Tamarra stood. "Best friends are for something more than just holding the toilet seat up while you puke your guts out after a night of partying together," she joked in an attempt to lighten the mood a bit.

"So I hear," Paige played along. "Although it sounds like you speak from experience."

Tamarra chuckled. "Well, yeah, but that's a whole 'notha story." She reminisced back to her rebellion stage as a young girl. It had been her way of acting out after being raped by her brother and giving birth to his baby. "Anyway, please know that I'm here for you through thick and thin."

Paige nodded and tried to smile. Her facial muscles must not have been ready to smile because they immediately transformed into a sad frown, then the tears came . . . again. She hadn't realized that a person could cry so much.

"It's okay," Tamarra comforted Paige with a loving embrace as she rubbed her hand up and down her back. Tamarra didn't try to stop the waterworks, but once her friend settled down, she asked the million-dollar question. "Paige, can I ask you something?"

"Sure," Paige sniffed.

"Why? Why didn't you tell me that Blake was abusing you?" Tamarra continued rubbing Paige's back. "I mean, I was in disbelief listening to you tell those officers the history of abuse you've been enduring at the hands of your husband. And not only the physical abuse, but the verbal insults as well." Tamarra shook her head in wonderment. "I just feel like I failed you; like I wasn't the best friend I claimed to be. Why else would you have felt like you couldn't come to me? I could have helped you. I could have done something . . . anything."

"Oh no, you don't," Paige stopped her friend. "I'm not blaming myself for what Blake decided to do to me. I'm most certainly not going to sit here and let you try to blame yourself either." This was the most strength Paige had shown since pulling her car up in front of Tamarra's house at the wee hours in the morning. "If I've learned one thing from talking to Sister Nita, it's that the woman, or the man in rare cases, should not blame herself for what his or her abuser does to them."

Tamarra stopped rubbing Paige's back. "Sister Nita? You talked to Sister Nita?"

Paige could hear the disappointment in Tamarra's voice. She'd just voiced to Paige how she felt like an inadequate friend because Paige felt she couldn't come to her and talk to her about the abuse. Now, here Paige was telling her she'd talked about it to a church acquaintance. Tamarra had barely seen Paige say two words to Nita back when she attended New Day. What was up with that?

Deciding that right now was neither the time nor the place to get offended, Tamarra said, "Well, I'm just glad you were able to talk to somebody. Unless there is somebody else who can back up your claim of abuse—" Tamarra had a sudden thought. "You know, you might want to mention that to the officer; that you shared your abuse at the hands of Blake with Sister Nita."

"You're right," Paige noted.

And as if on cue, there was a rap at the door. A few seconds later, the door cracked open and the attending ER doctor who had examined Paige and done a rape kit on her peeked her head through the door.

"Is it okay to come in?" the doctor asked.

"Sure," Paige answered.

The doctor entered, followed by the officer who had questioned Paige earlier.

"Well, we think we have everything we need from you," the doctor told Paige. "Is there anything you need from us?"

"I'm fine for now," Paige replied.

"And you have someone you can stay with for a while, at least until we can issue a warrant?" the officer jumped in to confirm.

"Yes, she's going to stay with me," Tamarra interjected.

"Good." The doctor handed Paige several pamphlets. "Here is some literature that might help you deal with what you've experienced. There're even some counseling referrals. But what I want you to keep in mind, Paige, is that you are a survivor, not a victim."

The doctor's warm smile was a comfort to Paige.

"Just so you know, your husband will be arrested. He is probably going to be charged with assault, domestic abuse, and rape. But that's for the courts to decide," the officer told her. He reached down into his shirt pocket and pulled out a card, then extended his hand to Paige. "This is my card. If you have any questions or if you can think of anything else—"

"As a matter of fact," Paige interrupted, "there is something else." She went on to tell the officer how her church could vouch for the abuse Blake had been inflicting on her. She told the officer how her pastor had even referred them to a domestic abuse counselor. The officer took notes and told Paige how helpful all of that information would be in coming out victorious in her case.

"Thank you, Doctor, and Officer," Tamarra offered, "for taking care of my friend."

"It was our pleasure," the doctor smiled.

"And our duty," the officer added before tipping his hat and exiting the room.

As Tamarra helped Paige off the table and the two prepared to leave, the doctor said, "Paige, there is just one other thing I wanted to discuss with you, and that's this little pill right here." The doctor held out a little plastic cup with a pill in it. "Some people might refer to this as 'The Morning-After Pill.' It's—"

"I know exactly what it is," Paige cut her off, "and I'll pass." Paige's tone was stern.

"Wait a minute, Paige," Tamarra said. "Don't you even want to think about—"

"Did you think about it, Tamarra?" Paige snapped before she realized the question she had posed to Tamarra. She knew Tamarra had been raped by her own blood brother and had gotten pregnant as a result. Tamarra had been so young, though, and Paige didn't know whether Tamarra had considered ending the pregnancy. "I'm sorry. I didn't mean to bring up Raygene like that," Paige apologized, but it was too late for her to take the words back.

"No, it's okay," Tamarra told her sincerely. Tamarra was healed and delivered from the fact that she'd been raped by her brother and had gotten pregnant with her now-deceased daughter, Raygene, as a result.

"It's not okay," Paige stated. "But I am truly sorry. I know this isn't about you. It's about me." Paige turned to face the doctor. "And that pill is not for me."

The doctor nodded. "Okay, then, well, unless there is anything else I can do . . ."

"There's nothing else you can do, Doctor," Paige informed the physician as she and Tamarra walked toward the door. "The rest I have to do myself." And Paige knew that part of what she had to do was figure out how life would go on after divorce, because there was no way she was staying married to Blake.

Chapter Five

"She's carrying *whose* baby?" Eleanor shouted. Her loud screech ripped through the Family Café, causing every head to turn in her direction.

"Mom," Lorain gritted through both her teeth, embarrassed. "Can you hold it down?" Lorain self-consciously ran her fingers through her short, edgy-cut hair. The golden-honey highlights appeared to match her nail polish.

"No, I can't!" Eleanor confirmed. "If you were going to share news like that with me, then you shouldn't have brought me in this itty-bitty ole public place. You should have taken me somewhere where I'd have plenty of room for my voice to travel; some place like the Grand Canyon."

"Oh, for goodness' sake," Lorain said as she quickly fumbled through her purse. She guesstimated the cost of her and her mother's meal. After all, she'd eaten at the town's local restaurant enough times to pretty much know the menu prices by heart. She pulled out a twenty-dollar bill and several ones. That was enough to cover both the meals and have a little somethin' somethin' left over as a tip for their waitress, Zelda.

"Come on, let's go," Lorain ordered as she placed the money in the center of the table. She stood up, and then practically pulled Eleanor up with her and out the door. But Eleanor continued her rant all the way to the parking lot.

"Hey, I didn't finish my coffee," she complained. "Don't be mad at me because you've decided to use the *ghetto* girl from the sit-com *Girlfriends* to serve as a surrogate and have your baby."

"Which one? All the girls on *Girlfriends* are ghetto," Lorain spat.

"Why can't you find a man like God intended and have your own baby?"

Lorain knew that lying to her mother, lying to the world, was the wrong thing to do. But perhaps she should have reconsidered exactly what lie she was going to tell. Was letting the world believe that Unique had agreed to carry a child for Lorain via in vitro fertilization too over the top? Did black people even do that kind of stuff? Lorain now wondered. But then she realized that a whole lot went on in the African American community that its own members didn't even know about . . . or want to face.

Anyway, right now, all she knew was that she couldn't tell her mother that Unique had backslid, gotten drunk, and then gotten pregnant yet again by a man who wasn't thinking about marrying her. She couldn't tell anybody; Unique had made her promise not to. True enough, Unique was the natural and biological mother of the child. The father, at least, wasn't some stranger she decided to go home with one night. He was already the father of one of her other children, the oldest child. But none of that was going to stop people from talking—from condemning and convicting Unique.

As Unique's biological mother, Lorain wanted to be there for her daughter and help her any way she could. She couldn't change the past. She couldn't change the fact that she'd left Unique, a newborn baby, in a trash can to die, never going back to reclaim her. Had she, then she would have learned that all these years, the child she thought was dead was very much alive. And even though she couldn't change what happened, she could try to make up for it. Lorain couldn't think of a more perfect way to make up for it than to raise Unique's baby as if the child were her own. Not only would this gesture divert some of the negative talk from Unique's direction, but it also would allow Lorain a second chance at motherhood.

Sure, people would reason that Lorain was still young; in her mid thirties, as a matter of fact. God would provide her plenty of opportunities to be found by a husband and bear a child of her own flesh and blood. But this child, the one Unique was carrying, the one Unique would hand over to her after giving birth, was Lorain's flesh and blood, only no else knew it. Right now, outside of the restaurant, Eleanor was having a fit—so much so that Lorain didn't know whether it would make a difference if her mother knew the entire truth.

"Now can you just quiet down and listen?" Lorain asked her mother.

"Humph," Eleanor moaned, crossing her arms and rolling her eyes. "I'm listening."

"Mom, just try to understand where I'm coming from on this one," Lorain pleaded.

"Oh, daughter of mine, I may not know where you're coming from, but if you and that girl see this thing out, I know exactly where you might end up—the both of yous."

Lorain closed her eyes, counted to three, and then threw her hands up. They fell down to her side like weighted down sandbags. "Forget it. I knew you wouldn't understand. That's why there are some things I choose not to tell you. This should have been one of them." Lorain walked away from her mother and over to the driver's side.

"Just a minute, young lady. Are you referencing the fact that you didn't come to me and tell me that Broady had been molesting you? Is *that* what you're trying to insinuate here?" Eleanor's voice cracked, and she was on the verge of tears.

Lorain knew that was a low blow she'd just thrown at her mother. "No, Mom, that's not what I was trying to say." Another lie. That's *exactly* what she had been trying to say. "I was just speaking in general." Liar, liar, pants on fire.

There was silence as Lorain stood at the driver-side door and Eleanor stood at the passenger-side door of Lorain's car. "Let's just talk about this later, okay?" Lorain said.

"From the sounds of it, there's really nothing left to talk about. Sounds like you've made your mind up."

"You're right. I have. But you're my mother. You're my best friend. I'd like to talk about it with you. I'd like you to be there for me. After all, you're going to be a grandmother," Lorain smiled. Little did Eleanor know, she was already a grandmother; a great-grandmother as well.

Eleanor couldn't fight the smile that forced her lips to part. "Okay, we'll talk. I'll try my best to understand some of the mess you young folks scheme up." Eleanor pointed a stern finger at her daughter before the doors unlocked and they got into the car. "But I'm not making any promises," she warned.

"Thanks, Mom," Lorain said as she put the key in the ignition and started up the car. She'd gotten over the first bridge barely unscathed, but there were many more to come.

Living out this lie was not going to be easy, of that Lorain was sure. She knew if she focused and put her mind to it, that it could be done. She could live this lie the same way she'd lived many others in the past. She only hoped this time God would give her a pass because at least this lie was helping out someone besides herself. Still, even if she could manage to pull this thing off, just how long she could do it was yet to be determined.

Chapter Six

"Let me make sure I understand what you're trying to say," Margie said to Mother Doreen, who was sitting in a chair on the opposite side of her desk. "You not only want to start up the Singles' Ministry again and take on the role of being the leader of the ministry, but you want me to join as well?" Margie tried not to look at Mother Doreen as if she had two heads, but that was no easy feat, considering what else Mother Doreen had posed as well. "And not only do you want me to join the ministry, but you want me to serve as the co-leader?"

Mother Doreen nodded with excitement as she awaited her pastor's reply. Only the reply wasn't anything near what she was expecting as Margie burst out laughing.

"Oh my goodness, please do forgive me, Mother Doreen," Margie apologized while still laughing. "But are you serious?"

Mother Doreen was offended. "Well, I thought I was being serious, but obviously I should take my show on the road if it's going to get that type of reaction."

Margie placed her hand on her chest as she began the effort of ceasing her laughter. "Whew, oh my. Again, I apologize, Mother Doreen. But a pastor joining a Singles' Ministry? I know your intentions are good, but I just don't think it's going to happen; not with this pastor anyway." Margie, no longer laughing, shook her head firmly.

"But why not, Pastor? I mean, you're single. What better way to show New Day how important and serious this ministry is than for the head of the house to support it?" Mother Doreen decided to pull out her ace in the hand. "You *do* support it, don't you, Pastor?"

Margie stood. "Mother Doreen, now you know if I didn't support the New Day Singles' Ministry, then I would have never okayed its creation in the first place."

"So you do believe it's an important ministry to have in the church?" Mother Doreen pushed.

"Ye . . . yes, I do," Margie responded.

"And you do believe that a ministry supporting single men and women of God is a necessity in the kingdom?" Mother Doreen waited.

"Well, uh, of course, I do."

"And you agree that the sheep follow the shepherd? So if the single members see you supporting the ministry and taking it seriously, then they'd be more apt to do the same."

"Come on now, Mother Doreen." Margie was on to Mother Doreen's tactics. "I see where you're going with this, and I get it. But in essence, are you trying to say that a pastor should be a part of every ministry that falls within the church just to set an example for the congregation? Because if you are, Mother Doreen—"

"No, Pastor," Mother Doreen stated, cutting Margie off. "And let me apologize for the way all of this is coming out. But I just really want this ministry to work. Not only do I think that your support could give it a boost, but, Pastor, you *are* single. Single pastors have it hard, and not just the single male pastors. Yes, there are a lot of women out there who would love to hold the title of first lady, but don't think for one minute there aren't men out there who would love the title of first man."

Margie nodded her head in agreement.

"Let the Singles' Ministry be your covering in that area of your life, Pastor," Mother Doreen pleaded.

Margie exhaled as she walked around from her desk and over to the sitting area in her church office. "I guess I never really looked at it that way before."

Mother Doreen remained quiet, praying that she wouldn't have to talk her pastor into it anymore; that if she shut up long enough, her pastor would talk herself into it.

"Look, I'll tell you what, Mother Doreen. Let me pray on it. Like I said before, let me pray on the issue of even allowing the Singles' Ministry to function at all. Then we'll move forward from there."

"Okay, Pastor." Mother Doreen stood up with a gleam of hope in her eyes. "That's all I'm asking. I know ultimately it's about what God says."

"Yes, it is," Margie agreed.

"Alrighty then, Pastor." Mother Doreen moved toward the door. "I better let you get back to taking care of kingdom business. I guess I'll see you at home; that is, unless you need me to do anything around the church while I'm here."

Margie thought for a minute. "Hmm, I can't really think of anything off the top of my head."

"Well, I'll just look around; go check the ladies' room or whatnot to see if there's any cleaning or anything I can do, although I know Sister Nita stays on top of things like that."

"Yes, she does, but I'm sure she'll appreciate any help she can get. I know I always do."

"Yes, Pastor," Mother Doreen smiled. "See you at home." Mother Doreen exited her pastor's office, closing the door behind her. With her hand still on the doorknob and her back leaning up against the door, she let out a loud sigh.

"Thank you, Jesus," she said under her breath. "Getting Pastor to even think about it was half the battle, and now I need to prepare for the other half."

Mother Doreen began her trek through the church to see if there was anything she could do around there. She needed to keep busy, very busy. In the past, she'd kept busy by relying on the assignments she claimed were from God. No one had seen through her façade in all these years. She couldn't risk being exposed now. Being exposed meant the skeletons of Mother Doreen's past would come tumbling out the closet.

Pastor had once preached to the congregation, "If for once some of you would just put your own mess aside and go help somebody with theirs, you'll be surprised to find that when you finally turn around to take care of your own mess, that it's gone. That God took care of it for you."

Now more than ever, Mother Doreen was hoping that was true, because she'd spent years helping folks clean up their messes. Now that it looked as though she was about to run out of other people's messes to clean up, Mother Doreen could only pray that hers really were gone.

Chapter Seven

"It seems like just yesterday I was the one being shown getting arrested all over the television and the Internet," Paige said to Tamarra. "Funny how things change."

Tamarra sat next to Paige on the couch in Tamarra's living room. Her hand rested on Paige's shoulder for support as the two watched scenes of Blake being hauled off from his job in handcuffs.

"Malvonia's golden boy, who not too long ago graced the cover of a national magazine for his major success in the commercial real estate market, now faces jail time," the news anchor reported. "The details of the charges are not known to us yet, but we'll inform our viewers as we continue our investigation."

"I can't believe they humiliated him by going to arrest him at his job," Paige said, shaking her head. "They could have at least waited until he got home or something."

"What do you care as long as they arrested his butt?" Tamarra replied. "He didn't look any more humiliated just now than you did when I found you sitting outside of my house in the middle of the night."

"I know, it's just that—"

"It's just that there is no reason for you to feel sorry for that rat bastard," Tamarra spat, removing her hand from Paige's shoulder. "What he did to you was awful, and he deserves to pay. Don't go letting your emotions make you feel a certain kind of way about that man. You heard what the cops said; you are their key witness. They need you to win this thing. You have to stay strong."

Paige was a little thrown off by Tamarra's harsh words and her tone. She could never even remember Tamarra being this upset when she talked about things that had happened to her in her own past.

"I hear what you're saying, Tamarra," Paige started, "but there is one thing you have to realize. That man," Paige pointed to the television screen although they were no longer showing footage of Blake's arrest, "is still my husband."

"And if you plan on having him locked up and the key thrown away, that's where you have to change your mind-set. He stopped being your husband when he started hurting you. He stopped being your husband when he started abusing you." A tear now trickled from Tamarra's eye. "He stopped being your brother when he raped you!"

Paige stared at her best friend who seemed to be on the verge of going into a fit. But it was at that moment—the moment when Tamarra said the word *brother* instead of *husband*—that Paige knew what was going on. It was then that Paige realized that Tamarra's anger wasn't just toward Blake. It was the anger she wished she would have shown for her brother all those years ago. She wished she had told someone what he was doing to her, pressed charges, and sent her brother to jail. That way, it would have prevented other little girls from being raped by him. But she didn't.

Momentary silence lingered before either woman said anything. Finally, Tamarra was the first to speak. "I'm sorry, Paige," she apologized. "For a minute there, I almost forgot that this wasn't about me; that it's about you." She stood, embarrassed, as she looked down at the floor. "I know you're probably wondering if I've truly forgiven my brother because of the anger you just heard me ejecting. Well, I have. I've even forgiven myself for the most part. But now having to deal with this same thing with my best friend . . . This is crazy. I just don't understand why . . . why so many women have the common denominator of having been assaulted, be it physically, sexually, or mentally. That's not something I ever wanted my best friend and me to have in common."

"And that's not a statistic I ever wanted to be a part of either," Paige said.

Tamarra wiped the stain of the lone tear from her face. "Hey, look, we're not going to sit here and have a pity party." Tamarra walked over and turned off the television. "Let's go over to your house and pack up your things while we know Blake isn't going to be there. Then afterward, let's go to the Golden Coral Buffet. Looks like you need to eat."

Paige looked down at her figure. "Yeah. My size four-teens are even starting to get loose. All this stress."

"And I should have known something was wrong then when I noticed you losing all that weight. I just thought it was because you'd changed your eating hab-its in order to keep your diabetes under control."

"Well, at first, that is why I started dropping weight. Then Blake's and my marriage relationship just started getting out of control to the point where I was always worried that he might snap. I could hardly eat, always feeling so nervous and scared."

"Yeah, I know. That's one of the reasons why my parents couldn't tell I was pregnant at first. Instead of gaining weight, I was losing it, because I was so nervous and scared about what they would say once they found out I was pregnant."

"Well, I'm not going to hurt my body by not taking care of it," Paige declared. "Not eating at all is no way to keep my diabetes under control." She stood. "So let's go to my house, then grab something to eat like you suggested."

"Sounds good to me. Let me go grab you a couple of my suitcases just in case we need them." Tamarra headed toward her basement, where she kept her luggage.

"Oh, no. I don't think that will be necessary," Paige stopped her. "I don't plan on getting everything. Just enough stuff to tide me over for a couple of days before I . . ." Her words trailed off.

"Before you what?" Tamarra pressed.

"Nothing. Come on. Let's just go." She looked around for her purse that had her house keys in it.

"No. Go ahead and finish what you were about to say," Tamarra urged, but Paige remained silent, looking around for her purse as a distraction. "So you really don't have any intentions on leaving him, do you? Not for good anyway. You were about to say, '. . . Before I go back home,' weren't you?"

That's exactly what Paige was going to say. She didn't even know why she was going to say it. Immediately after the assault, before leaving the hospital, Paige was adamant about not wanting to stay married to Blake, but now, those feelings weren't so concrete anymore. "Look, Tamarra, I'm just confused right now. This is all like one bad dream. It's absolutely surreal. My husband raped me. How crazy does that sound? Well, that's how crazy I feel. Yes, what Blake did was awful, but I know in time I have to forgive him, the same way you ultimately had to forgive your brother."

"Yeah, but that took time. I didn't forgive him over-night like you are trying to do with Blake, literally."

"Okay, then, so how much time should I take?" Paige asked sarcastically.

Tamarra threw her hands up. "I don't know. But even then, just because you forgive him doesn't mean you have to go back to living with him. How could you possibly want to stay married to a man who did that to you?"

Paige wasn't sure, but she thought the look she saw in Tamarra's eyes was one of disgust. She looked down in shame as she began to have second thoughts about this entire ordeal. If her best friend was looking at her with disgust, then how would the rest of the world look at her?

She buried her face in her hands as she began to weep. Tamarra quickly walked over to her friend and embraced her.

"I'm so sorry." Tamarra was apologizing again for the second time in the last five minutes. "I'm just so angry that this happened to you, and I don't want to see it happen to you again. And on top of everything else . . ." Tamarra paused as she became choked up. "I'm the one who set you up with him. If I had never set you up with the likes of Blake Dickenson, then none of this would have ever happened." Tamarra looked at Paige with an intense look in her eyes. "I got you into this, and now I'm going to help get you out, if it's the last thing I do."

Paige was glad to have the support of her best friend. She thought having Tamarra by her side would make this entire ordeal easier. Little did she know, things were about to get more difficult than she could have ever imagined.

Chapter Eight

"So Ms. Eleanor tripped like that?" Unique questioned Lorain after Lorain had shared with her that she'd told Eleanor about Unique's baby.

"Yes, she did," Lorain confirmed. "She was not feeling it."

Unique sucked her teeth. "My family ain't even trippin' about it," Unique told Lorain as she sat on Lorain's bed Indian-style. "Now at first, when they thought I had run off and got myself pregnant again, I was all kinds of hussies and fake Christians. The minute I lied and told them I was carrying a woman's child for her, I was a saint. Even my own momma had looked at me cross-eyed, like I was some kind of ho or something." Unique let out a harrumph. "If that wasn't the pot calling the kettle black with her five different kids with five different daddies . . . and that don't even include me, the child she bootlegged adopted."

Unique's mind went back to when she'd been abandoned by her foster parents. She thought about how they'd left her with their neighbor and never came back for her. They'd decided they wanted to pick up and move to another state, but they didn't want to take Unique with them. What they did still want, though, was the check they received. It wasn't a welfare check. It was a check they received as a foster care stipend. Figuring something was better than nothing, that's when the woman who ended up raising Unique came into play. The foster parents talked her into keeping Unique and helping them out with the scheme, and in return, she got to keep half of the check. Figuring something was better than nothing as well, she agreed.

The foster couple moved away without forwarding their mail initially. Their neighbor got their mail and forwarded it to them every couple of weeks, minus the foster care check.

The system was either too stupid or didn't care enough about Unique to realize that the woman who raised her and was cashing the state checks being sent to care for Unique wasn't even the woman who they'd originally placed Unique with. Before moving away, the foster mother had allowed her neighbor to use her birth certificate and Social Security card in order to go get a picture ID with her face on it. That certainly made cashing the checks easy, not that the corner stores cared much about ID. All they cared about was getting the fee they charged to cash the checks. Unique herself thought that the scheme was brilliant that her foster mother and the woman she now refers to as "Mommy" had cooked up just to keep the checks coming.

The foster parents and the woman who raised Unique lived in a duplex. It was one of those double family homes where two families shared the same building. That made it easy for them to trick the new casework-er—when she came to check out things—into thinking somehow the system had the wrong address for where little Unique was staying.

Unique's new Mommy had intercepted the visiting caseworker on the porch, telling her she was going to the wrong address, that it was her place she needed to be at. With the building being a duplex, this made it seem more believable. Then, of course, Unique's new Mommy complained about how she'd called and asked them to correct it several times. And how her neighbor had even gotten her check and brought it over to her a couple of times. The new caseworker hardly asked any questions, penciling in what she thought was the correct address with a promise to correct it in the system for certain when she returned to the office. Caseworkers seemed to change every other month anyway, which made the scheme even easier to pull off. Cases got transferred; files got lost; and unfortunately, sometimes so did kids.

But out of everything, what Unique really thought about was how, even though Unique was absolutely no blood relation to the woman she called "Mommy," she'd followed in so many of her footsteps. Just like the woman she called "Mommy," Unique had ended up having multiple babies with multiple baby daddies. And even now, just like the woman she called "Mommy," she found herself caught up in a scheme of her own, with her biological mother, no less. And now, just like her biological mother, she found herself pregnant with a child she couldn't take care of. She was pregnant with a child she wouldn't raise as her own. *Life couldn't possess much more irony than that,* Unique thought.

"Not that it matters what people say anyway," Lorain said as she sat Indian-style across from Unique, giving her a Mary Kay make-over. "But at least you don't have to worry about folks thinking those bad things about you; not as long as they think you're doing a good deed and carrying a baby for me."

"People are still going to talk, even people up in New Day," Unique decided. "The men don't say too much, but you know how diva some of them New Day women are. Some of them think they are perfect and have lived life without ever making any mistakes; without ever doing anything they regretted or felt ashamed about."

Unique looked down and rubbed her protruding belly that had been growing for the last four months.

"Look up at me," Lorain said as she pulled Unique's face up by her chin with one hand, and held a bottle of mascara in the other.

"Oh, I'm sorry," Unique apologized. She'd gotten so caught up in the conversation that she'd forgotten Lorain was applying makeup to her face. She hoped she hadn't messed her up. Unique held her head tilted upward and closed her eyes.

"No, I said look at me."

Unique opened her eyes to see Lorain staring at her with an intense look on her face. "Don't you ever let people make you feel as though you need to walk around with your head down, not as long as you are serving the mighty God that you do; the all-forgiving God. The great and merciful God. Do you hear me?"

"Yes, ma'am," Unique nodded, feeling as though she'd just been scolded by her mother. A slight smile spread across her lips as she realized she was being scolded by her mother; her real mother; a mother whose veins pumped the same as hers. The DNA test they'd taken had proven it.

"What? What are you smiling about?" Lorain asked, now with a smile on her face matching her daughter's.

"Nothing," Unique replied.

"Good, then sit back and let me finish teaching you how to apply makeup. If you are going to start selling Mary Kay products, then you need to know how to apply it correctly," Lorain instructed. "Now don't blink your eyes." She swiveled the mascara brush around the bottle and prepared to apply it to Unique's lashes.

With her eyes looking straight ahead, Unique spoke as Lorain repeated strokes on each of her eyelashes. "Do black women really buy this stuff?"

"All women buy this stuff: black, white, Latino, Asian. You're going to be surprised at just how diverse both the women and men who actually use this product are. Just wait until you build up your clientele. And just think, you already have a few of mine lined up, the ones that didn't find another rep while I was going through my . . . you know . . . situation."

"Yeah, I know. Pretty much the same situation that caused me to be jobless in the first place," Unique sighed. "I sure did love working with Sister Tamarra." Unique shrugged. "Who knows, she just might give me a second chance one day."

"But in the meantime, you are going to be your own boss, Miss Mary Kay Representative."

"Thanks for doing this for me." Unique was grateful.

"Not a problem. I mean, I wasn't doing anything with the stuff. I was going to start up my business again when everything got back on track, but now that I have to prepare for a new baby in the house . . ." Lorain's eyes lit up at the thought. "God is so good. And He's definitely a God of second chances. This is a second chance to be the mother to your child that I wasn't to you." Lorain began to tear up.

"It's a second chance for me too; to finally do something right. I'm going to sell this Mary Kay, save up every dime I earn, then after the baby is born, I'm going to get me and my three boys a place of our own. Nothing is going to stop me this time—nothing!" Unique was adamant.

"Now *that's* what I'm talking about. You break that curse of lack in Jesus' name," Lorain declared.

"Amen to that," Unique concurred as she and Lorain high-fived.

Both of these women may have thought they had the master plan at getting their lives back on track and in order. But was that the Master's plan?

Chapter Nine

"I know that typically board meetings are closed to congregation members not holding a position on the board," Margie started, "but I asked Mother Doreen to join us for a reason. Now if all of the new and old business has been discussed, I'm going to ask her to join us in the conference room now."

There were a couple of mumbles and nods from the other seven persons in the room, all board members of the New Day Temple of Faith Board of Directors.

"Okay, then," Margie said when no one brought forth any other subject matter to be discussed. "I'll let Mother Doreen know it's okay to come in now."

She went and opened the conference-room door, then entered the lobby area outside of her office where Mother Doreen had been waiting for the last fifteen minutes. The board meetings usually ran no longer than an hour, so Margie had asked Mother Doreen to arrive toward the end. That's exactly what Mother Doreen had done.

"Good evening, Mother Doreen. I'm glad you could make it," Margie greeted the olive-colored woman with salt-and-pepper, ear-length hair.

"So am I." The shorter woman standing under five feet tall stood and greeted her pastor in return.

"Well, for the past couple of days, I've been thinking and praying, of course, about the Singles' Ministry and having you start it back up again, Mother Doreen."

"Uh-huh." Mother Doreen nodded her attentiveness to what Margie was saying.

"And so I wanted to discuss this matter with the board. And since the ministry was your vision, I wanted to include you as well. Is that okay?"

"Certainly," Mother Doreen replied, eager to hear the verdict.

"Then shall we?" Margie held out her hand for Mother Doreen to lead the way. A few seconds later, the two joined the others in the conference room.

"Good evening, Mother Doreen," Sister Perrin, one of the board members, greeted. "It's so good to have you back at New Day. How is that sister of yours doing? You know we prayed for her the entire time you were there."

"She's doing quite well," Mother Doreen replied. "I spoke with her this morning, and she was enjoying her grandbaby, my great-niece."

"That's good to hear," Sister Perrin smiled. "We know you were down there doing God's work, but we missed you," the heavyset woman smiled.

"And I missed my church family as well. It's good to be back indeed." Mother Doreen looked at Margie. "And to be rooming with the pastor temporarily is an added treat."

"I'm sure it is," another board member agreed. "Getting to step in that constant overflow of anointing from Pastor is truly favor indeed."

"Oh, gosh now, y'all cut it out," Margie jokingly blushed. There were chuckles throughout the room. "But seriously, Mother Doreen, could you have a seat?"

"Yes, Pastor." Mother Doreen found an empty seat next to Sister Perrin.

After she was seated comfortably, Margie began. "I've asked Mother Doreen here concerning matters regarding New Day's Singles' Ministry."

There were immediate sighs and even some eye rolling. Noticing the board members' reaction to just the mention of the ministry made Mother Doreen doubtful that things would go the way she'd wanted.

"I know there have been issues in the past regarding the ministry," Margie continued, "but the Singles' Ministry was a vision from God given to Mother Doreen. And we know that if God gives us a vision, then He also gives us provision. I believe the provision is what the ministry was lacking, which explains why it began to function out of order."

"Those women are why it started to function out of order," a male board member begged to differ. "My niece, Joy, was part of that ministry for a minute there. She said she wanted to quit after only a couple of meetings. That's when she realized that most of the women in the group weren't there for the same reasons she was there, which was to get support and learn how to live as a single Christian. They were there because they thought the group could help them find a man. She didn't quit though. The only reason why she stayed a member was because she said the meetings were more interesting and entertaining than anything on television Friday night."

"I bet," Sister Perrin stated.

"Pardon me, if I may," Mother Doreen requested with the raising of her hand.

"Go right ahead," Margie insisted.

Mother Doreen cleared her throat. "When I walked into this room, I had no idea I would be having to defend the Singles' Ministry itself."

"No blame on you, Mother Doreen. We know you had no idea the ministry would become such a joke when you left it," Sister Perrin told her. "You are a mighty woman of God. That fact not even the devil himself can dispute. We know had you still been running things, it would have maintained order. You would have stopped at nothing to see God's vision through, for we know that you are not one to walk in disobedience."

"Well, amen to that," Margie agreed behind a couple of other Amens.

"Thank you, Sister Perrin. I'm glad you feel that way." Mother Doreen looked around the room. "I'm glad most of you feel that way, because if you truly believe that, then you will have no qualms about me taking over the ministry once again and leading it under the direction of the Holy Spirit."

"Well," "uh," "but," "um," were just a few of the murmurs that could be heard from the board members.

"Sounds that way to me too," Margie smiled in support of Mother Doreen.

Sister Perrin noticed the evil eye a couple of members gave her who were not in support of the reinstatement of the ministry. It was kind of like one of those thanks-a-lot looks. When she'd made those compliments about Mother Doreen, she was just speaking the truth from her heart, not realizing she was making the case for Mother Doreen. She had her own opinions about the Singles' Ministry, and they weren't all that good.

She herself was a single woman who wanted no part of the ministry. Once, she had planned on joining and even came out to attend one of the meetings. She was running late and the meeting was already in full swing by the time she entered the church. She could hear one of New Day's former members ranting and raving about her ex-husband who had cheated on her, resulting in a child being born outside of the marriage. All the other members were ooohing and ahhhing and throwing in their two cents.

Standing outside of the room, Sister Perrin turned on her heels and exited the church just as quickly as she had come, without anyone ever knowing that she was there. She remembered thinking, *I could have stayed home and watched Basketball Wives for all this.* So needless to say, she was not in support of the ministry itself, but she was in support of Mother Doreen.

"Look," Sister Perrin started, "some of us may not be in support of the Singles' Ministry itself, but I believe we've all just made it clear that we support Mother Doreen. We know our sister in Christ to be a woman who clearly hears from the Lord. So if God gave her this vision . . ." Sister Perrin looked at Margie, ". . . and if Pastor believed in the vision enough to allow it to get off the ground in the first place, then I say the same way we serve a God of second chances, then perhaps we should give the ministry a second chance as well."

Surprisingly, there were hand claps in support of Sister Perrin's statement. She smiled proudly.

"Wow, Sister Perrin," Margie stated, "I'm going to have to get you to speak during women's month." Next, she turned to face Mother Doreen. "Well, Mother Doreen, it sounds like the board is in favor of the Singles' Ministry's reinstatement."

"Yes, thank you, Jesus," Mother Doreen responded, raising holy hands.

"Then I guess this is just confirmation of what God already told me," Margie stated. "Because I'd already made up my mind that I would reinstate the ministry; well, God made up my mind for me. I was just hoping for the support of the board as well."

"Thank you, Pastor," Mother Doreen said smiling broadly. "Your support means a lot to me."

"You're welcome, Mother Doreen," Margie smiled. "And please just let me know if there is anything you need from me."

"Well, actually, Pastor, there is that one other thing we discussed," Mother Doreen reminded her pastor.

Margie thought for a moment but came up empty. "I'm sorry, Mother Doreen. Will you enlighten me?"

"Well, Pastor, not only did I come to you asking that you consider reinstating the Singles' Ministry, but I also asked that you consider showing other members your support of the ministry by joining it yourself."

"Okay, now you're pushing it," Sister Perrin blurted out without thinking. "What would it look like having our pastor be a part of a group like that? She'll seem desperate. It's bad enough she's single in the first place, but to be single and desperate on top of that." Sister Perrin shook her head, adamantly against the idea of her pastor joining the Singles' Ministry. "No way, Jose."

"Although I value your opinion, Sister Perrin," Mother Doreen told her, "this is about Pastor and her opinion; what *she* wants to do."

Every eyeball in the room was honed in on Margie. "Well, I kind of didn't take that one to the Lord, Mother Doreen," she admitted. "But you already know how I feel about joining the ministry. I kind of agree with Sister Perrin." Margie looked at Sister Perrin. "But that statement about it being bad enough that I'm single—I'm not quite sure I get that."

Now every eye in the room zoomed in on Sister Perrin for an explanation.

"Well, uh, Pastor, I was just saying," Sister Perrin stammered. "You know, congregation members talk all the time about your status as a single woman."

"Is that so?" This was news to Margie. "What exactly does the congregation say all the time about my status as a single woman?" she mocked.

"Well, uh . . ." Sister Perrin's eyes darted from one board member to the next, begging someone to help her out. No one volunteered. She was on her own. "Well, that uh—and know that this ain't me saying it— I'm just repeating some of the things I've heard."

"And what have you heard?" Margie inquired again.

"Well, that perhaps you're, you know, maybe one of those undercover . . ." Sister Perrin cleared her throat. ". . . that you're possibly gay. Some members say that even if you're not gay, being single puts you in the same position that it does with some of the male pastors."

"And what position is that?" Margie probed.

"Well, you know how some male pastors are tempted by their female congregation members. I guess some folks are afraid that by you being single, you'll indulge in the same temptations with your male congregation members."

Now every eyeball rolled back in Margie's direction. Mother Doreen and the board members were expecting some type of reaction from their pastor, but instead, all they got was a, "Humph, is that so?"

"Yes, it is so," the only male board member vouched. Heck, Sister Perrin had already said the worst parts. He couldn't see how cosigning would hurt him any. "But even though some folks frown upon a single pastor, whether male or female, and they have no right to do so, I just don't feel broadcasting that you are single by joining the Singles' Ministry is a good idea, Pastor."

A thick sheet of silence floated across the room until Mother Doreen sliced through it with her voice. "Well, Pastor, again, I'm just going to ask you to pray on it."

"And I will, Mother Doreen," Margie assured her. "In the meantime, I want you to pray about God's agenda for the Singles' Ministry. Put it in writing, and then at next month's board meeting, have something to present to me. If we all agree that everything is decent and in order, then we'll move on with determining a start-up date for the Singles' Ministry. How's that sound?"

"Sounds good to me," Mother Doreen said, although she'd lost some of her enthusiasm. She was ready to dive back into the duties of the leader of the Singles' Ministry right away. A month was too much idle time. She needed to keep busy now; right away. She needed some hands-on assignments to be involved in. As the saying went, idle hands were the devil's playground. Well, hopefully, Mother Doreen had been doing a little warming up just in case, because the devil was ready to play. And it wasn't going to be some friendly game of school yard dodge ball either. Nope . . . the devil was ready to play hardball!

Chapter Ten

Paige sat in the courtroom next to Tamarra feeling all kinds of ways. She felt scared. She felt hurt. And then when she saw Blake being escorted into the courtroom, donned in jailhouse garb and wearing handcuffs, she felt guilty.

"Oh my God," she gasped at the sight of her husband. "He looks so . . . so . . ." Paige couldn't even find the words to describe the man looking like a complete stranger in the courtroom. But then Tamarra reminded her that just a few nights ago, he'd also been a stranger in her bedroom; someone she didn't know and had never met before. Because the man she married would not have been doing those god-awful things to her.

"He looks bad," Tamarra finished Paige's sentence in a whisper. "But not as bad as you looked with that busted-up lip and black eye he gave you."

The reminder stung Paige enough to shift the pity back to herself. "Yeah, you're right about that." Paige touched her eye. "Even with all this Mary Kay makeup that I bought from Sister Lorain months ago piled on my face, you can still see the bruises." That's why Paige had yet to return to work. Mentally, she wanted to get back to work to keep her mind off of the rape, but physically, she couldn't do it. She worked with the public. All it would take was for one person to complain about her job performance and her job could be at stake. She'd worked too hard and put in too many hours to jeopardize her livelihood, especially since there was a chance it would soon be her only income.

"Your Honor," the bailiff started, bringing order to the court, "this is the case of the State of Ohio versus Blake Dickenson."

The judged flipped through a few papers, and then said to Blake, "Mr. Dickenson, you've been charged with assault and battery, rape and domestic violence. How do you plea?"

"Dannnnnngggggg," could be heard from someone sitting behind Paige and Tamarra. When they both turned around, there sat a young man approximately twenty-five sitting next to a girl about that same age. He wore a white T-shirt that was so big that it could have doubled for a dress had he been a female. "Dude 'bout to get some time," he said to the girl sitting next to him. "'Cause remember that time I had to go upside your head when you was runnin' off at the mouth? Shoooootttt, they wanted to give me like three years for that. Thank goodness you ain't show up in court to testify against me, 'else I'd be dude's cell mate."

Paige and Tamarra turned their attention back to the proceedings at hand. Even though Paige was trying to focus on what was going on, she just kept hearing the words from the young man behind her play over and over again in her head. Was it possible that the judge could lock up Blake and throw away the key? Could a man who'd once had it all now risk losing everything— and it all be Paige's fault?

He was already basically starting from scratch when it came to his finances thanks to that lawsuit his mother, Barnita, had brought up against him. Barnita was the woman who Blake thought was his mother anyway. He'd agreed to pay her hundreds of thousands of dollars just to get that frivolous lawsuit she'd brought against him done and over with. Apparently before Blake's father had died, Mr. Dickenson had won and received a huge settlement from a lawsuit against his former employer. He'd been badly injured on his job. Once he died, Blake took over all of his father's assets.

Even though Barnita had abandoned Blake and his father, taking only his sister with her the day she left them, Blake's father and Barnita had never officially gotten a divorce. All these years later she came back to claim what she felt was rightfully hers. Instead of participating in a long-drawn-out trial, Blake settled out of court, being forced to pay Barnita a ridiculous amount of money. But Blake had felt it was worth it. The dealings with his estranged mother had been causing way too much stress in his life, so much so that he was starting to become abusive to Paige—mentally and physically.

Paige honestly thought things would get better once the lawsuit was settled, but they only got worse. Blake was too busy to go to the counseling their pastor had suggested, and Paige was stressed out about the secret Blake's so-called mother had shared with her only moments before Blake signed over his life fortune to her. She'd admitted to Paige that she wasn't Blake's biological mother; that the woman who gave birth to him died immediately after doing so. She was the woman with whom her husband, Blake's father, had been having an affair.

Blake's father, who, to this day, Blake felt could do no wrong, being the biological father, had legal rights to the child. He therefore had to take the baby home from the hospital, the baby being Blake. Barnita loved her husband more than life itself. She loved him to the point where she'd do anything to make him happy. That included adopting her husband's mistress's child and raising him as if he were her own . . . That is, until the day she couldn't take it anymore. Then she packed up her daughter and left, leaving Blake and his father to fend for themselves.

Carrying this secret had been hard on Paige. She'd become distracted in her marriage and withdrawn, so much so that Blake began to think she was having an affair. That's what he'd accused her of the night of the rape.

"I know you're cheating on me," Blake had fumed as the two argued in their bedroom.

"I am not!" Paige had become so furious that she began to cry hysterically as she defended herself.

"Not only are you a cheat, but now you're a liar. Just tell me the truth, Paige."

Paige wanted to pull her hair out. How could Blake accuse her of such a thing as loyal as she had been to him? But that's when a light went off in her head and she realized that she hadn't been so loyal. She'd been keeping something from Blake. It was something that she knew, if the shoe were on the other foot, she'd want to know. And that's when she decided to tell Blake the truth—the truth about Barnita. Unfortunately, her words hadn't come out right when she started to tell him.

When she'd said to Blake, "You're right, Blake, there is something I need to tell you," she hadn't meant that he was right about the affair. She'd meant that he was right about her being a liar. She was lying by omission by not telling Blake the truth about Barnita. But he never gave her the chance to clarify things and explain.

The next thing Paige remembered was a sucker punch to the face with an impact that knocked her back on the bed. She was dazed. She was stunned. She felt another blow, this time to her mouth. She could taste blood.

Then after that, it was all a blur as she floated in and out of consciousness.

"I'm sorry, baby," she heard Blake saying. "Let me make it better. Let me make it better just like all the other times."

All the other times, after Blake had done something hurtful to Paige, he'd smooth things over with intimacy. But this time Paige wasn't going for it. This time Paige didn't want to be one with her husband. At this point, she didn't even want a husband, but Blake didn't care as he ripped off her gown. Blake didn't care as he yanked her underwear to the side. Blake didn't care as he rammed himself into her body. Blake didn't care that Paige was screaming the word "No" over and over again.

With her hands pinned above her head by the strength of only one of Blake's hands, Paige was defenseless. She couldn't even push him off of her. So she just lay there. She lay there and closed her eyes, praying that it would be over soon.

She squeezed her eyes so tightly that not even the tears could break through. She squeezed her eyes so tightly because she didn't want to see the light. She didn't want to see the light of the fact that, just like Nita had warned her, things wouldn't get better until Blake had decided that he wanted to be better. Until Blake decided in his mind that he wanted to seek the resources, the help, and the counseling that were necessary for him to get better. But even with her eyes squeezed as tightly as they possibly could be, she had finally seen the light . . . and it was blinding.

As Paige sat in the courtroom looking at the back of Blake's head, she became sick to her stomach recalling all that had taken place that night. She recalled lying there with Blake still inside her for at least an hour, because he'd worn himself out raping and ravaging her. He had actually fallen asleep on top of her. She'd been too frightened to move. And when he finally rolled off of her, she silently pulled on some jeans, grabbed her car keys, and quickly left the house. The next thing she remembered was Tamarra tapping on her car window.

Just as all these thoughts were whizzing through Paige's mind, she realized that she was no longer staring at the back of Blake's head, but instead, she was staring him right in the eyes as he'd turned around to scan the courtroom in hopes of seeing his wife.

"I'm sorry," he lipped before his attorney elbowed him to face the judge.

Paige's hands immediately began to tremble.

"Are you okay?" Tamarra asked upon noticing Paige's shakiness. Paige didn't respond. She just sat there shaking, still staring Blake's way. Tamarra followed Paige's eyes to Blake, who just so happened to turn and look over his shoulder again. He quickly winked at Paige before turning back around to face the judge.

Paige shot up out of her seat and darted from the courtroom. It happened so quickly that Tamarra didn't know how to react at the disturbance that caused everyone to look in her direction. This time when Blake turned around it was Tamarra's eyes his locked with.

The two stared each other down without even blinking once. They would have continued their stare off had the judge not called order back to the courtroom. Tamarra was so disgusted with herself. How could she have ever allowed her best friend to get involved with a man like that? Even worse, how could she have let herself get involved with him? Would Paige ever forgive her for dragging her into the messy bed she'd made with Blake, literally? As far as Paige knew, Tamarra had known Blake from a catering affair she'd done for him. It just so happens, though, that that wasn't the only affair the two had been engaged in.

Chapter Eleven

"It's a girl. We're having a baby girl," Lorain shouted as she stared at the monitor.

"Yep, she opened her legs for us," the nurse confirmed as she performed Unique's ultrasound. "See right there . . ." the nurse pointed with her index finger.

"There's nothing there," Lorain observed while squinting.

"Exactly," the nurse chuckled. "If there had been something there, then you'd be buying blue sleepers instead of pink."

"This is so exciting," Lorain exclaimed, fighting back tears. "God's doing it. He's giving me my daughter back to raise." Lorain wanted to shout and do a praise dance right there in the middle of the examination room, but she refrained.

"A girl, huh?" was all Unique had to say.

"Yep, it's a she," the nurse confirmed again as she finished up the ultrasound, wiping off the gel she'd placed on Unique's belly. "You can go ahead and get dressed, Unique, and we'll see you at your next prenatal checkup visit."

"Thank you," Unique said as she sat up, pulling her shirt down over her stomach.

"Can you believe it's a girl?" Lorain asked as she helped Unique up off the table.

"Sure I can. I've always wanted a girl, and finally the one I have to give away, God makes a girl." She looked upward. "Oh, He's got jokes. He's full of them nowadays." This time, Unique sounded somewhat agitated.

Lorain picked up on her tone. "Is everything all right, Unique?"

"Oh, yeah, everything is fine. You just heard what the nurse said. The baby is doing—"

"I know everything is fine with the baby," Lorain interrupted her. "I'm talking about you. Is everything fine with you? Are you still okay with our plan? Because if you want out—"

Now it was Unique's turn to interrupt Lorain. "Oh, no, I don't want out. Trust me, there is not a single bone in my body that has a desire to keep and raise this child. I mean, even if I wanted to keep the baby, I couldn't. You should have seen my sister's face when I told her I was pregnant. The first thing she started yapping at the mouth about was how me and my boys were only supposed to have been staying with her for a little bit. 'And now you tryin' to bring yet another body up in the house,'" Unique mocked. "Oh, she was not having it. But once I told her about . . ." Unique used her two forefingers on each hand to make air quotations, ". . . *our plan*," she was cool. I could see the look of relief on her face when she learned that the baby wouldn't be taking up residence in her home."

"Yes, but the plan is that you'll be getting your own place soon. You'd have plenty of room for the baby then," Lorain reasoned. She wasn't trying to give Unique any ideas. Lorain wanted nothing more in the world than to raise the baby growing inside Unique's womb. But on the same token, she only wanted to go through with it if Unique was 100 percent certain of her decision. The last thing she needed was to form a bond with the baby, and then, out of the blue, Unique decided she wanted it back.

Taking the baby back would be easy for Unique, because part of the plan was that no legal paperwork would be filed. They weren't involving the system at all. Unique didn't trust the system, not after the way they'd handled her case. Reluctantly, Lorain agreed, relying solely on Unique's word. After all, even though Lorain was going to raise the child as her own, they'd planned on telling the child the truth once she was old enough to understand. They pretty much had no choice, considering the birth certificate would list Unique as the child's biological mother. In the back of Lorain's mind she had doubts about that part of the plan being bulletproof, especially now that Unique had learned the baby was a girl. It was the girl she never had but more than likely wanted after having three boys.

"Look, if you're worried about me changing my mind about this whole thing just because I learned the baby was a girl, don't worry. That's not about to happen. Besides, the last thing my son's father wants to do is to have to throw me some change for another baby," Unique explained.

"Oh, yeah, about that, what's he saying about you being pregnant? Does he have any suspicions that the baby is his?"

Unique sucked her teeth. "Please, even if he did have any suspicions, he sure ain't gon' speak on 'em. You think he wants another mouth to feed? That fool tried to act like he didn't even notice I was pregnant. I guess he figured 'Don't ask, don't tell.'" Unique chuckled. "But like I said, don't worry about a thing. He ain't claiming this baby. He don't care if I gave it away to the tooth fairy to raise as long as he wasn't the one who had to leave money under the pillow."

Now Lorain chuckled. "Girl, you a mess."

Unique sighed and closed her eyes. "I know. Believe you me, you don't have to tell me that."

"Oh, sweetie . . ." Lorain walked over to Unique and embraced her. "I didn't mean it like that."

"I know, I know." Unique wriggled out of Lorain's embrace. "I just need to get it together in life, you know? I was doing so good just trying to stay saved, and now look at me. It all seems like it's in vain; like I have to start over from scratch proving myself to God, you know?"

"Yeah, I know. But, fortunately, God doesn't operate like that. You don't have to go back and start over. All you have to do is move forward."

"Well, I better get to moving forward and get back to the house and get my kids. My sister has to go to work in a few. Besides that, I want to get busy on her computer and create me an e-mail address and get my Mary Kay Web page together. And by the way, thanks for loaning me that hundred dollars to start my Mary Kay business. I promise I'll pay you back like ten dollars a month from my county check until I start bringing in an income from my sales."

"Don't worry about it. Consider it an investment into the millions you are about to make. You don't have to pay me back a dime. All I ask is that I get to ride shotgun in your pink Cadillac once you earn it. Deal?" Lorain smiled.

"Deal," Unique agreed as the two exited the doctor's office.

"Do you really believe I can make a million pushing cosmetics?"

"Yes, I do, but you can't look at it as just *pushing* cosmetics. You have to look at it as pressing forward into that entrepreneurial spirit; just like Sister Tamarra did."

"It seems like such a risk to invest so much time and energy into pressed powder and face cleanser."

"I once heard someone say that you know you are headed in the right direction if your only transportation to getting there is a leap of faith."

"Hmm. I like that. That's good," Unique nodded as the fall weather briskly greeted them as they stepped outside.

"Yes, it is good, but God is better. Just meet Him at the promise. Do your part and meet Him at the promise and see what will happen."

"You're right. Psalm 112 says that wealth and riches shall be in my house. Well, if I expect to receive that word, then I have to do my part." Unique rubbed her hands together. "Thanks, Lorain. I'm so excited. Please keep encouraging me."

"I plan to. Because Psalm 112 also says that your seed shall be mighty upon the earth. You are my seed, Unique." She pointed to Unique's belly and finished the scripture. ". . . the generation of the upright shall be blessed." She stopped walking and looked at Unique, who had also stopped walking. "We are a blessed generation, and we can't forget it. Generational curses, no more. No more! I declare it in the name of Jesus!"

"And I receive it in the name of Jesus," Unique declared with authority as she began speaking in tongues. "Whew." She grabbed her belly.

"Are you okay?" Lorain was concerned.

"Yeah, I think the little one got caught up in the spirit too. She's in there leaping like Elizabeth's baby."

Both women laughed as they continued walking and approached Lorain's car and climbed inside.

"Thank you, Lorain," Unique said once the car was started and they'd pulled off.

"For what?" Lorain questioned.

"For everything; for just being there for me through this. For being my friend." Unique paused and then mumbled, "For being a good mother."

"Thank you, Unique, for forgiving me, which ultimately cleared the path so that I could be a mother to you."

"Yeah, but it's too bad nobody else knows what a good mother you are to me."

"It's not about what anyone else knows. It's about me and you," Lorain assured her as she drove.

"Yeah, I guess you're right. What other people think doesn't matter at all."

"Not one bit. Even if the entire world knew I was your mother, it wouldn't make a difference to me."

Hopefully Lorain truly meant those words, not because the entire world was about to find out that she was Unique's mother. No, only the members of New Day Temple of Faith were about to find that out.

Chapter Twelve

Mother Doreen was deep in prayer when she heard the doorbell ring. She thought about not opening the door, considering it wasn't her house. She knew whoever it was wasn't there for her. But then considering that perhaps it was a package or something for her pastor, she decided she'd at least go check it out.

"If it's a Jehovah Witness or a foot salesman, I ain't answering that door," she spoke out loud.

Being only four feet eight, Mother Doreen could barely look through the peephole. But as she balanced on her tiptoes, there was no mistaking who was on the other side.

"In the name of Jesus!" Mother Doreen exclaimed under her breath as she quickly turned, leaned back against the door, her hand flying up to her pounding heart that threatened to explode. There was more knocking, only she couldn't tell if it was her heart or the unannounced and unexpected visitor on the other side of that door.

Mother Doreen remained as stiff as a board against that door. Even though it wasn't a Jehovah's Witness or a foot salesman, she was not about to answer that door. In her opinion, what stood on the other side of the door was worse than any solicitor or deliverer of the "good news." She didn't want to have anything to do with this person. Well, that was a lie. The truth was that she couldn't have anything to do with this person. Forming a bond and connecting with that person would only lead to one thing: her being exposed.

She had seen or heard about it happening all too many times. She'd witnessed what happened to women like her firsthand. Devils came out of the woodwork in the form of jealousy to expose women like her for who they were; to uncover their past. To uncover their history just so they'd look like a hypocrite. But as the knocking ceased and the sound of footsteps could be heard receding, Mother Doreen couldn't help but question herself. *Was* she a hypocrite?

Realizing that sweat beads had formed on her forehead, Mother Doreen wiped them away. That hadn't happened in a long time. Once Mother Doreen had begun to walk in her God-given authority and in holy boldness, that sweating of the forehead thing had gone away. Once upon a time, a sheet of perspiration announcing itself on her forehead had been a dead giveaway and the first sign of her uneasiness. Was she starting to lose some of her authority?

Slowly, Mother Doreen walked away from the door and made her way over to the couch, where she sat down while slowly shaking her head. "You are up to no good, Satan. You are up to no good," she spoke into the atmosphere.

Looking down at her hands, Mother Doreen noticed that they were slightly trembling. "Oh, no, you don't," Mother Doreen continued her talk with the devil. She shook her hands as if she were shaking the devil off. "You will not have me all bound up and hindered," she told the devil. "I ain't gonna let you shake me up, devil. No, siree." Mother Doreen stood and began pacing back and forth as if she were stomping on the devil.

"I'm wiser. I'm stronger. I'm not that ole girl whose mind you once got a hold of. Who you once convinced to get out of God's will and do ill will." Mother Doreen's heart began to palpitate once again as past memories began to cash themselves in to her memory bank.

"In the name of Jesus, I have been forgiven. I have been convicted and forgiven. Satan, I've done my time. I won't let you start pointing your wicked finger at me, accuser. I'm not that person anymore. I'm better, and I partly owe it to you, Satan."

There might as well have been smoke seeping out from underneath Mother Doreen's feet, because she was pacing at record speed. "Oh, Satan, you should have took me out when you had a chance. You should have never let me call on Jesus. You should have never let me know that He is all who He said He is. No, devil, you should have took me out when I was downtrodden, clasping the metal bars of the prison as a captive." She pointed to the ground, thrashing her finger. "Devil, you should have took me out. It's too late now. You are defeated. Hallelujah." Mother Doreen's feet now began to move almost in a two-step. There were no church musicians playing instruments to aid in her praise. No drummer to egg on her Holy Ghost dance. No way did Mother Doreen need all that. Nope, she danced on the devil like she was squashing a roach.

A couple of minutes later, she collapsed on the couch. She breathed heavily as she wiped more sweat beads from her forehead. This time the sweat beads were from all the dancing in the spirit she'd just done. She closed her eyes and tried to think of a scripture to meditate on, one that would help her get through this pending situation. Try as she might, though, Mother Doreen couldn't focus to save her life. And her life being saved is just what she needed right about now. And she knew just the lifeguard on earth she could call upon.

Standing up, Mother Doreen located her purse and keys, then walked toward the door. Just as she was about to pull the door closed behind her, the phone rang, causing her to hesitate. As the phone rang a second time, she contemplated on whether to answer it. Nine times out of ten it was for Pastor anyway. But then again, it could have been Bethany. She'd called there for Mother Doreen a couple of times. Mother Doreen tightened her lips at just the thought of Bethany being on the other end of that phone line. Something told her that Bethany didn't have everything to do with the surprise visitor at her doorstep just a minute ago. "But she's got *something* to do with it," Mother Doreen suspected as she marched over to the phone.

"Just as I expected," Mother Doreen said, looking at the caller ID screen, and then answering the phone. "How dare you?" was her greeting into the phone receiver after she'd picked it up.

"My, my, my, somebody woke up on the wrong side of the bed today," the caller teased.

"Bethany Lou Ellen Tyson. I promise if I was right there in Kentucky, I'd turn you over my knee and light your behind up," Mother Doreen spat. And she meant it.

"I take it your *special visitor* called upon you today." Bethany let out a schoolgirl chuckle.

"Do you think this is funny?" Mother Doreen shouted. "How dare you meddle in my life!"

"Please, coming from you, Sis—the woman who invented the word *meddle*."

"So is that really and truly what you felt about my visit down there to Kentucky? That I was meddling? Well, I'll have you know that I was on an assignment from God and—"

"Blah, blah, blah," Bethany interrupted. "So why is it you feel that you are the only one who God gives assignments to? Who's to say He didn't give me one this time?"

"'Cause God ain't gon' give the devil's employee work to do." Mother Doreen was fuming. Bethany, on the other hand, knew her sister was only blowing steam.

"Oh, so now I'm the devil's advocate?"

"If you had anything to do with that man showing up at my doorstep today, you are."

Bethany paused for a minute. "You're serious, aren't you? You really are upset with me."

"You dang right I am, Bethany. You had no right. And to not even warn me . . ."

Realizing that her sister really was displeased, Bethany's tone became apologetic. "Sorry, Reen. I really didn't think this would make you so upset. I honestly thought I was doing a good deed. I mean, I saw the way the two of you were becoming—"

"Listen, Bethany." Mother Doreen lowered her tone and became somewhat apologetic as well. "Just please, stay out of this. You have no idea the size of the fire you're messing with here. Now I have to go right now. I have an urgent matter I have to tend to, thanks to you. But we'll talk later."

"All right, Reen. I still don't know why you're bent this much out of shape."

"And it's not meant for you to know either. Like I said, I've got to go. I love you, and I'll talk with you later." Mother Doreen hung up the phone. This time she grabbed a paper towel to mop up the sweat on her forehead. Marching out the door she said out loud, "It's not meant for anybody to know; at least, it wasn't until today."

She closed the door, then went to her car. She never thought this day would come. She'd hope to be dead and buried before things ever got to this. But now she had to do it. She had to tell someone about the thing she'd only spoken to God about. She just hoped that she didn't find herself out on the streets afterward.

Chapter Thirteen

"Oh, excuse me, Pastor, I didn't know you already had someone in your office," Paige stated as she stood in Margie's office doorway.

"Come on in, Sister Paige. I was expecting you." Margie stood up and walked toward the doorway to greet Paige with a warm hug.

"Never mind me. I was just leaving," Paige could hear the church secretary say. "I was just helping Pastor with some things for the church calendar, but it can wait until later."

Some shuffling around could be heard behind Pastor. A few seconds later, both Margie and Paige could hear the church secretary exiting the office and the door gently closing. But still, they kept their embrace. With eyes closed, they were wrapped in a Holy Ghost hug. It was a hug that Paige needed. It was a hug that Margie knew her sheep needed. That simple hug was just what the doctor had ordered for Paige at that given moment. The doctor, of course, being Jesus.

Sounds of weeping crept from Paige's throat, but they never made it out of her closed mouth. Stifled in her throat, she felt as though she might choke on her cries.

"Oh, ba, sa, ye, ah toh, yam bey, syo." Margie spoke in tongues as she rubbed her hand up and down Paige's back. "Give her strength in the name of Jesus," Margie whispered. "Oh, ba, sa, ye, ah toh, yam bey, syo. Give

her strength in the name of Jesus." Margie continued to not only speak in tongues, but to interpret her
tongues as well. "Oh da sa ey ye byo. Oh da sa ey ye byo.
Rest in me, daughter. Oh da sa ey ye byo. Rest in me,
daughter."

After a couple more minutes, the two women parted.
"Have a seat," Margie instructed Paige by holding out
her hand toward the sitting area in her office. Just as
Paige sat down on the sofa, there was a light knock on
the door.

"Oh, yes. I hope you don't mind," Margie said to Paige
as she walked to the door and opened it. "But I asked
someone to join us."

Just then, Paige looked up to see Nita standing in
the doorway. Nita's eyes were bloodshot red, as if she'd
been crying just as much as Paige had. Funny thing
was, she had. Ever since Nita had seen Blake's arrest
on television, she'd been fasting, praying, and crying
out to God on her sister in Christ's behalf. She'd even
taken the last three days off from work in order to stay
in constant prayer for Paige.

Instinctively, she'd wanted to call Paige, to go see
about her. But all she could hear from the Spirit man
was "Drop to your knees and pray." So that's what she'd
done. She was well prayed up and had been standing in
the gap for Paige. And good thing too, because the last
few days, Paige hadn't even had the strength to pray.
She hadn't any words to say to God; not because she was
angry at Him or anything. She just couldn't even muster
up the words to have a talk with her heavenly father.
But God knew her heart; that's why He put it on Nita to
stand in the gap and keep Paige covered.

As soon as Nita locked eyes with Paige, she made a
beeline to the couch and sat down next to her. She was
barely seated before Paige's arms were flung around

her neck and Paige was wailing like an injured sea lion. Before Margie knew it, both her members were wailing, crying, and shouting out to God. Margie just stood at the closed door with her hands lifted in the air. Her lips mumbled a silent prayer for only God's ears.

"Thank you, Jesus, for bringing her out of this situation alive," Nita cried out. "I bless your name, Lord. I never doubted that you would bring her out, God. Because I know if you did it for me, you would do it for my sister. And you did, Lord. You did it for her, God. Thank you! Thank you, God!"

"Hallelujah." Paige finally gave God some praise, and she'd given Him the highest praise. "Hallelujah. Thank you, God. Thank you." This went on for five more minutes before the atmosphere in Margie's office was calm.

"I should have listened to you, Sister Nita," Paige said, wiping the last of the tears from her face. "I should have taken heed to your warning that things could get worse. I just . . . I just loved him so much." She looked into Nita's eyes. "I still love him." Paige sniffed. "I know this may sound like a crazy question, but after your husband did what he did to you, did you still love him?"

Nita thought for a moment, and then nodded. "Yes, I did. Every time he hit me, spit on me, called me out of my name, raped me—afterward—yes, I still loved him. I loved the idea of him getting better; changing. But after he murdered my babies, cut my throat and left me for dead—no, my sister; the being in love with him went away. Not immediately. Love was not the emotion I had for him. So much so that . . ." Nita's words trailed off. She looked over at Margie who still had her hands extended in the air, her eyes were closed, and she was mumbling a prayer.

"You don't have to talk about it if you don't want to," Paige told Nita, sensing some reluctance.

"I do have to talk about it," Nita insisted. "Like I always say, I know the purpose of my story is to save someone else." Nita finished what she had started to say. "I felt so much hate for that man that the day of his sentencing I showed up at court with a nine millimeter. I had it tucked down in my panty hose. Media cameras were everywhere because the story, as you might recall, had made national news. I'd carried a key chain with a bottle of mace on it as a distraction. I knew the metal detector was going to go off. I figured if I acted like I was a distraught mess, weak, and could barely stand, they'd just hurry up and figure that it was the mace that had made the metal detector go off and just let me be. That's exactly what had happened. Once they took the mace, they let me go on without having me go back through the metal detector, patting me down, wanding me, or anything."

Nita shook her head. She couldn't believe she was telling this. She'd told nobody but God up until now. "Anyway, I got in the courtroom with the gun. I'd made my mind up that I was going to do the sentencing. I wasn't going to wait for some man in a black robe to hand out the punishment for what had been done to me and my children. I had more of a right than he did."

"But vengeance is mine, thus sayeth the Lord," Paige interrupted.

"Exactly. That's exactly what a still small voice kept whispering in my ear."

"So what did you do?"

"I got up and exited the courtroom, even before they began sentencing."

"Didn't you at least want to know what the judge was going to do?"

"Nope, because the real judge had just told me that He had this thing, and I believed Him. God's Word has never come back void. Ever." A smirk spread across Nita's lips. "That man will never see the light of day." Nita shrugged. "Of course, had I put one through his skull, he never would have seen the light of day either." She faced Paige and took her hands into hers. "But I might not have either. And then I wouldn't be here today to share my story with you."

Once again, Paige's eyes began to fill with tears. "And I'm glad you're here. I thank God for you, Sister Nita." Paige hugged Nita. That's when she looked up and realized that her pastor was still standing there. "And you too, Pastor."

Margie exhaled and opened her eyes while she lowered her hands to her side. "And I speak for both Sister Nita and myself when I say that I'm glad you're here too, Sister Paige."

Paige's eyes cast downward.

"But there was a moment when you felt as though you didn't want to be here, didn't you," Nita surmised.

Paige nodded and folded her lips under her teeth.

"It's okay, Sister Paige. Don't you let the devil influence your mind. You are here, and you are here until the good Lord says otherwise, do you hear me?"

Paige nodded.

"Good." Nita let out a sigh of relief. "In the meantime, just stay strong. I know as you wait for this whole trial and everything that it can be a mean time. But know that I am here. Pastor is here. You have a church family who loves and adores you. More, and most importantly, you have an ever-loving God who is going to protect you. Okay?"

"Okay," Paige said. And hopefully God would protect her, because as she spoke, Blake was being released from jail. He was being released with only one thing on his mind, and that was to get his wife back.

Chapter Fourteen

"Come here, child, let me look at you," Eleanor said to her daughter as they walked through the church foyer. She cupped Lorain's face in her hands, then roughly moved it from side to side, examining it. She then lifted Lorain's head upward and looked up her nostrils.

"Mama, are you crazy?" Lorain swatted Eleanor's hands from her face. She then looked around at the eyes that seemed to be piercing both her mother and her.

"I was just checking to see if you had sleep in your eyes, a booger in your nose, something," Eleanor explained. "Unfortunately, you don't."

"What do you mean 'unfortunately'?"

"Because otherwise, that would have explained why everybody is staring at you like you're the one who decided to take Gary Coleman off life support."

"Mama, that was just ugly," Lorain seethed.

"Good morning, Sister Lorain," one of the church members greeted as she walked by wearing a hat that the average person wouldn't be caught dead in. She then nodded and smiled at Eleanor as she kept it moving to her seat.

"Whew, now that was ugly." Eleanor twisted up her nose.

"Mother, what has gotten into you? Why are you cuttin' up like this in the Lord's house?"

"I'm not the one cuttin' up. Are you blind or something? Look around." Eleanor swept the room with her arm. "It's all these folks in here cuttin' up; well, cuttin' their eyes at you anyway. Something's up."

"Oh, Mother, please. Word is just getting around about how Unique's carrying my baby is all. As a matter of fact, Pastor and I had a talk in her office after Saturday morning prayer. She warned me that some folks weren't going to agree with what Unique and I are doing, but that's just how folks are. Christian or not, everybody has their opinion."

Lorain had prepared herself for the various reactions she would get from her church family. She wasn't really looking for their full support, especially since no one knew the full story. Actually, as of yesterday, Margie knew. Lorain and Unique had decided to tell their pastor everything. They felt it necessary in order for their shepherd to lead them properly through the pasture of the journey they were embarking on.

"So, Pastor, do you feel Unique and I are living a lie? That we are being manipulative?" Lorain had asked Margie as she met alone with her pastor.

"How I feel should not affect your choice and actions," Margie had replied. "I can say that I might have done things a little differently had I been in your shoes, but I'm not. I can say that I feel Sister Eleanor needs to know the entire truth of the matter."

"I agree, Pastor, and I plan on telling her soon."

"Soon is better than later, because you wouldn't want her finding out from someone other than yourself. And you certainly wouldn't want her to feel as though she's the last to know. On top of everything else, you certainly don't want the devil to beat you to it."

"*I agree, Pastor. I guess I need to talk to Unique about that. I feel it's something I think I'd like us to do together.*"

"*If you think that would be best, then I support that. Just ask God to open up that window of opportunity for you to be able to share everything with your mother. And ask God to prepare her heart to receive it.*" Margie chuckled. "*Because I know how Mama Eleanor can be.*"

"*Tell me about it,*" Lorain had agreed before reassuring her pastor that she'd tell Eleanor the truth about Unique being her daughter soon.

Unfortunately, it would not be soon enough.

"Look, I'm about to go to the bathroom real quick before deacon what's his name opens up in prayer," Eleanor told Lorain. "That man prays longer than the pastor preaches. And he don't be praying about nothing."

"Just go, Mom. I'll save you a seat next to me." Lorain hurried her mother along, hoping that by the time she got back, service would start and she'd have to keep her mouth shut.

Lorain entered the sanctuary and found some seats for them. After a bit, she saw the deacon approaching the pulpit in order to open up service in prayer. *Good,* Lorain thought. *Mother will have no choice but to be quiet and behave with service in progress.* But as Lorain looked over her shoulder just in time to see Eleanor entering the sanctuary, she couldn't have been more wrong.

Just as the deacon was about to ask the congregation to rise, Eleanor came flying down the aisle. "I'm a granny? I'm a grandmother?" she spat at Lorain. "Say it ain't true. Say I didn't have to find this out from two women running their mouths in the bathroom."

Lorain was embarrassed. If she hadn't noticed how everyone had been eyeing her before, she certainly noticed it now. "Mother, will you calm down? You knew darn well that that baby Unique is carrying is mine; that you're going to be a grandmother. Now sit down, please."

"That's not what I'm talking about. I'm talking about that girl—that project chick." Eleanor scanned the sanctuary, and then pointed where her eyes landed. "Her. Her right there." Eleanor turned her eyes back toward Lorain and glared at her. "Is what that woman in that god-awful ugly hat said true? Is that girl your daughter?"

Every eye in the sanctuary followed Eleanor's trembling, pointing finger and saw that it had targeted Unique.

"Mama, why are you making a scene?" Lorain asked, trying to whisper. "You know the baby girl Unique is carrying is mine." Lorain let out a nervous laugh.

"Don't you play with me, child." Eleanor got in Lorain's face and now pointed her finger close to her nose. "I will snatch you up and give you to the Lord all right . . . literally. I'm talking about *her*." Eleanor jabbed her pointed finger in Unique's direction again. "Unique . . . is Unique your daughter?"

Lorain felt heat rising in her body and a sickness in her stomach. A wind gushed through her body. She could only thank God that she was sitting down; otherwise, Eleanor's words would have knocked her flat on her rear end anyway.

"Answer me!" Eleanor shouted.

"Mother, this isn't the time or the place." Lorain was looking down. She couldn't dare look up and face anybody, especially her mother. "Let's just sit through service, and then we'll go have a nice lunch afterward and talk."

"I don't want to go nowhere and eat," Eleanor declined. "Besides, I'm already full. You've been feeding me enough bull—"

"Sister Eleanor, please," an usher pleaded, gently tugging Eleanor by her arm. "Let's go to the kitchen and get you something to drink so you can calm down."

Eleanor jerked away from the usher, not once taking her eyes off of her daughter. "You better honor your mother and answer me right now!" Eleanor demanded. "Is Unique your daughter?"

After a few seconds, Lorain closed her eyes. Upon closing them, a tear fell from each eye. All she could do was nod her head. She couldn't see her mother's response, but she could hear it. A loud gasp escaped Eleanor's mouth as she stood trembling so much so that the usher had to support her. This time, Eleanor didn't fight the usher as the woman dressed in a white top and black skirt led her away. But before Eleanor could take a third step, she stopped and turned to Lorain. "Then if she's your daughter, who's her father?"

Chapter Fifteen

Shortly after Eleanor had been led away by the usher to the kitchen, Mother Doreen joined them.

"You can go ahead," Mother Doreen told the usher. "I got her."

Without argument, the usher left Mother Doreen to tend to a distraught Eleanor.

"Oh, Lord Jesus. Oh, Lord Jesus," Eleanor repeated over and again as she leaned on the counter.

"Here, sit down." Mother Doreen escorted Eleanor over to a little nooklike seating area. "Let me get you some water." Once Mother Doreen got Eleanor seated, she went and retrieved a bottled water from the fridge. After twisting the cap off, she handed it to Eleanor.

"Thank you, Mother Doris," Eleanor said as she began to sip the water.

"Doreen," she corrected her.

"Oh, no, my name is Eleanor."

"I meant that my name is Doreen. You called me Doris. It's Mother Doreen."

"Oh, please forgive me," Eleanor apologized. "I'm just a little out of it is all."

"It's okay. It's quite all right. I wholeheartedly understand." Mother Doreen joined Eleanor in sitting. The two older women sat there in silence while Eleanor sipped water from the bottle.

"My baby has a baby who's having her baby." Eleanor shook her head. "If that ain't about some Jerry Stringer sh—"

"Sister Eleanor, please."

"Oh, God, forgive me." She looked up, then she looked back at Mother Doreen. "I don't even cuss, so I don't know where this is coming from." Eleanor buried her face in her hands. "God, make me understand all this, please." Eleanor let her hands fall and bang on the table.

Mother Doreen patted Eleanor's hands gently. "Now, now, it's going to be okay. You and Sister Lorain just need to talk and get everything straightened out."

"Mother Doreen is right," Margie said, entering the kitchen.

"Pastor, aren't you supposed to be out there giving the word?" Mother Doreen asked.

"Elder Simmons is prepared to do so," Margie replied. "Right now, I have a sheep I need to tend to, so the other ninety-nine will just have to wait. Besides, hopefully, they all came to get a word from God and not me. And if that's the case, I'm confident Elder Simmons will relay God's message just fine."

"Amen to that," Mother Doreen said. She stood and gestured for Margie to take the seat she'd been sitting in across from Eleanor. "Here you go, Pastor, you take a seat."

"Thank you, Mother Doreen." Margie took the seat and gave her full attention to Eleanor. "You and your daughter need to talk, Sister Eleanor, but not in a church-filled sanctuary."

"And I do apologize for that," Eleanor said with humility. "I had no right to disrespect God's property like that. You just don't know how it felt to find out something like that from bathroom gossip. I mean, she's my daughter. I thought I raised her to let her know that I loved her. Why doesn't she trust me enough to tell me things?" Eleanor shook her head as her eyes watered.

"No no no!" she told herself. "I'm not going to sit here and get all emotional and cry. No, indeed. I'ma stay good and pissed off so that—" Eleanor put her hand to her mouth. "Oh, no." Her eyes traveled from Margie to Mother Doreen. "Is that another bad cuss?"

"Look, Eleanor, I can only imagine how you feel finding out this way—" Margie said.

"Then why, Pastor?" the voice came from the doorway. Margie, Eleanor, and Mother Doreen looked up to see Lorain standing in the doorway. "Why'd you share what I confided in you?"

Shock was an understatement to describe the look on Margie's face. "Pardon me." She stood, placing her hand over her chest.

"Pastor, I don't mean to accuse you of anything, but nobody else knew. Nobody but you, me, Unique, and God."

"And *I* didn't tell it," Unique said, walking up behind Lorain.

"Hold on just a second here." Mother Doreen put her hands up in defense. "I'm not going to sit here and allow y'all to disrespect Pastor like that." Mother Doreen was offended by what Lorain was insinuating. "In all my years, and of all the things I've confided in my pastor, not once has anything ever gotten back to me."

"Tsk," Unique said, rolling her eyes. "Let's be honest, Mother Doreen; your life is not all that exciting. I mean, everybody knows you keep yourself too busy with other folks' lives so that you don't have to live one of your own. So I'm sure anything you've told Pastor over the years wasn't worth repeating anyway . . . no offense."

"Well, that's where you're dead wrong," Mother Doreen countered. "Just the other day I was in Pastor's office and shared the most—"

"Mother Doreen." Margie cut off her church member and her roommate. "You don't have to explain yourself, nor defend me, although I do appreciate it."

"I'm just saying, Pastor, if they knew like I knew, the thought of you telling people's business wouldn't even cross their minds." At least that's truly what Mother Doreen hoped and prayed, because just a couple days ago, she'd made a visit to Pastor's office and shared something with her that she'd never before felt compelled to share. It was after the visit she'd received, and she knew she had to go to her pastor. She could no longer do this thing alone. And although her pastor didn't judge her after her confession, she'd never forget the look on Margie's face.

Margie had leaned back in her church office chair. For the first time since she could recall, she was speechless. She honestly had no idea what to say. Well, her flesh had a lot of ideas, but she knew that at a critical time such as this, her words needed to be sensitive and orchestrated by God.

After a few seconds, Margie had opened her mouth to speak, but nothing came out. So she went back into thought, waiting to hear from God. After a few more seconds, she opened her mouth to speak again. Still, she had nothing.

This act was driving Mother Doreen, who sat in a chair on the opposite side of Margie's desk, out of her mind. Every time she thought her pastor was about to say something, she'd lean in to listen. But each time, nothing came out of her pastor's mouth, so she'd rest back against the chair.

But this time after Margie fixed her lips to say something and no words came out, Mother Doreen couldn't take it any longer. She broke the silence. "If you want me to leave your house, I'll understand. If you want me to leave your church, I'll understand."

Still, Margie was silent. Finally, she spoke. "First of all, this is not my church. It's God's church. Second, there is no way I'd put you out on the streets because of something you did in the past. Besides, you've paid your debt to society. Who am I to hold that against you?"

Mother Doreen had been so happy to hear her pastor say that, because she needed her on her side with this battle. But right now, it looked as though Margie needed Mother Doreen on her side to help fight the brewing battle that was now taking place.

"Look, right now, it really doesn't matter who told what," Margie said. "What matters is that the two of you . . ." Margie looked from Eleanor to Lorain. But then she looked at Unique as well. ". . . or perhaps the three of you, should go home and talk."

"Unique, if you'd like, I can get the kids from Children's Church for you," Mother Doreen offered.

Lorain looked at her mother. She tried to read her expression to see if that was something she was willing to do.

Eleanor shrugged. "I guess I can do that, although it seems a day late and a dollar short."

Margie looked at Lorain. "Sister Lorain, what do you say?"

"Of course," Lorain agreed. She then looked at Unique. "Unique, I'd like for you to be there too." She quickly turned her attention back to Eleanor. "But, Mother, no matter how upset you are, I won't stand for you hurling any insults at my daughter; no more than you'd stand for somebody talking bad about me."

Unique fought like the dickens to keep that smile from splitting her lips. It felt good to hear Lorain stand up for her. Nothing Eleanor said at that point could steal the joy she felt in that moment of time.

"Okay." Eleanor stood. "Let's do this then." She walked past Lorain and Unique, but stopped and looked back at them once she realized they weren't budging. "Well, what are you waiting for? Come on, daughter," she said to Lorain, then looked at Unique. "You too, Shanaynay." Then she headed for the car.

Lorain shook her head and looked up at Unique. "Well, you heard her, Shanaynay. Let's get a move on it." Lorain grabbed Unique by the arm as the two exited the kitchen a few seconds behind Eleanor, leaving Mother Doreen and their pastor behind.

Margie let out a huge breath and then flopped back down in the seat. "And you want me to join the Singles' Ministry? And then other members even want me married off. Who has time for all that and at the same time be available to deal with what I have to deal with?"

"I understand, Pastor," Mother Doreen said, taking the seat Eleanor had vacated. "But you still have to take care of you. If you don't, who else will?"

Margie thought for a minute before saying, "Hopefully God will, Mother Doreen. Hopefully God."

Chapter Sixteen

It had been a week since Paige had been to work. It was a much-needed leave of absence. Not only did her bruises need to heal, but she had to get her mind right as well. Mentally, she was going through so many emotions she felt schizophrenic at times. One minute she felt guilty about Blake having been thrown in jail, the next minute she was afraid because he was no longer in jail.

When she'd received the phone call from the detective letting her know that Blake was being released, she was surprised. Not knowing much about the court system, Paige had just assumed he'd stay in jail until after the trial and sentencing.

Another part of Paige felt worried. She worried whether Blake would just be able to pick back up where he'd left off at work, or if he even had a job to go back to. For the life of her, she couldn't figure out why she even cared. Her main concern should have been whether she'd be able to function at her own place of employment.

As she parked her Lexus that Blake had bought her after she'd totaled her car in the accident, she walked inside the theatre. She was feeling nervous, as she didn't know what to expect from her coworkers. How much did they know? What had they seen on television? Or on the Internet, even? With all those social networks, folks chatted about everybody's business under the sun, whether they knew the person or not.

Most of Paige's concerns disintegrated as she looked at the ticket window and saw a smiling Norman waving at her. She smiled, and then waved back. Next, he began to wave her inside the booth. She held up her index finger, letting him know she'd be in there shortly. First, she wanted to go inside to her office and check on some things.

"Good morning, Mrs. Dickenson," one of her employees greeted her.

"Hi, Sam. How are you?" Paige returned the greeting.

"Fine, and yourself?"

"Just fine, Sam. Just fine." Paige waited to see if Sam was going to give her a funny look or anything or be intrusive and ask her personal questions about the situation she was dealing with. That never happened. Sam just went on as if everything were everything. This made Paige smile even more. She had nothing to worry about. At least, not at the moment.

After checking e-mails, Paige decided she would check phone messages. Just as she went to pick up the phone, it buzzed. "Paige Dickenson, how can I help you?" she asked.

"You can help me by coming out to this ticket booth and letting me lay eyes on you. I need to know that you are okay," Norman stated.

Again, Paige smiled. His concern for her was warming. Norman was her buddy. He may have been a white man, but he understood her sista ways like nobody's business. He'd been there for her while she was both saved and unsaved. He'd been there for her even at times when Blake wasn't, which almost got her into trouble. After spending so much time with Norman, an attraction had formed. But Paige nipped that in the bud, and the two were able to resume their close friendship without awkwardness.

"Give me a minute, would ya?" Paige chuckled. "I know I'm the best boss in the world, and you could probably barely function around this place without me, but I have been gone for a week. I have things to do besides sit out there in the ticket booth and watch you get phone numbers. Especially with this being the first week that *Sex in the City 2* has premiered. I know you've run out of room in your Rolodex," Paige joked.

"See, now," Norman countered, "it's not even about that. I honestly wanted to see about you."

"I know you did. I'm just joshing with you. But really, give me a minute and I'll be out to see how things are going."

"I'll be waiting."

"I know you will." Paige ended the call with a smile on her face. "Shoot, perhaps I should have come back to work sooner," she said as she began checking her phone messages. After checking about four messages, her phone buzzed again.

"Paige, I need you to—" Norman started before Paige cut him off.

"Okay, already." Paige let out an exhausted breath of air. "I can see right now you're not going to let me get through these phone messages. So you win, Norman. I'm on my way out." Paige hung up the phone. She stared at it for a minute before shaking her head and smiling. After dealing with so much mental, physical, and emotional torment from a man, Paige was relieved that God had created good, kind, loving men . . . like Norman. "All right, Norman," she said into the air as she stood up from her desk, "I'm coming to you."

Before Paige could even take a single step she gasped, falling back down into her seat.

"So he calls and you come running, huh?" Blake said with cold, steely eyes as he stood in her office doorway carrying a bouquet of roses. "Here I've been calling your cell phone for a week, and you won't even talk to me. But you will go running for the white man." Those spike-sharp eyes nailed her to the chair. "So is it him? Is it Norman? Is he the one you are having the affair with? Is that what you were going to tell me the night I . . ." Blake's words trailed off.

He didn't know the exact words to say. The way he saw it, he'd made love to his wife that night, but the courts felt otherwise. And considering Paige didn't run to his defense to clear the matter up, she must have felt the same way that the courts did.

"And just to think, I came up here to let you know that I forgive you and—"

"You forgive me?" This was the first time Paige had spoken. "For *what?"*

"For the affair, for you not telling that stupid judge that I didn't do to you what they are accusing me of doing. I mean, how ludicrous is that? You are my wife, for Pete's sake. How can a husband be accused of taking something that is his in the first place? I mean, the Bible says so."

"Don't you dare twist the Word of God to justify what you did to me," Paige countered.

"Paige, honey, so *are* you serious?" Blake looked dumbfounded. "You actually agree with the courts and that judge? You feel that I . . . that I . . ." Again, Blake couldn't even fix his lips to say it.

"That you raped me." Paige helped him out. "Yes, that's exactly how I feel, because that is exactly what happened. You raped me, and you hit me, Blake. And *you* came to forgive *me?* Get out!" Paige pointed. "Get out!"

Any fear that she might have had seeing Blake in her office had now been replaced with unadulterated anger.

"I'll get out." Blake remained calm. "But not until you tell me when you're coming home. You're my wife, Paige. I love you." Paige was unmoved. "Look, if it means anything to you, I'll be the one to apologize. I'm sorry. I'm sorry for every wrong I've ever done to you, Paige. I mean that. I'll do whatever I have to do to get you back. I'll do counseling with Pastor, with the domestic abuse counselor, with Jesus Himself. I don't care. I just want my wife back." Blake inched toward her. "I can't live without you, honey."

"Is everything okay in here?"

Both Paige and Blake looked to see Norman now standing in the doorway.

"Everything is just fine, no thanks to you," Blake seethed, moving in on Norman. "Since I'm here, I might as well confront you face-to-face, man-to-man." Now Blake stood towering over Norman with his six feet tall, 230-pound build. All that compared to Norman's slinky build. "Stay away from my wife."

Norman didn't back down. "I find that impossible considering your wife is my boss. I have to work with her."

"Don't be a wise guy. You know exactly what I mean."

Norman showed no sign of intimidation. "Speaking of working with Paige . . ." Norman looked at her. "Mrs. Dickenson, there's an issue out in the ticket booth that I need your help with."

Paige looked at Blake to see what his next move was going to be. He stood still for a moment, and then raised his arm. Paige flinched, but Norman still stood strong. "Here, these are for you." Blake placed the flowers on her desk, and then headed toward the door. He brushed past Norman, who still didn't flinch. "Like I said, Paige, I'm willing to do whatever I have to do to get you back." And on that note, he exited the office.

Just as soon as Norman figured the coast was clear, he nearly collapsed into the chair in front of Paige's desk. Paige rushed around to his aid. "Norman, are you okay?"

"No, I think I'm losing my mind," he gasped, staring straight up at the ceiling as his slinky body sprawled across the chair. "I must be out of my mind. Even back in elementary I didn't stand up to Betty the Bully, and she was a girl who was three inches shorter than me, might I add. And here I just stood up to a big black dude." All of a sudden, Norman perked up with a starry-eyed look. "I'm the man," he proclaimed with pride.

Paige smacked him behind his head and stormed back over to her chair.

"What?" Norman asked.

"Nothing, Norman," Paige trembled.

Norman walked over to her. "You afraid?" he asked her. She nodded her answer. "Then look, first things first; you need to take a restraining order out on him for protection," Norman suggested.

Paige thought for a minute. "Yeah, I think you're right," she agreed. "I'm going to call the police now." She retrieved the business card of the police officer she'd dealt with at the hospital. That particular officer wasn't available, but she got the information she needed from another officer on how to go about filing a restraining order. On her lunch break, she drove down to the courthouse to do just that. She was nervous, scared, and still somewhat embarrassed. But thank God Norman had volunteered to go with her for support.

"Well, now that that's done, do you want to grab some fast food on the way back to work?" Norman asked.

"No, I don't really have an appetite. I'm too nervous and afraid to eat."

"There's nothing to be afraid of now. You've filed the restraining order, so Blake has to stay away from you. He's not permitted to come to your place of employment or Tamarra's house, where you're staying."

"Yeah, you're right. I don't know what I'm so worried about."

"Good, now let's go get something in your stomach. That might help calm your nerves. Then your day can get back to normal."

Paige agreed, allowing Norman to stop at McDonalds for one of their salads. He was right. Putting something in her stomach had helped calm her nerves, and the rest of the day ended up getting back to normal. But that was just one day. It was the rest of her life she was concerned with.

Chapter Seventeen

"Mom, it's me again. Call me back. I love you. Bye."
Lorain hung up the phone and rested her head back
against the headrest of her car. She'd just pulled up
in her driveway after a long day at work. It had been a
rough day; too many deadlines, too little time to meet
them. On days like this, she liked calling her mother,
who always had some crazy, twisted piece of wisdom
or advice to give her. So just like she'd normally do, she
called her mother. Only this time, her mother wasn't
answering. She wasn't answering because she wasn't
home or she was in the shower and couldn't hear the
phone ringing. No, Lorain knew that Eleanor was sitting right there by the phone staring at the caller ID,
deliberately allowing Lorain's calls to go to voice mail.

Ever since Eleanor, Unique, and Lorain had their
talk after leaving church this past Sunday, Eleanor and
Lorain hadn't spoken two words to each other. Lorain
had plenty to say to her mother. Eleanor had nothing
else to say and couldn't bear listening to anything else
her daughter might fix her lips to say.

"A bad mother," "inadequate," "blind," and "stupid,"
were just a few descriptions Eleanor had rattled off,
describing how her daughter's lies and secrecy had
made her feel as a mother. "I can see you not telling
me that you tried pot, drugs, or alcohol, but to feel as

though you couldn't share all of this with me, I just don't understand," Eleanor had sobbed.

"As a child, I can even see it. Perhaps you were scared—intimidated," Eleanor reasoned. "But once you reached adulthood, there is no reason why you could not have come to me."

"Mom, by the time I reached adulthood, I had blacked all that out. I didn't want to relive it by retelling it," Lorain told her.

"What's crazy is that I'm not really sure I wish that you were telling me now," Eleanor replied. "At this point, what harm would be done by you taking it to your grave?" Just then, a shiver ran down Eleanor's back. "I'm just so disgusted is all."

Up until this point, Unique had been sitting quietly while mother and daughter went back and forth. But now she had something to say. "Are you disgusted at me?" Unique bluntly asked Eleanor.

Eleanor looked over at Unique. She wanted to speak, but she didn't have the words.

Unique let out a sarcastic chuckle. "Don't get all speechless on us now. You've not had a problem once speaking your mind. Why stop now?"

"Don't you dare speak to me that way, young lady," Eleanor snapped. "I am your grandmother, and you best show me some respect. I don't care how old you are and how many babies you got. No granddaughter of mine is too big to get turned over my knee."

The room fell dead silent in an instant. Lorain's eyes bucked with a glimmer of hope. Had her mother just claimed her daughter? Had she just taken on the title of grandmother? Had Eleanor just given Unique the title of being her granddaughter? Was acceptance brewing in the air? Was God about to turn around for good what the devil meant for evil? For her mother's *good? For her daughter's good? For her own good and the good of her grandchildren?*

"You said grandmother," Unique said, almost in disbelief. "You called me your granddaughter. You claimed me."

"I . . . I . . . I did no such a thing," Eleanor recanted.

"Yes, you did. I heard you," Unique exclaimed, almost getting angry. "Don't try to take it back now. I heard you. You said that you are my grandmother, and that I'm your granddaughter. You said it. I know you said it." Unique looked at Lorain frantically. "Didn't she? Tell me you heard her say it too. Tell me I'm not going crazy."

"Okay, look, calm down," Eleanor ordered. "I said it. I said it, okay, but that's not what I meant."

"What else could you have meant by it, Mother?" Lorain asked. "After all, it is the truth."

"Truth? Truth?" Eleanor spat in an indignant tone. "Who knows what the truth is anymore, especially coming from you?" She nodded toward Unique but continued looking at Lorain. "And who says this is the baby you threw away? Have you even gotten a DNA test?"

"As a matter of fact, we have," Lorain informed her mother. Although Lorain knew in her heart, and from all the evidence she'd gathered, that Unique was her child, they decided to go ahead and get a DNA test done anyway. The results were 100 percent that Lorain was Unique's mother.

"Okay, so maybe she is your baby then," Eleanor replied, refusing to bow out gracefully. "But you still haven't told us who the daddy is." Eleanor had a smug look on her face. "Who's to say you even know who the father is? That's probably why you haven't said two words about him."

"I'm to say," Lorain declared, on the verge of becoming insulted.

"Tah, and we all know the value of your word nowadays," Eleanor said. "Besides, it could have been anybody's baby. Don't think I didn't know about you changing into revealing clothes once you got to school. Kids talk to their mothers, and then their mothers talk. Word got back to me how if I didn't keep a watch on you, you were gonna make me a grandma early." Eleanor rolled her eyes. "See how right those people were about you?"

"Now wait a dangon minute," Unique jumped in.

Lorain put her hand up to cut Unique off, who was fully ready to defend her mother. After all, those words hit close to home for Unique. Those were some of the same things people used to say about her when she was coming up. So what if some of it had come to pass? Still, no one had a right to judge anybody else.

"It's okay, Unique; let her finish," Lorain suggested. "This is why we're having this talk; to get it all out in the open."

"Really, Lorain?" Eleanor begged to differ. "Are you really going to get it all out in the open this time? Or next week are you going to tell me that you used to sleep with your real daddy too and perhaps that's why he left? Perhaps he left because of you and not me. What? Were you throwing yourself at him too? Heck, who knows? She might be his baby."

Right then and there, Lorain stepped out of herself. A demonic presence rose up in her and began to control parts of her body, like she was the puppet and it was the puppeteer. Lorain tried to fight it off, but it was too late. It had control of her hand, and the next thing she knew, that hand was stinging Eleanor across the face.

The smack was hard. It was so loud. It sounded like two rough hands clapping together instead of a woman's soft, gentle hand connecting with another woman's soft, gentle cheek. Lorain was in shock; Eleanor was in shock; and even though she wanted to slap Eleanor herself, Unique was in shock.

Lorain was immediately convicted. She felt sick to her stomach about what she'd just done. She felt guilty and sorry, yet her lips wouldn't move to apologize. Once she finally came to her senses, Eleanor was already out the door. Lorain went charging after her, but Unique had grabbed her arm. "No, let her go," Unique suggested.

"But . . . but, she's my mother," Lorain stammered. "How's she gonna get home?"

"We'll call a cab to pick her up. I'm sure she's not going to go far." Unique led Lorain over to the couch, and then went and called Eleanor a taxi.

Lorain just sat there on the couch with tears falling from her eyes, the same way she was now sitting in her car with tears falling from her eyes. "Oh, Mom, will you ever forgive me?" she cried.

Lorain sat in the car a couple more minutes, reliving the scene that had taken place in her living room. Eventually, her ringing cell phone brought her mind back to reality. She quickly said a silent prayer that it was her mother finally returning her call. When she looked down at the caller ID she was slightly disappointed to see that it was not Eleanor. As a matter of fact, she had no idea who it was. She didn't recognize the number.

"Hello," Lorain answered.

"Lorain, this is Renee."

"Hi, Renee. How are you?" Lorain was surprised that Unique's sister, the one she lived with, was calling her.

"Oh, I'm just fine. But it's Unique you might want to come see about," Renee stated.

Fear immediately tried to infiltrate Lorain's mind, but she fought it off. She needed to stay calm just in case Unique needed her. What good would she have been to her if she was a mess herself? "Wha . . . what is it? Is it the baby?"

"I think she might want to tell you. You should get to the hospital . . . now."

Chapter Eighteen

"Well, I'll definitely keep you all in prayer," Margie said before ending her call with Lorain. Margie stood up from the table in her study and made her way to the kitchen, where she could smell Mother Doreen whipping up something delicious.

"Evening, Pastor," Mother Doreen greeted her. This was Mother Doreen's first time seeing Pastor that day. Pastor had been awakened from her sleep at around four that morning by the Holy Spirit. He called for her to go to her prayer room and pray for the saints of New Day. After praying for a few hours, she went to her study to work on the sermon that had been dropped into her spirit during prayer. After that, she felt led to call Sister Lorain, one of the saints that had specifically been dropped in her spirit to pray for. Initially, she'd gotten no answer.

Next, Margie showered, dressed, and went to visit a couple of New Day's sick and shut-in members. Lastly, she went to the church to handle some church business and to do some counseling. She'd finally made it back home where she went to her study, worked on some Bible study topics, then placed another call to Lorain. That time she got Lorain on the phone, but she was on her way to the hospital, so they could only speak briefly. They spoke just long enough for Margie to find out that things between Lorain, her mother, and Unique were worse off than when they'd left the church on Sunday.

"You've been on the move today, Pastor," Mother Doreen noticed. "But then again, you're on the move every day. It's no wonder you're single." Mother Doreen stirred up the pot of greens on the stove. "But there is nothing wrong with being single. I say as a pastor, you should embrace it. Let folks know that they don't have to be married to have an enjoyable, happy life."

Margie smiled. She knew what Mother Doreen was up to; that she was still justifying cause for her to join the Singles' Ministry.

"So is it safe to say that you've lived a happy and enjoyable life without being married as you did when you were married?" Margie questioned.

Mother Doreen stopped stirring. "Well, uh, I guess you could say that." She continued stirring. "I mean, being married to Willie was not always a bed of roses." She looked up. "God rest my Willie's soul." She drew an invisible cross across her heart with her index finger and then continued. "But there was more good than bad, I reckon."

"So have you ever considered remarrying?" Margie asked.

"Ouch!" Mother Doreen shouted.

"Are you okay?" Pastor asked with much concern in her voice.

"Yeah, just burnt myself is all." Mother Doreen hadn't burned herself cooking in years. Not since her mama was first teaching her how to do it. She placed her burnt finger in her mouth to sooth it. That's when the doorbell rang.

"I'll get it," Margie said. "You just get some ice on that finger."

"Yes, Pastor," Mother Doreen said, even though she didn't follow her pastor's instructions. She just stood there in a daze, still trying to suck the pain away from her finger.

"Mother Doreen, it's for you." Margie had a peculiar look on her face as she returned to the kitchen.

At first, Mother Doreen had a peculiar look on her face as well. Then she remembered that the person in charge of New Day's SWATC Ministry, which catered to sheltered women and their children, was supposed to come by and pick up some things Mother Doreen had purchased to donate.

"Oh, shoot. I forgot Sister Nita said she was going to stop by after work today or tomorrow to pick up those toiletries I purchased for the SWATC Ministry," Mother Doreen recalled. "By the way, Pastor, I think that was a fine idea; Sheltered Women and Their Children."

"Thank you, Mother Doreen, but—"

Margie couldn't finish her sentence before Mother Doreen was out of the kitchen and into the living room to greet Nita . . . or so she thought.

"Good evening, Mother Doreen. I do apologize for calling upon you so late, but it's the only time I figured I could catch you. I've already apologized to your pastor for my intrusion as well."

Mother Doreen just stood there staring at Pastor Frey as if he weren't really real.

"I, uh, stopped by the other day," said Pastor Frey. "I thought I saw your car out there, but I suppose I was mistaken. Or perhaps you could have been with your pastor or something."

Mother Doreen still said nothing.

"Which is okay, because it just gave me more time to pray and to hear from God. You know, to make sure I was hearing Him right about my assignment." Pastor Frey leaned in and whispered. "You know how it can be when God gives you an assignment. You gotta make sure you're hearing Him clearly. That you're not confusing God's assignment with that of your own." Pastor Frey winked, and then straightened himself back up.

Still, Mother Doreen just remained silent.

"Anyway, I guess I'll just get right to the point as to why I'm here." Pastor Frey took a step toward Mother Doreen. "I came here on assignment from God." He took another step. "I came here out of obedience." He took a third step. "I came here to get something."

Mother Doreen swallowed, and then finally spoke. "And, what might that something be."

Pastor Frey paused before answering her. "I guess it would be more like a someone versus a something."

Mother Doreen swallowed hard again. "Oh, yeah? And what might . . . I mean, who might that someone be?"

Pastor Frey took two steps toward Mother Doreen, leaving just inches between them. "I came to get what God said is mine. I came to get something I should have never let go in the first place. I came to get my wife. And I'm telling you now, woman, I ain't leaving without her." Pastor Frey closed up those few inches that had separated him and Mother Doreen. "I came for you."

Chapter Nineteen

"The nerve of him," Tamarra spat as she listened to Paige tell her about the incident with Blake earlier that day.

The two women were in the kitchen. Tamarra had a catering event earlier and had brought in all of her warming pans to clean. She stood at the sink washing out a pan as Paige sat at the table picking at a plate of food Tamarra had brought back for her.

"I would have picked up the phone and called 911 right then and there," Tamarra added. "Good thing Norman showed up when he did or no telling what that fool might have done to you."

"I know," Paige agreed. "Norman saw Blake when he arrived at the theatre. He tried to call and warn me, but I didn't listen." Paige shook her head as she thought back to her encounter with her husband. "I honestly don't know who that man is anymore, Tamarra. I honestly don't."

"Well, I know who he's not, he's not the man I thought he was at first either." Tamarra stopped washing the pan and thought for a minute. "I knew he was too good to be true. How slick and sweet talking he is. How he can just woo a woman right into bed." Tamarra continued washing the pan. "Huh, I knew you'd be a match for him; knock his ego down a peg or two."

With a mouthful of Tamarra's specialty, macaroni and cheese, Paige asked, "What do you mean?" Her best friend's comment had piqued her interest. "Blake doesn't have an ego." As far as Paige was concerned, Blake was one of the most humble men she knew. He'd always tried his best to pretty much stay under the radar. She wanted to know what Tamarra was talking about, and she wanted to know now. That's why she couldn't even wait until she swallowed her food to ask.

Tamarra nearly dropped the pan, realizing she'd said too much.

With that same mouthful of food, Paige began to speak. "Back when I told you that Blake had proposed to me, you know, when you confessed to me how my meeting with Blake wasn't chance; that you and he had set the entire thing up," Paige reminded Tamarra, "you told me that you just knew that if I would only give him the time of day, the two of us would hit it off just fine. Remember? That's what you told me."

There's one thing Tamarra had learned from her parents, and that was if a person tells one lie, they have to keep covering it up with another. But if a person just tells the truth in the first place—the entire truth—then they won't have to worry about keeping up with all the lies they've told. It was now that Tamarra wished she'd just told Paige the truth—the entire truth—in the first place. Because now she had to keep lying.

"Uh, yeah, I did say that back then," Tamarra admitted. "But you know, I still had my doubts, because, well, you know your history with dating back then." Tamarra swallowed hard. "Hey, how's that macaroni and cheese?"

Paige looked down at her plate. "Oh, yeah, it's delicious. Thanks for thinking about me and bringing me a plate home. I haven't eaten good since . . . well, you know."

"I know. It shows." Tamarra laid the pan down on a towel she had spread across the counter. "You're going to need to go shopping for some smaller clothes."

Paige looked down at her droopy blouse. "I know."

"Hey, do you have to work tomorrow?" Tamarra asked.

"Yes, I do," Paige nodded.

"Oh, yeah, that's right. This was your first day back since . . . you know."

"Look, can we just get one thing straight?" Paige pushed her plate away and stood up. "I know what happened to me, Tamarra. You know, Pastor knows, and anyone who can put a news story together and knows that I'm Blake's wife knows what happened to me."

Even though when Blake's arrest had been shown on television and they didn't mention that the woman who'd been assaulted was his wife, Paige knew it wouldn't take a rocket scientist for people to start eventually putting the pieces of the puzzle together. It was clear that most of her employees at her job hadn't figured it out. They didn't really know Blake. Because Blake had attended church with her on many occasions, she knew a couple of New Day members might figure it out as well. But she still took comfort in knowing that at least no one knew of the long-term abuse. That way, she wouldn't get the sideways glances and have to read the questions in people's eyes: "Why did you stay that long? Long enough for him to do that to you?" Paige would have no answer for them.

"I was raped . . . by my husband . . . by Blake," Paige said boldly. "If you're going to talk about it, just say it. It's not going to bring up any type of memories. Trust me; the memories are already there, right in the front of my mind. So there is nothing you or anyone can say to ignite or trigger something in me. I haven't forgot-

ten. I will never forget. But I do know that through the
strength of God, I will get to a point where when I wake
up in the morning, it's not the first thing I think about,
and when I go to sleep at night, it's not the last."

"I'm sorry, Paige. I didn't mean to—"

"You don't have to apologize. Just don't talk about
the rape around me like I'm a child who you don't want
to find out the truth about Santa Clause. Okay?"

Tamarra smiled at Paige's comparison. "Okay, friend."
She walked over and hugged Paige. "Oh, I'm so glad
you're here. I feel like we're young ladies who just got our
first place together and are living by ourselves for the first
time."

"I'm glad I'm here too." Paige didn't sound too con-
vincing.

"You don't sound so sure about that."

Paige turned away from Tamarra. "I just can't help
that there is a part of me that still wants to be a wife—
Blake's wife." She turned back to face her friend. "And
I hope you don't think this sounds sick or anything, but
there is a part of me that misses being with my husband . . . I mean being with him . . . being one . . . being
intimate. After all, when I married Blake, I was a vir-
gin. He's the only man I know." Paige tried to shake the
thought, the feeling, away. "How can I think that way?
How can I want to have sex again with my rapist?"

Tamarra left that one alone. She did not have the
answer to Paige's question.

"You're awfully quiet over there." Paige wiped a tear
that had escaped her eye. "You must think I need help."
She let out a nervous chuckle.

"Well, I do think you need help," Tamarra admitted.

"Huh?" Paige was stunned by her reply.

"I think you need help in understanding your feelings. It might be beneficial if you knew why you were

having the feelings that you are having. If maybe other women in your shoes have experienced the same feelings . . ." Tamarra suggested.

"Friend, I think you might be right. I'm going to go look at the pamphlets the doctor at the hospital gave me and see if I can't find some type of women's group to attend or something. You know what they say; misery loves company. I suppose I should go keep misery company."

"I wouldn't look at it that way," Tamarra said. "I just think you need to be around women who know how you feel, who know what you're going through." Tamarra thought for a minute. "I can only imagine how different my life could have been had I gotten some type of help after my brother raped me. After I ended up pregnant and gave birth to his child," she corrected herself. "My daughter—after I gave birth to my daughter." Tamarra lightened up. "But thank God that He is a deliverer, and that He is a healer. Because if it had not been for Him, no telling how deep and messed up in myself I'd be right now."

"I just wish you hadn't had to go over to Power and Glory Ministries to get delivered." Paige had a sudden thought. "But now that you are delivered, why don't you come on back over to New Day?" she joked.

Tamarra laughed. "No, it's not even like that. And it's not that I couldn't have gotten delivered at New Day. Many folks have gotten delivered at New Day. Remember that breakthrough Sister Deborah had awhile back?" Paige nodded. "It's just that that wasn't my appointed place. For all my stuff, I needed the leadership and guidance of an apostle and a church that operates in the prophetic. Not saying that New Day's pastor isn't an awesome woman of God. But God had something else for me, somewhere else, and He needed to use someone else. And that He did, in the form of Dr. Apostle Maurice Broomfield."

"Amen," Paige touched and agreed.

"But let me make it clear. It's not the man who brought me out. Yes, Apostle is a powerful man of God, but he's not God, and he's not bigger than God."

"Hmm, I don't know about that. Apostle Broomfield is a nice-sized man." Paige raised her eyebrows.

"Girl, you know what I'm saying." Tamarra sucked her teeth, and then got serious. "But for real, don't be talking about my apostle. I don't allow that."

Paige raised her hands in defense. "My bad, I repent."

"But anyway, it's like if you need surgery, you don't go to just any old doctor. You pray about it and ask God to lead you to the person He has equipped to help fix your particular sickness. Well, it just so happens that for me, it was Apostle Broomfield. Again, not taking anything away from your pastor."

"I know, I get it," Paige said. "And I know exactly what you're talking about. It's like with me, when my issues with Blake first started, God used Sister Nita instead of Pastor. I thought that was strange at first. But then just like you said, God has His chosen vessels to help you with your particular issue." A dreadful look fleeted across Paige's face.

"What? What is it?" Tamarra inquired.

"Umm, nothing, I guess. But I was just thinking. Do you find it strange that God chose not to use Pastor for either of our situations? What do you think that means?"

Tamarra shrugged. "I don't know, Paige. But you and I both know now that you've posed the question, God's gonna answer it."

Chapter Twenty

"Is everything okay?" Lorain asked in a calm panic as she entered Unique's hospital room.

The doctor was just leaving. "Yeah, I think the girls are going to be fine." The doctor looked over his shoulder at Unique. "Mom here just needs to take it easy."

"Yeah, yeah. I hear you, Doc," Unique stated.

"Keep an eye on your sister here for me, would you?" the medium height, dark-skinned, mini-Afro-wearing doctor whispered to Lorain.

"I'll try, but I'm sure you've figured out by now that that is not going to be an easy feat," Lorain replied.

"Hmm, you might be right about that." The doctor looked over his shoulder again and playfully glared at Unique with his soft brown eyes. "We'll have to think of a way to get her tamed." He looked back at Lorain. "At least for this last trimester."

"Well, Doc," Lorain said, repeating what Unique had referred to him as, "if you come up with any ideas, I'm open for suggestions."

"Is that so?" The doctor looked Lorain up and down. His eyes were doing anything but being discreet. "Then I'll make sure that I definitely come up with something and get back to you. Is that all right with you?"

Lorain was a little thrown off. Something about this doctor's eyes told her that the conversation had just turned serious. "Yeah, uh, well, I guess so," she stammered.

"I take it your sister here will know how to get in touch with you?" The doctor stared into Lorain's eyes while she stared right back into his.

"Uh, hello? Pregnant woman who just found out she's having twins over here," Unique called out. "Besides, she's not my sister. She's—"

"Twins?" Lorain yelled, walking past the doctor and over to Unique's bed. "Did you say that you are having twins?"

"Yes, that's exactly what I said," Unique replied. "Although I'm surprised you even heard that the way you were hanging on to Dr. McHottie's every word," Unique spat as the doctor quietly slipped out of the door to let the two women talk.

"Why didn't you call me?" Lorain asked as she stood over Unique's hospital bed.

"My sister called you," Unique reminded her.

"No, I mean, why didn't you call me when you were on your way to the hospital? You could have gone into early labor or anything. I want to be here for the baby." A huge grin stretched across Lorain's face. "I mean, the babies."

Unique wasn't smiling. "Oh, so, just being here for me isn't enough?"

Was that a tinge of jealousy Lorain was sensing from Unique? "That's not what I meant. I want to be here for you as well," Lorain added.

"Yeah, well, everything turned out to be just fine. The girls were in there fighting or something, because I started having the worst pain, and they were moving around like crazy." Unique rubbed her stomach. "Come to find, one little mama had been covering the other all these months."

"Wow, if they aren't one of the family, then I don't know who is," Lorain snickered. "Covering for each other . . . fighting. They got it honest."

Unique caught on to the pun and let out a chuckle of her own. "Yeah, you're right about that. Speaking of which, have you and granny made up yet?" Unique asked. "Which is another reason why I didn't want to bother you—I knew you had enough drama going on with you and Eleanor."

Lorain sighed, and then sat down in the chair near the foot of Unique's bed. "She still won't take my calls."

"Do a drive-by," Unique suggested. "You know how you New Day Divas will do a drive-by in a heartbeat."

"Hmm, as you'll get to know hopefully one day, Eleanor Simpson is not somebody you want to do a drive-by on."

"From what I saw, you the one somebody don't want to do a drive-by on." Unique began throwing fake punches. "You might sneak on 'em once or twice for showing up unannounced."

"Unique, this is serious."

"Okay, my bad." Unique regained her composure. "But she did have it coming, and I can understand how you snapped and all."

"I can't, not if I call myself a Christian."

"Well, she's kind of sort of a supposed-to-be Christian too." Unique shrugged. "So I'll pray that she turns the other cheek."

"Really?" Lorain asked.

"Sure. Grab my hands. I'll pray now." Unique closed her eyes and extended her hands out to Lorain.

Lorain felt all warm inside that even though Unique was laid up in the hospital bed, she had the energy to pray for Lorain and Eleanor's relationship. Lorain closed her eyes and placed her hands inside Unique's.

"Father God," Unique began, "I pray right now in the name of Jesus that you touch Ms. Eleanor's heart. That you soften it so that she might forgive Lorain's flesh for rising up and slapping her."

"Yes, Lord," Lorain mumbled.

"I ask that you would have Ms. Eleanor do as your Word says to do and to turn the other cheek."

"Yes, God. Please, Lord."

"Have her turn the other cheek, God," Unique continued, "so that I may slap her on that one. In Jesus' name I pray, amen."

"Unique," Lorain spat, opening her eyes and quickly removing her hands from Unique's.

Unique couldn't stop laughing.

"I do not touch and agree with that," Lorain spat. "I rebuke that prayer in the name of Jesus," she declared.

"Oh, God, I'm sorry." Unique looked upward. "Really, God, I'm sorry," Unique laughed. "I just couldn't help it. Besides, I'm only keeping it real. The way your mama was running off at the mouth, the hurtful things she was saying to you . . . Childddddd, I am not mad at you for decking her."

"Well, I'm mad at myself. A daughter does not hit her mother under any circumstance."

"Then don't look at it as though you hit her. Look at it as though you laid holy hands on her. And they were holy all right, because you knocked the holy—"

"Okay, that's it. That's enough." Lorain stood. "I see you're all right. The babies are all right, so it's time for me to go." Lorain headed for the door.

"No, no, don't storm off. I'm sorry," Unique pleaded, trying to stifle her chuckling. "I'll cut it out."

With furrowed eyebrows and doubtful eyes, Lorain decided to give Unique a second chance. She walked back over to the chair and took a seat.

"I hear the drama ministry at New Day is putting on a play here soon. You should try out." Unique seemed to be making small talk.

"Drama?" Lorain had a questionable look on her face. "I didn't even know we had a drama ministry."

"Yeah, and Tyler Perry is the leader. He's redoing *Madea's Family Reunion,* and he wants you to play the part of the girl who slapped the snot out of her mother played by Lynn Whitfield." Unique could barely get her laugh out when Lorain went barreling out of the hospital door.

"Call me when you've come down off the high from whatever meds they've given you up in here," Lorain said as she walked out the door, closing it behind her. She was genuinely upset, but as she stood outside of Unique's hospital door, she had to let out a chuckle or two. Who was she kidding? Unique had pulled some funny stuff in there. Besides, people say that laughter is the best medicine. Maybe laughing about the situation would help her feel better about it. But that reasoning was quickly thrown out of the window when Lorain's laughter turned to tears.

What was going down between her mother and herself was no laughing matter. It was a praying matter. So Lorain decided that's just what she would do; pray and fast until God put His hand on the situation. But just as Lorain went to walk off so she could go get started, she felt a hand on her all right, but it wasn't the hand of God.

Chapter Twenty-one

At first Mother Doreen was speechless. She shook her head and blinked her eyes as if she could shake away that very moment. As if after each and every blink, Pastor Frey would no longer be standing there right in front of her. Neither the shaking nor the blinking worked, because there he still stood in front of her, proclaiming he'd come all the way from Kentucky to Malvonia to get his wife. Supposedly that wife was Mother Doreen.

"Well, aren't you going to say something?" Pastor Frey asked a stunned Mother Doreen.

Mother Doreen opened her mouth, but it took a few seconds for words to actually come out. "Wha . . . what do you want me to say?"

"I don't know, whatever God is leading you to say would help."

"What's God got to do with it?" Mother Doreen put her hands on her hips and tilted her head. With puckered lips and squinted eyes, she repeated, "What's God got to do with you coming all the way here to Malvonia, then showing up on my doorstep talking about you came for your wife . . . blah, blah, blah?"

"Oh, Doreen, surely I don't have to explain that one to you. I mean, certainly you know what it's like to be on an assignment from God, don't you?" He looked at her knowingly with a smirk.

"Don't play with me, Pastor Frey. What's your deal? I can't see you traveling all this way to hit me with this when a phone call would have sufficed."

"Would a man propose to a woman over the phone?" Pastor Frey went into his pocket.

Mother Doreen sucked in a huge pocket of air, placing her hands over her mouth. Was this man about to do what she thought he was about to do?

Pastor Frey began to kneel down as he fished around in his pocket. "Doreen, will you . . ." One knee was already on the ground when he retrieved the mini Bible from his pocket. ". . . pray with me?" His other knee hit the ground.

Mother Doreen exhaled loudly. Her hand drooped down to her side, and disappointment covered her face.

Pastor Frey gave a knowing little grin. "What? What did you think I was going to ask you?"

Mother Doreen stared at the man, now down on both knees, who was over ten years younger than she. To be in his upper fifties, the man didn't have a gray hair on his head. He was, though, balding on top, but it was kind of, sort of, becoming. His shiny brown face housed a beard and mustache and sideburns. It also housed the deepest, brownest eyes Mother Doreen had ever stared into. They were hypnotizing. And right about now, she was being caught up in their spell. Realizing she was being pulled in by Pastor Frey's antics, Mother Doreen pulled back . . . her feelings . . . her emotions.

"Look, I don't know what you're up to, but I'm not down with it," she spat. "I'll pray with you. But I'm gonna do it from a distance. Now, my pastor and I were about to have dinner, so I think you better get to getting . . . all the way back to—"

Catching the tail end of what Mother Doreen was saying, Margie entered the room and cut her off. "Oh,

Mother Doreen. This man says he's your friend all the way from Kentucky. A friend of yours is a friend of mine." She looked at Pastor Frey, who was still down on his knees. She then looked back at Mother Doreen. "I don't mind if he joins us for dinner."

"Oh, now, I wouldn't want to intrude," Pastor Frey said, lifting one knee and placing his foot flat on the floor. He extended his hand to Mother Doreen, hoping she'd assist him up off the floor. She simply folded her arms and turned her nose up. Chuckling, and attracted to the older woman's actions, Pastor Frey managed to get up all by himself. Mother Doreen knew he could all along. He had the body of someone ten years his junior, who'd taken good care of himself.

"Nonsense. You won't be intruding," Margie assured him. "Isn't that right, Mother Doreen?" Not waiting for her roommate to respond, Margie grabbed Pastor Frey by the hand and led him toward the kitchen. "Now let's go. You can save your prayer to bless our meal. How's that sound?"

"Sounds fantastic," Pastor Frey smiled as Margie led him across Mother Doreen's path. His smile was one of victory.

Mother Doreen remained in the living room with a frown of defeat. She didn't like the way she was feeling right now, and it had nothing to do with Pastor Frey. It did, though, have everything to do with her pastor. For the first time ever, Mother Doreen was slightly upset with her pastor. How could she interfere like that? Just inviting this man to have dinner with them? Not just any man, but Pastor Frey, a man who was interested in making Mother Doreen his wife.

"A pastor's wife," Mother Doreen said under her breath. "The devil sho' is a liar, because, God, I know you don't have nothing to do with this. You know better than anybody that I'm not fit to be no pastor's wife . . . to be a first lady. I mean, with the way congregations rip apart, dig around, and try to find stuff on the first lady . . . Why, it wouldn't take long at all for folks to find out that I—"

"Mother Doreen, you coming?" Margie asked, peeking her head into the living room. She'd just interrupted the conversation Mother Doreen intended to be having with God, but was actually only having with herself.

"You know what, Pastor? I'm not really hungry. Why don't the two of you go ahead and enjoy the meal?" Mother Doreen turned and walked to the guest room she'd been staying in. "Give Pastor Frey my regrets."

Mother Doreen stomped by with such an attitude, Margie could sense that there was some tension in the air, and it was directed toward her. With a downcast look on her face, she returned to the kitchen.

Pastor Frey stood from the chair he'd been seated in upon Margie entering the room. Noticing the look on her face he asked, "Is everything okay?"

"No, I don't think so." She was honest in answering his question. "It looks like Mother Doreen won't be joining us after all. She sends her regrets. And to be honest with you, I think she's a little upset with me that I asked you to stay." Margie sat and looked at Pastor Frey. "Is there something going on between you two that I don't know about? Because, forgive me for saying this, but she doesn't seem nearly as excited about seeing you as you do her."

"I'm sure you know Doree . . . Sister Dor . . . Mother Doreen," Pastor Frey had a time figuring out just how to refer to Mother Doreen under these circumstances. She was no longer the woman attending the church he had temporarily pastored. She was now the woman he was seeking to be his wife. So what he really wanted to call her, and some day soon, was First Lady Frey.

Margie put her index finger up, cutting Pastor Frey off. "Sorry, Pastor Frey. I don't mean to cut you off. But will you excuse me for a minute?" Margie didn't really even wait for Pastor Frey to respond before she rose up from her chair.

Pastor Frey stood as Margie stood and exited the kitchen, making her way to Mother Doreen's room.

Approaching the door, Margie tapped softly on it. There was no response. She tapped again, this time while simultaneously saying, "Mother Doreen, it's me, Pastor." Within seconds, the door opened and Margie could see Mother Doreen's back as she walked away.

Closing the door behind her, Margie stepped into the room. "Are you feeling okay?"

"Sure, Pastor, why would you ask that?"

Was that a hint of sarcasm Pastor was detecting from Mother Doreen? Mother Doreen was one of the most respectful people at New Day. She was one of the most respectful people Margie knew, period. She was truly surprised by her tone.

"Well, for one, you decided to skip dinner. Is it because you don't want to have dinner with your gentleman caller, or is it because you don't want to have dinner with me?"

"Would I offend you, Pastor, if I said it was a little of both?"

Margie was offended. "In all honesty, yes, it would. I'd like to know where all this is coming from."

"Pastor, you know where all this is coming from. Remember our talk the other day in your office? Remember everything I shared with you about my past?"

"Yes, but what does that have to do with anything?" Margie was truly confused. She recalled the story

Mother Doreen had shared with her; an intense story it was. But she had no idea what that had to do with Pastor Frey.

"It has everything to do with it, Pastor." Mother Doreen pointed at the door. "That man isn't just a gentleman caller. That man is someone who, during my stint back in Kentucky, I got close to." Mother Doreen turned her back to Margie in embarrassment. "Too close."

Margie cleared her throat. "Are you saying that you two—"

"Oh, for heaven's sake, no, Pastor," Mother Doreen replied sharply, turning back around to face her pastor. "I mean, I took a strong liking to the man, and he took one to me as well."

"Still, I don't see anything wrong with that." Margie paused and thought for a minute. "He's not already married, is he? He's not one of those men of God who claim that God told them even though they're already married, that another woman is their wife, is he?"

"No, Pastor Frey is a decent man," Mother Doreen confirmed.

"Then, once again, I'm in the dark on this one. I need you to shed some light on it for me."

"Pastor, that man wants me to be his wife."

"And let me guess. You being his wife would mean you can't head the Singles' Ministry that you have all these big plans for."

"No, well, uh, yeah . . . I guess I never thought about that."

"Oh, Mother Doreen, I was just kidding." Margie swished her hand. "What's really going on? What is it that scares you so much about that man?"

"He only knows *this* Mother Doreen; the one he met in Kentucky," she answered. "He doesn't know about the *other* one."

"And good thing too because it's this one that he wants to marry." She pointed at Mother Doreen while saying, "Not the other one."

"Pastor, you know what I mean," Mother Doreen pouted.

"Mother Doreen, I've known you for years. And that woman you used to be, I thank her."

"You thank her? For what?"

"Because I know she has everything to do with how the woman standing in front of me now turned out." Margie shook her head. "I've seen it once, and I've seen it time and time again—folks running from their past. You don't have to run from it. All you have to do is just leave it behind. Period. If someone decides to pick it up and remind you of it, what you do in return is show them who you are today."

"And that's all fine and dandy when it's just you, Pastor," Mother Doreen countered. "But I can't bring someone else into it, especially not no pastor. I just can't do it. I can't take the chance of someday ruining that man's ministry because of a stupid, stupid mistake I made in my past."

"So, I guess you think he doesn't have any mistakes he's made. I guess you don't think I have made mistakes in my past that I once thought could ruin my ministry," Margie explained. "I assure you, that is the furthest thing from the truth. Remember when I jokingly mentioned something about feeling like I was back in my college days? Well, the woman of God standing before you now is definitely not the same young woman who used to sell drugs on the college campus back in the day."

This information about her pastor was not news to Mother Doreen. Pastor had given her testimony a time or two to the New Day congregation.

"Not only did I sell them, but I used them. I used to eat pills like they were Sweet Tarts from the penny candy store. But that's not who I am now. And had I let my past keep me in bondage and keep me in fear, then I would not be a part of the ministry I'm in today." Margie looked at Mother Doreen. "You've not let your past keep you from doing what God has called you to do before. Perhaps God is calling you higher. Perhaps God wants to put you in a position to minister to even more people. As a first lady, just think of all the women you could bless and all the women you could save with your story.

"Remember the first time I gave my testimony? All the folks who got saved and rededicated their lives to Christ? There is a time and a purpose for everything under heaven, Mother Doreen. Perhaps your time is now. I'm sorry if I upset you by inviting Pastor Frey to stay for dinner. I honestly didn't look that far back into your past and that far ahead into your future to connect the dots. I honestly didn't mean any harm, and I'm sorry."

"Oh, Pastor." Mother Doreen embraced Margie. "It's okay. I overreacted. I let the devil do something I haven't let him do in a long time, and that's to get inside my head and influence my thoughts."

"So what are you saying, Mother Doreen?" Margie waited excitedly for Mother Doreen's response.

"I'm saying that no devil in hell, on earth, or in high places is going to keep me from what God has for me." Confidently, she walked past Margie and went over and opened her door.

"Are you referring to your ministry?"

"Heck, no. I'm referring to my man!" And on that note, Mother Doreen whisked out the door, leaving an elated Margie with hands clasped.

"Yesss!" Margie said, pumping a fist in the air. This was a victory for both her and Mother Doreen. Mother Doreen would get her man, and Margie would get out of having to partner with Mother Doreen in the Singles' Ministry . . . or so she thought.

Chapter Twenty-two

"It felt good having you back, Sister Paige," the choir leader said to Paige after closing prayer. They'd just wrapped up their Saturday morning choir rehearsal, and Paige was now on her way to work.

"And you have no idea how good it feels to be back." Paige meant that with all her being. Singing to and for the Lord had just done something to her. It had ignited the fire in her belly again; renewed her spirit. Without a doubt, she knew that God was going to bring her out of her trials and tribulations unscathed. She just had to trust Him. And that's just what she declared after singing "I Trust God" by Johnny Sanders. "See you guys at service tomorrow," Paige said smiling as she left the church.

"Hey, I heard you in there singing," Sister Nita said, coming out of the women's bathroom with mop and bucket in hand. "And I believed you. I believed your every word."

"Me too, Sister Nita. Me too." Paige smiled, and then exited the church. "Glory," she said under her breath. "Hallelujah. I thank you, Lord. I thank you, Jesus." The anointing was still on her, and Paige couldn't shake the feeling of admiration she had for God. But in a moment's time, she'd be needing to shake off something else—the devil.

"That's right, praise Him."

A chill seized her as Paige heard a familiar voice coming up beside her. She turned to see Blake approaching her.

"He's worthy to be praised," Blake declared. "After all, it is He that I give all the honor and glory to for blessing me with such a wonderful wife. You know what the scripture says, 'He who finds a wife finds a good thing.'"

"Yeah, and she who finds a husband should have never been looking for him in the first place," Paige shot back.

Blake chuckled. "That was a good one."

"It wasn't a joke," Paige snapped.

"And neither is our marriage." Blake was serious. "So don't treat it like a joke with this frivolous charge that's pending."

"Look, Blake, I think you better go. There's a restraining order on you, you know," Paige reminded him nervously.

"Oh, you mean this?" Blake pulled out a pink and yellow piece of paper. "This thing that tells me that I'm supposed to keep away from your job and Tamarra's place?" Blake looked around. "Well, it didn't say anything about the church."

"You know what it means, Blake. Don't try to play games. It means stay away from me, period; wherever I am."

"But this is my place of worship. It doesn't say I can't come to my place of worship." Blake chuckled. "Oh, so what? Does God have a restraining order against me too?"

Paige shook her head in disgust. "Tamarra was right; you are egoistical, and I don't know why I never saw it until now."

"So that's what this is all about. Tamarra is over there feeding you garbage. This is why you haven't come back to me. You're over there taking advice from a bitter, middle-aged woman who couldn't keep her own husband, or even her fiancé, for that matter. She's just jealous."

"You know that couldn't be the furthest thing from the truth," Paige retaliated on her friend's behalf. "She's the one who hooked us up in the first place, and boy, oh boy, does she regret it."

"I bet she does," Blake said with a raised eyebrow.

"And just what is *that* supposed to mean?" For some reason, a knot the size of a peach pit formed in Paige's belly. She suspected that she was treading water that, if she got any deeper into, she'd need a life jacket.

"You're stupid. You used to be fat and stupid, but now you're just plain old stupid."

Not too long ago, those words would have cut Paige like a knife. Sadly to say though, she was immune to Blake's personality shifts now. "Well, if I remember correctly, you didn't have any problems with me being fat and stupid before."

"Then that just goes to show how good of a memory you have. Because as I recall, it took me forever and a day just to stomach seeing you naked, let alone making love to you."

That was the straw that broke the camel's back. Paige, with a raised open hand, went charging at Blake. He quickly wrapped his hand around her wrist and fought off any blow she might have intended on swinging his way. Then he grabbed the other wrist just in case.

"Come on, sweetie. You don't want to do this," Blake said as he began kissing Paige's neck. "You don't want to hurt me. Not after all we've been through. Not after all I've given up for you. Besides, if you hit me, then I'd have to take a restraining order out on you. You'll be the one being charged with assault and end up back in jail . . . again. You don't want that now do you, honey?"

"Let me go! Get off of me," were the orders that seethed through Paige's teeth. "You've given up nothing for me."

"Are you serious? I've given up my life savings pretty much, just so I could sweep that ridiculous lawsuit under the rug and move on with our lives together. I did that for us, not for me. And now, here we go with another legal issue. This one brought on by you."

"This is not my fault!" Paige screamed, still struggling to free herself from Blake. "What you did to me is not my fault." She finally loosed her hands free from him. "Go away! Go now before I call the police and you'll be doing the perp walk on live television again."

"So this is how we're gonna do this, huh?"

"You're darned right," Paige said, pounding her fist on the top of her car as she shot out an explicit, "You crazy son of a—"

"Yeah, I probably would agree to that last statement. But that just goes to say that I married someone just like my mother."

"Please," Paige spat in rage. "You don't even know your mother." Then she sarcastically said, "Oh, yeah, that's right. You think Barnita is your mother." Paige let out a wicked laugh. "I forgot. She didn't let you in on her little secret, or should I say, her little scam, to take you for everything you had."

Paige had Blake's attention now more than ever. It was as if her words had shrunk him down to size. She hated to admit it, but she loved the feeling of superiority she had over him at that moment. She decided to run with it. "Yeah, you heard me right. Barnita isn't even your real mother. You turned over your life savings to a woman who only deserved about a quarter of what you gave her, *if* that." Paige put her hands on her hips, leaned into Blake, and said, "Now who's the stupid one?"

She didn't even have time to blink before his hands were gripped around her throat. She felt as though her eyes were going to pop out of their sockets. She tried to plead with Blake to let her go using her eyes, because no words could escape her throat.

"You knew all of this?" he shouted in rage as veins popped from his forehead. "You let me sign my life away, and you *knew* all of this? Who else knew? Oh, I bet you and Tamarra are over there laughing it up. I'm sure I'm the butt of every joke. Well, while you and Tamarra are over there playing comedians, did she tell you the one about the best friend who slept with the other best friend's husband?"

Paige's eyes bucked out even further.

"Yeah, I thought so," he snickered. "Well, ha-ha. I guess the joke's on *you* now." And with that, he released Paige. She fell to the ground. She was still gasping for air when she heard Blake's tires peel off.

Chapter Twenty-three

Two weeks had gone by, and Eleanor still refused to take any of Lorain's calls. Lorain had driven over to Eleanor's house earlier in the day unannounced, but Eleanor had refused to answer the door. Lorain would have used her spare key to let herself inside, but the screens were locked. Fearing that something might be wrong inside, she had called the police to have them come over and check things out.

When they arrived, Eleanor didn't hesitate to respond to their knock on the door. Lorain watched the police chat briefly with her mother. She stood in the driveway by her car, waiting for the police to come back with their report.

"Ma'am, your mother is fine," the police officer assured Lorain after talking with Eleanor. "She says she just doesn't want to be bothered . . . by you." The officer acted as if he hated to relay those words to Lorain. "And, uh, she also said that she'd like for you to stop calling her and coming by. And to tell you the truth, I did have to be honest with her and let her know her rights as a citizen."

"Her rights?" Lorain questioned.

"Yes, that if you continue to do these things after you've been instructed not to, she can charge you with harassment."

Lorain looked over the policemen's shoulders at Eleanor, who was still standing in the door, watching the long arm of the law pass on instructions to her daughter. She didn't think for one minute her mother would go that far.

"Your mother also says that she wants you off of her property . . . now. She says if you refuse to leave, she'll press assault charges on you from an incident that happened the other day . . ." The officer's words trailed off. He looked at Lorain knowingly.

Lorain felt like a fool. Her mother had told this man their family business. Second, Lorain had just told herself that her mother would never go as far as pressing harassment charges against her. Now Lorain was reminded that she'd gone as far as smacking her own mother in the face. Things could go further than anyone ever meant for them to.

"You should probably leave now, Miss," the officer suggested to a confused and emotional Lorain.

Lorain didn't know what to do. She didn't know if she should just pull off and leave, or if she should insist that she and her mother work this thing out.

"Ma'am, you should leave *now*." The officer made the decision for her.

"Yes, sir." Lorain looked over her shoulder again at Eleanor. "As long as she's okay. I just wanted to make sure that she was okay."

"She's just fine. Oh, and she says you have spare keys to her house. She'd like them back."

Okay, now Miss Eleanor has gone too far is the thought that popped up into Lorain's head. The taking of keys was too final; like in a relationship where the couple have been living together. There is something about making the other person give the keys back that is a sign that there is no chance in the world that they will ever have a relationship again; not the kind of relationship they once had anyway. Lorain wasn't about to let that happen.

"No, I won't give the keys back," Lorain shouted. Without thinking, she began walking toward her mother's home. "Mama, this has gone too far for far too long. You get out here and talk to me now."

"See? See what I mean, Officer," Eleanor began to say in a panic as Lorain continued her strut toward her.

"Oh, cut out the drama, Mother. We need to talk. And I'm going to keep calling and keep coming by until we settle things and get back to normal. As a matter of fact, I don't care what you or these officers say. I'm not going anywhere until you come out here and talk to me right now!"

It all sounded good at the time, and Lorain had meant every word. She had no intention of leaving Eleanor's home, but a few minutes later she did. Not on her own accord though. She was escorted, in handcuffs, down to the county jail.

"Watson!" a guard called out to the holding cell that Lorain shared with three other women at the time.

The guard's voice rattled Lorain's thoughts back from the incident earlier that day to the present. "Yes, that's me." Lorain stood and walked over to the bars.

"Let's go. You've made bail."

The guard couldn't let her out quickly enough as Lorain exited the holding cell and was processed out. "Thank you so much, Pastor," Lorain said as she was free at last.

Margie stood from the seat she'd been waiting in for Lorain to be released. "What on God's green earth is going on?" She looked so confused, hurt, and disappointed. This was the third one of her congregation members that had been jailed in the past few months; Paige and Blake being the other ones. "I mean, really, what's going on with the saints of New Day? Should we just start holding Sunday services at the jail? I mean,

this is *not* what the church had in mind with the incep-
tion of a prison ministry."

"I'm sorry, Pastor. I can't make any excuses. There is
no mistake. I deserved to be here," Lorain confessed,
and on the ride to get her car from Eleanor's driveway,
Lorain confessed everything else that had gone on between her and her mother.

By the time they arrived at Eleanor's house, Lorain
was in tears, crying out for help. She wanted help from
the pastor, help from God, help from anyone who was
willing to give it. If someone asked Lorain, let her tell it,
her mini stint in jail wasn't long enough. She'd struck
her mother; the ultimate no-no. Then she had the
nerve to show out in her mama's driveway after she'd
refused to see her.

"Now just calm down and get yourself together,
Sister Lorain," Margie instructed as she rubbed her
hand down Lorain's back. "God hears your cries. He's
pleased that, according to His word, you have acknowledged your transgressions."

"That's in Psalm 51," Lorain recalled.

"Yes, that is correct. Psalm 51 verse three," Margie
confirmed.

Lorain continued breaking down the scripture. ". . .
that thou mightest be justified when thou speakest, and
be clear when thou judgest.'" She paused and looked up
at the sky. "Lord, whatever punishment you see fit for
my transgressions, even if it's more time in jail, I deserve
and receive your judgment in this matter, God," Lorain
confessed. She continued shedding tears for a couple
more minutes before she calmed down.

"Are you going to be okay for the night?" Margie
asked. "Are you okay to drive?"

"Yes, Pastor, I'm fine," Lorain assured her as she
wiped the wetness from her eyes and face with her
hands.

"Here . . ." Margie opened her glove box and pulled out a napkin. She handed it to Lorain.

"Thank you." Lorain accepted the napkin and wiped her face dry. "I better get going before she looks out the window and calls the police again. Then we both might end up in jail."

Margie smiled at Lorain's attempt to make light of the situation. "Why don't you come to the church tomorrow, during your lunch hour or something, so we can talk, and pray," Margie suggested.

"Yes, thank you, Pastor," Lorain agreed as she opened up the car door. "And again, thank you for bailing me out. I'll bring the money I owe you with me tomorrow." Lorain got out of the car. Before closing the door she said, "I know this pretty much goes without saying, but I'd appreciate it if no one found out about this incident."

"Of course." Margie had a strange look on her face. It was an expression that tried to cover up the one that lay beneath—one of offense. Why would Lorain say that to her? In all her years of pastoring, no one had ever had to just come out and ask her to keep their business under wraps. They'd always just expected that of her as a pastor, and they'd received what they'd expected. So what was changing now?

As Lorain went and got in her car and drove off, Margie sat in her car still trying to figure out why Lorain had made such a request of her; then it hit her. She thought back to the scene in the church kitchen where both Lorain and Unique had insinuated that Margie was the one who must have leaked the information about Unique being Lorain's daughter.

"The devil is a liar," was all Margie had to say about that as she pulled off and returned home.

Perhaps the devil was a liar. Then how would that explain why the members of New Day truths were starting to get put on full blast? Maybe Satan was getting credit for something he had nothing to do with . . . nothing to do with at all.

Chapter Twenty-four

"Just call him," Bethany spat through the phone receiver. "Quit calling me to find out if I've seen him or talked to him and just call the man himself. Hold on. I've got his number just in case you've lost it or something."

"No, no. No need for you to go and do all that. I'm not calling that man," Mother Doreen replied as she sat in her room on the edge of the bed, talking to Bethany on the phone.

"Oh, so now he's 'that man'?" Bethany let out a harrumph.

"Look, I don't know why I even called you."

"The same reason why you've called me every day for the past two weeks," Bethany said. "To pick me for information about your could-have-been husband."

As much as Mother Doreen wanted to tell her baby sister that she was wrong—dead wrong—that wasn't the case. Bethany could not have been more right. Ever since that day Pastor Frey had showed up at her pastor's house two weeks ago proclaiming his intentions to make Mother Doreen his wife, Mother Doreen couldn't stop thinking about the man. She couldn't stop missing him and thinking about what could have and should have been had she not initially acted so stubborn. But once again, her stubbornness had run off another man. But she knew she couldn't make the same mistake twice, unlike the mistake she'd made with her deceased husband. She knew in her heart of hearts that she had to let this one go. Going after him could prove to be just as deadly as the last time she went after her man.

Shaking past thoughts from her head, Mother Doreen decided to end the call with Bethany. She also decided that the only reason she'd be calling her sister again was to check up on her and her family. No more calls about Pastor Frey and his disappearing act. Mother Doreen had to be honest with herself, though. She had to admit that the day he'd shown up at the house, after her talk with her pastor, she'd been all set to go into that kitchen and not only join Pastor Frey for dinner after all, but to let him know that there was nothing more she'd rather do than join him in holy matrimony.

She'd honestly felt with everything in her being that God was leading her to do just that. But when she arrived in the kitchen to see Pastor Frey's chair empty, her heart dropped. Then she thought that perhaps he'd just gone to the bathroom or something, but that hadn't been the case either. Neither was he waiting in the living room for her. Mother Doreen raced over to the window. She looked out of it to find that his car was gone. He was gone.

"Guess I got my signals crossed again on this one, God," Mother Doreen told herself as she exited her bedroom. "Now what?" And just like that, the answer to her "now what?" came to her. She grabbed her purse and keys, turned down the pot roast she'd been cooking in the Crock-Pot, and then left speedily, headed toward her destination.

Twenty minutes or so later, Mother Doreen arrived at New Day Temple of Faith. There were several cars parked outside in the parking lot. That's when it dawned on her that noon prayer was taking place. Looking down at her watch, however, she observed that it was a quarter after one o'clock, which meant noon prayer should have been over, considering it was scheduled to be only an hour long. Mother Doreen knew as well as the next saint that the Holy Spirit didn't care anything about someone's time frame. When He was moving, He didn't expect for man to cut Him off. That was one of the reasons why Pastor had removed clocks from New Day's sanctuary. She didn't want people to get caught up in time. After all, the folks at the casinos never seemed to worry too much about time.

Entering the church, Mother Doreen could hear soft talking. Assuming prayer was still in session, she decided to wait in the foyer for a bit; then she realized that she should just go ahead and join the prayer warriors already in tune with the Lord. Creeping inside the sanctuary, Mother Doreen noticed that those in the sanctuary were all sitting up front and they were talking among each other. Prayer was clearly over and a few people had decided to hang around and perhaps do some catching up.

Walking closer, Mother Doreen was about to greet her fellow churchgoers when she heard her name. That slowed her pace. Then she heard the words "jail," "murder," and "felon." That made Mother Doreen not only stop in her tracks, but let out a gasp.

Hearing a deep exhale behind them, several of the parishioners immediately looked in the direction from which it came. The looks on their faces to see Mother Doreen, the topic of their discussion, standing right behind them was priceless.

"Oh, Mother Doreen," the church secretary stood and spoke nervously. "Good afternoon."

What Mother Doreen shot back was no greeting. It was a penetrating glare and the words, "And in God's house, no less." Her eyes met each person's in the room. "Each and every one of you should be ashamed. Gossiping and backbiting. I guess saints are getting bolder and bolder these days. So much so that they can't even wait until they at least get in the parking lot to start allowing their tongues to do evil." No one said a word, so Mother Doreen kept the words coming. "I just hope since you were all sitting here talking about me, that you at least prayed for me too." On that note, she turned and exited the sanctuary.

"Mother Doreen, I didn't know you were coming up for prayer today."

Mother Doreen extended the same glare she'd just extended to her church mates to her pastor, who now stood in front of her. "I bet you didn't, Pastor. Otherwise, your opening remarks wouldn't have been about me and my past." Mother Doreen was so hurt. She felt as though a knife had been deeply stabbed in her back by her pastor. "And just to think that I defended you when Sisters Lorain and Unique tried to accuse you of telling their business. Looks like I owe those two ladies an apology."

"Mother Doreen, what are you talking about?" Margie placed a hand to her forehead that housed a confused mind.

"I'm talking about what all of them were talking about in there." Mother Doreen pointed to the sanctuary. "They were talking about me, Pastor." Mother Doreen's eyes watered. "I trusted in you when I told you those things about my past. I confided in you as my pastor. I never thought in a million years you'd tell someone. I know you are a pastor, and that you are a woman first. I know you need someone to confide in. I understand that some of our burdens may weigh you down at times and you need to release. On top of that, I know how women are—"

Margie had been the one to preach one Sunday that people who always get offended should take a look at themselves, because perhaps they walk in offense. She never pegged herself as a person who walked in offense, but she'd sure been getting offended a lot lately, and by her own church members. "Are you saying that female pastors can't be trusted? That we can't hold as much water as a male pastor?" Margie asked Mother Doreen.

"Oh, on the contrary. I'm not speaking about female pastors in general at all," Mother Doreen affirmed. "I'm speaking about *you*."

Okay, *now* Margie was *really* offended. Mother Doreen could tell too, because she watched her pastor turn as red as a tomato. "I think we better take this into my office," Margie suggested.

"No, Pastor," Mother Doreen declined, "that won't be necessary. I think enough has been said already." She sadly made her way past her pastor. "I probably won't be at your house by the time you get there."

"Mother Doreen, this is crazy. We really need to talk about this. Besides, your tenant doesn't move out for another week."

"I'll find a nice hotel that will have me . . . and where the walls don't talk." After throwing that low blow, Mother Doreen was on her way out the door. She kept her composure all the way to her car while she was unlocking it, while she sat inside it, and even when she started it up. It was right when she was about to put the car in reverse and back out of her space that she broke down in tears. Mother Doreen couldn't believe it herself. It had been years since she'd been broken. She thought she was all better . . . all fixed. Guess she was just some fancy vase that had been broken, glued together, and was now leaking through the cracks. It was only a matter of time before she'd fall through the cracks completely.

Chapter Twenty-five

"Are you sure I'm not putting you out, Sister Nita?" Paige asked as she stood in her pajamas folding up the covers she'd slept on. After doing so, she laid them on the arm of the couch. This had been her second night sleeping at Nita's place.

"Not at all," Nita assured her, fully dressed for work. "When I told you that I was here for you, I meant it."

"Yeah, but you have no idea how many other people have said that to me and I thought they meant it," Paige huffed, and then sat down on the couch.

"Are you referring to your husband?" Nita asked, taking a seat on the couch as well.

"He's one of them. He's *definitely* one of them." But Blake was not exactly who Paige had in mind when she'd made that statement. The person she'd had in mind was her supposedly best friend Tamarra.

All Paige could think about were the words Blake had shot out at her. "*Well, while you and Tamarra are over there playing comedians, did she tell you the one about the best friend who slept with the other best friend's husband?*" What exactly had he meant by that? Paige had so desperately wanted to know once she was able to get herself up from the ground and pull herself together. While doing so, a couple of the parishioners had come outside and questioned Paige regarding her condition.

"It's just my diabetes acting up," Paige had lied out of habit when it came to her and Blake. "My sugar is low, and so I'm feeling a little weak. But I'll be okay."

After the two women fussed over her until she assured them she was fine to drive, Paige got in her car and drove toward Tamarra's. On the drive there, she played with the idea of whether she should confront Tamarra with the words Blake had spoken. For all she knew, he could have been speaking out of pure rage in an attempt to cause tension between her and Tamarra. Running back and accusing Tamarra of sleeping with her husband was probably exactly what Blake had wanted her to do.

On the other hand, she'd spoken some things to Blake about his mother out of anger, but all that she'd spoken had been true. What if the same could be said about Blake?

When Paige arrived at Tamarra's, she was packing up to go to a catering event. With only a couple minutes to spare, Paige knew that if she struck up the conversation, they wouldn't have time to finish it, so she kept it to herself. She'd wait until Tamarra returned home to mention it. So for the next few hours, Paige sat playing Blake's words over and over in her head. She concluded that nine times out of ten, there wasn't any truth to them. So by the time Tamarra returned home that evening, any ideas Paige had about confronting her were no more.

Later as Paige lay in bed, her eyes would not close as she stared into darkness. Something deep in her spirit wouldn't let her rest. Once confused about Blake's words, now the mere thought of her husband and her best friend having slept together had Paige out of her bed, pacing madly.

"Lord, help me," Paige had prayed. "Please relax my spirit, Lord. Calm me so that I'm operating in the spirit and not the flesh," she pleaded, but it was to no avail, it seemed, because the more Paige paced and prayed, the more her flesh fought to rise up. "Guide, me, Holy Spirit, about what I should say and what I should do."

Paige didn't know how much time had gone by, but eventually she exited the room. The next thing she realized, her hand was pounding on a door. After pounding several times, the door eventually opened a crack.

"Sister Paige, is everything okay?" Nita asked after opening her front door.

"No," was the reply that came out of Paige's mouth. "I need a place to stay."

Nita looked down at the bags that sat at Paige's feet. They were bags Paige had managed to pack before exiting the bedroom at Tamarra's where she had been laying her head. "Come on in." Nita moved to the side, allowing Paige to enter. "I . . . I don't have an extra bedroom, but I do have a couch."

"That will be fine," Paige replied dryly, heading over to the couch.

"Let me go get you some sheets and covers." Nita walked to her linen closet, and then returned a few moments later with a sheet, two thin covers, and a pillow. Next, she proceeded to make the couch presentable for sleep.

Still in her pajamas, Paige lay down. She hardly even acknowledged the couch's owner.

"Did something happen between you and Sister Tamarra?" Nita asked.

"No, but I think something happened between Sister Tamarra and my husband." Again, Paige's tone was dry.

"Did he, did he come to the house?" Nita was getting more and more concerned by the moment. "He didn't try to hurt you or Tamarra, did he?"

Paige shook her head. "No, it's nothing like that." She exhaled loudly, and then closed her eyes.

"Okay. Well, I guess as long as everybody is okay, I'll let you sleep, and we can talk about this in the morning."

"Good night, Sister Nita."

"Good night, Paige," a confused Nita said, returning to her room.

The next morning before leaving for work, Nita had expected Paige to speak about the situation, whatever the situation was that had brought her to her door late last night. She didn't, though. Paige woke up, got dressed, and left for work as if it were just another ordinary day. From the looks of things, that's exactly what it looked like she had planned on doing this morning as well, but not if Nita could help it.

"Might I take a wild guess and assume that Sister Tamarra might be another person you are referring to? A person who says that she is there for you but doesn't mean it?"

Paige thought for a minute about whether she should go there with Nita. After a few seconds, she decided that if she was going to speak to anybody about it, that it was going to be Tamarra.

"You know what, Sister Nita? With all that's going on, with my court date with Blake tomorrow, I just really want to try to focus on that."

"I completely understand." Sister Nita stood. "Well, I have to get to work. I may be my own boss, but there's still always somebody else writing the checks. In my case, that somebody is my clients."

"I have to get myself ready for work as well." Paige stood.

"Just lock the bottom lock," Nita advised her as she grabbed her keys and a couple of things and walked to the door. "I'm going to try to remember to get an extra key made for you while I'm out today."

"Oh, thank you. I appreciate it. Have a good day."

"You do the same." Nita exited the house, closing the door behind her.

Paige had a couple of hours to spare before she had to actually clock in at work. Out of her element in Nita's one-bedroom apartment, she wasn't quite sure what she should do to kill time. "It's been awhile since I've taken a nice, long, hot bath," Paige told herself, deciding to do just that.

After going through her bags, picking out what she was going to wear and ironing it up, she made her way into the bathroom. The entire time she worried if Nita had a clean bathtub or one with old, permanent stains or dingy little decals sticking everywhere. She was pleasantly surprised to see that the latter wasn't the case. It was then Paige realized that Nita cleaned for a living. Of course she'd have a clean tub.

Paige turned on the water and rinsed out the already-clean tub. Locating some scented bath gel under Nita's sink, she allowed that to serve as her bubble bath, pouring it under the water faucet. Paige cut the water off after it filled three-fourths of the tub.

For the next half hour, Paige sat relaxing in the tub. At first her thoughts rested on all the negative things that were going on in her life. Then, for a change, she decided that she'd only allow good stuff to settle. She thought about everything good she could possibly think of: all the things God had blessed her with in life, not all the things she'd seen as a curse.

She thought about all the things she liked to do: watch movies, go for walks, talk to her mom on the phone. She thought about the things God had blessed her with: a nice church home, a voice to praise Him with, a best friend she could— That's when she realized that some of her gifts could possibly serve as a curse.

A chill now forming in the water, Paige decided to get out. Right as she stepped out, the doorbell rang. She was a little startled at first, considering she'd just spent the last hour in a quiet house. She grabbed a towel and was going to at least look through the peephole. She didn't even make it out of the bathroom before stopping in her tracks.

"Oh, no, you don't," she said to an invisible Satan. "I remember what happened the last time I took a long, hot bath, the doorbell rang, and I was wearing nothing but a towel." Paige was referring to the incident when she was arrested, handcuffed, and led out of the house wearing nothing but the bath towel she'd wrapped around her after just getting out of the tub.

The doorbell rang again. Paige quickly dried off and threw on her clothes in less than a minute. She figured she'd go back and put her lotion and deodorant on before going to work.

Halfway to the door, Paige heard a voice. "I know you're in there, Paige. Your car is out here. Open the door. We need to talk. I'm worried about you."

Paige stopped once she was at the door. The worry in her friend's voice nearly melted her. It certainly didn't sound like the voice of someone who would betray her as Blake had insinuated.

"Please, Paige. I'm your best friend. You can talk to me," she heard Tamarra plead through the door.

By the time Paige got up enough nerve to at least look through the peephole, Tamarra had dropped her arms down to her side in defeat and was making her descent from off the porch.

In a split second, Paige's mind began to question whether she should let Tamarra go or open the door and get to the bottom of things. She watched Tamarra walk down the walkway and to her car. Time was running out. She had to think fast . . . think very fast. So Paige closed her eyes, and that's exactly what she began to do: think. In a moment's time, she finally opened the door. She opened the door just in time to see Tamarra's car pull away. She hadn't thought fast enough.

Closing the door and locking it, Paige returned to the bathroom to finish getting ready for work. A half hour later, she too was in her car, pulling off. Digging her cell phone out of her purse, she placed a call. "Hey, Norman, I couldn't remember off the top of my head whether you are on the schedule today," she stated after dialing his cell number.

"Sure am," he replied. "I'm at work now."

"Good. Can you cover for me? An emergency came up. I'm going to be a little late."

"Not a problem. I'll see you when you get here."

Ending the call, Paige made a detour from the path to her job to the path to her best friend's house. There was no way she would have had a productive day at work with thoughts of the possibility of her best friend and her husband having slept together. She needed to find out the truth, and she needed to find out now.

On her drive to Tamarra's house, Paige really didn't have any concerns about whether Tamarra would tell her the truth once she confronted her with the subject matter. Her concern was that once Tamarra did tell her the truth, if it wasn't what she wanted to hear, would she be able to handle the truth?

Chapter Twenty-six

Lorain almost wished she hadn't answered the phone. The loud screech on the other end gave her an instant headache.

"I'm not gonna believe you went to jail and haven't called me and said boo about it. Why is that?" Unique spat, without giving Lorain an opportunity to answer. "I have to hear it from Sister Helen."

"Sister Helen?" Lorain said. "How would she know?"

"Beats me. She told me while I was giving her a complimentary Mary Kay makeover."

"What?" Lorain said angrily. "I offered a free makeover to Sister Helen over a dozen times, and she declined every time. You ask her, and she's all for it?"

"Yep, and she bought over a hundred dollars worth of products too," Unique said proudly. "But don't go trying to change the subject Tweety Jailbird. The kids are at school, so I'm listening without interruption."

"Ugh, it's nothing," Lorain sighed. "Besides, I'm at work. That's not something I want to talk about here."

"Well, just so you know, the word is that Pastor had to bail you out of jail. But not only did Pastor have to bail you out of jail, but she had to do it with church funds."

"Are you serious?" Lorain asked loudly. She then lowered her tone and repeated the question.

"I'm very serious, but remember, you can't talk about it."

"Yes, you're right. I can't," Lorain acknowledged. "But what I will say is that is a dog-faced lie. And besides, I paid Pastor back the bail money already. But that's neither here nor there. Like I said, I can't talk. I'm at work."

"Uh-huh. Likely story." Unique sounded as if she wasn't buying Lorain's reasoning for not wanting to talk. "Anyway, I guess I'll let you go. You can't afford to lose your job. You have two babies to feed. Deuces."

Unique hung up the phone, and for some strange reason, Lorain sat at her desk with a smile on her face. Actually, it wasn't for a strange reason at all. Hearing Unique remind her that in a few months she would be caring for her two granddaughters, who she would raise as her own daughters, put a big smile on her face.

Lorain had to be reminded that life was greater than her and her woes. Although it was important to her that she and her mother mend their relationship, she had to stay focused on what lies ahead. Lorain raised her hand and smacked herself on the forehead. Thinking about her new endeavor of raising children, she was reminded of the parenting classes she had signed up to take. With all that had been going on, she'd already missed the first class that had started yesterday.

"I am not going to start this raising babies thing out on the wrong foot. No, I'm not," Lorain told herself, making a mental note as well as vowing to herself not to miss another week of the six-week session.

Deciding to dive back into her work, Lorain's cell phone rang again. "Darn it, Unique," she mumbled to herself without even looking at the caller ID before actually picking up the phone. "You just don't give up, do you?" Lorain assumed it was Unique calling her back to pick her for more information about her county jail stint. "I promise I'll talk to you on my lunch break," Lorain said into the phone.

"In that case, I'll see you at, let's say, around noon-ish," the masculine voice on the other end of the phone stated.

"Dr. Wright, is that you?" Lorain asked.

"Yes, this is Dr. Wright, but like I told you before, call me Nicholas."

Twice in the last few minutes a smile made Lorain's lips its dwelling. Just hearing the good doctor's voice lifted her spirit. She'd given him her number almost two weeks ago. That day outside of Unique's hospital door when he'd stopped her, he'd offered her his business card. She'd accepted as well as offered him one of hers. He'd not called her until now. Quite frankly, she'd forgotten all about the exchange.

"Doctor, I mean, Nicholas, I'm surprised to hear from you," Lorain informed him.

"I would have loved to call sooner, but it's been crazy here at the hospital," he explained.

"Oh, I can only imagine."

A four-second period of silence filled the phone line.

"Sooo, uhh, are you going to keep that promise?" Nicholas asked.

"Promise?" Lorain was confused, to say the least.

"Yes. When you answered the phone you promised that you'd talk to me at lunch. Any chance we can talk over soup and salad?"

Lorain was yet again surprised. Perhaps not so much surprised as she was caught off guard.

"Hello? Are you still there?" Nicholas asked when Lorain didn't reply.

"Uh, yes, I'm here. I was just looking at my calendar is all," she lied. She quickly began to scan her desk calendar so that she wouldn't be lying after all. "And it looks like I'm available. How does 12:30 P.M. sound?"

"Sounds good to me," Nicholas said with a smile in his tone. "I know a hospital cafeteria doesn't sound too thrilling for a first date, but I'm on call so I need to stay close. Any chance you can meet me here at the hospital?"

"That won't be a problem."

"Good, I'll see you then."

"Bye-bye," Lorain said, then ended the call. "Oh my God," she screeched under her breath. And just like that, once again, she'd forgotten about all her woes. As Lorain worked the morning away, she knew eventually she'd have to try to reach out to her mother, but right now, she wasn't going to allow that situation to keep her in bondage. She was going to keep things moving forward in her life. No looking back.

God, you're just going to have to touch my mother's heart, Lorain prayed. *When she's ready to smash this thing, I'll be waiting.* And how Lorain saw it, at this point, her mother would have to come to her. Not that Lorain had much of a choice. Considering her mother had a restraining order against her, Lorain certainly couldn't go to her.

At around 12:15 P.M., Lorain wrapped things up at her desk and left her office to walk to her car. She'd not eaten all day, so that soup and salad was sounding good. But just being in the presence of Nicholas was sounding even better. She couldn't wait to meet up with him. But as she approached her car, she realized then that she just might have to wait after all.

Chapter Twenty-seven

Margie paced back and forth across the conference-room floor. Her hands were folded, and her lips were moving. No words could be heard, not by man anyway. Only by God.

"Pastor, let me know if you all need anything else."

Margie had forgotten all about her secretary even being in the conference room until she spoke. "Oh, thank you." Margie scanned the room. "But everything looks fine. You can go ahead and make calls to this past Sunday's first-time visitors."

"Will do," the secretary said as she left the room.

Margie continued pacing . . . and praying. "Please, God, let her show up." The "her" Margie was referring to in her prayers was Mother Doreen.

Just like Mother Doreen had warned Margie, she had vacated her house. The entire situation between them just didn't sit well with Margie, not at all. She stayed up all that night praying for answers and direction from God. Although God didn't immediately penetrate her spirit with the answers, by the next afternoon He had. Operating in instant obedience, Pastor began her search for Mother Doreen. With there being only one hotel and one motel in the small city of Malvonia, after figuring out that Mother Doreen wasn't staying with any of her other parishioners, Margie began her search.

She found out Mother Doreen was staying at the hotel. After having the operator transfer her call to Mother Doreen's room, the call went to the hotel automated voice messaging system. It was then that Margie left a message informing Mother Doreen that a board meeting had been called concerning the Singles' Ministry and that she needed to be there. Knowing that the Singles' Ministry was Mother Doreen's project, her baby, so to speak, it was Margie's hope that Mother Doreen would show up to tend to it.

"Looks like I'm the first one here," a voice said, interrupting Margie's pacing . . . and praying.

"Mother Doreen." The relief could be heard in Margie's tone. "You're here."

"Why wouldn't I be?" Mother Doreen held a puzzled expression on her face. "Since when have you known me not to show up for God? As much as He shows up for me, I wouldn't dare miss showing up for Him." Mother Doreen made her way to a conference-room chair. "This *is* about God, isn't it?" Her eyebrows raised.

"Why, yes, of course," Margie assured her.

Mother Doreen was just about to sit down before she asked, "Oh, did I need to wait out in the lobby area first like last time?"

"No, no," Margie replied. "Please sit down."

"This is the day that the Lord has made. We shall rejoice and be glad in it."

Both Mother Doreen and Margie looked at the doorway to see Sister Perrin leading the way of the other board members into the conference room. "Praise God, Pastor, Mother Doreen."

The members, Margie, and Mother Doreen took a minute to greet one another. Once everyone was seated, a prayer was said and the meeting was brought to order.

"The last time we met we discussed the matter of the operation of the Singles' Ministry," Margie reminded them all. Everyone nodded, signaling they all recalled the subject matter. "Well, after prayer and direction from God, I motion that we allow the ministry to begin operating again, effective immediately."

"If that's what God has spoken, Pastor, then I second the motion, of course," the only male board member declared. He then looked around. "All in favor say 'Aye.'"

"Aye," was heard from every board member.

Mother Doreen's facial expression remained neutral, even though she wanted to do a Holy Ghost dance right smack on the middle of the conference-room table.

Margie looked at Mother Doreen. "Well, Mother Doreen, it looks like it's time for you to see God's vision through. I trust you'll operate completely in the provision He's given you as well."

A smile that Mother Doreen couldn't contain settled on her face.

Just then, Sister Perrin cleared her throat. "Uh, well, uh, Pastor . . . are you saying that Mother Doreen here is *still* going to be in charge of the ministry?"

Margie looked around at the other board members whose eyes and facial expressions seemed to be asking that same question.

"Perhaps she can just be like the overseer or something; kind of just remain in the background. But I was thinking someone else could be the face of the ministry."

"Maybe even *you* could be the face of the ministry, like Mother Doreen suggested in the last meeting," one of the board members called out.

Margie looked at that member. "But I thought the last time you were against me having anything to do with the ministry."

"Well, uh, yeah, maybe so. But that was before we found out about . . ." Her eyes wandered to Mother Doreen and then back to Pastor. ". . . you know." She nodded her head discreetly toward Mother Doreen.

The silence that filled the room was deep and heavy.

"Well, I still am against it," Sister Perrin spoke up. "To some degree. But right now, it doesn't look as though we have much choice."

"Look, I don't know what's going on here, but—" Pastor started.

"I think I do, Pastor." Mother Doreen stood. "What's going on is that obviously the board has heard about my . . . well, my past."

Almost every board member's eyes were cast downward, confirming they'd lent their eager ears to church gossip.

"She's right," Sister Perrin confirmed, now lifting her eyes and stiffening her broad shoulders. "I just don't think, knowing what I know now, that Mother Doreen would be the wisest choice to lead the Singles' Ministry. I think it should be someone who . . . who . . ."

"Who doesn't have a jail record?" Mother Doreen finished the sentence for her.

"Exactly," Sister Perrin said matter-of-factly. "As a matter of fact, Pastor, I was going to suggest, in light of this new information we now have on Mother Doreen, that before we place anybody in leadership, that we do a background check. I mean, look at that situation with Sister Lorain and her mother's deceased husband. He was a pedophile operating in his church's youth ministry."

"Oh my," one board member said, shocked.

"Are you serious?" another asked in disbelief.

"Yeah, I heard about that too," one replied.

By this time, Margie was appalled, shocked, and on her feet. "Who told you that?" she demanded to know from Sister Perrin. Her loud and fierce tone had startled everyone in the room. Even when she was preaching God's Word, Margie had never used such a tone. "Who told you all that?" Margie's eyes scanned the room after her fist hit the table.

At this time, Mother Doreen stood. "God is not the author of confusion." She gathered her things. "Right now, I have to really seek God to determine if I'm even going to be a part of this." And on that note, she moved toward the door.

"Do you mean a part of the Singles' Ministry?" Margie asked for clarification.

"No, a part of this church," Mother Doreen replied before leaving.

Margie's body sank back down into her seat. She shook her head in disbelief that New Day seemed to be turning into a playground for the devil himself.

"Pastor, I think we should discuss—" Sister Perrin started.

"Shhh," Margie ordered, holding up her hand to silence Sister Perrin. She rubbed her eyes with her fingers. "Look, I think we need to adjourn for right now, but I need it to go on the record that I still intend to allow the Singles' Ministry to operate, and I still intend on assigning Mother Doreen as the leader of the ministry; that's if she even wants to do it now."

"But, Pastor, you honestly can't believe God really called her to serve in that type of capacity. Her entire crime resulting in a stint in jail was concerning her relationship with a man. So who is she to tell folks how to handle relationships in a godly manner?"

"Who better to lead a drug addict than an ex-drug addict?" Margie declared. "Who better to lead an alcoholic than an ex-alcoholic? Who better to lead a gang member than an ex-gang member?" Margie shook her head and said. "And here I thought all this time I was dealing with mature Christians. My, my, my. Looks like what I need to reconsider is who the face of this church is as far as its board." She stood. "Meeting adjourned." She excused herself and walked to the ladies' room.

"Jesus, Jesus, Jesus," she repeated as she stood over the bathroom sink, still shaking her head in dismay. "Lord, you said no weapon formed against me shall prosper. Well, God, I'm giving you back your Word that it may not return void. No weapon formed against me, the church, or its members shall prosper. I declare such in the name of Jesus. Not even old weapons, Lord. Not anything from the past. I'm asking you to do a new thing, Lord. Do a new thing in my life, oh God, that the church might benefit. Your Word says that my help co-meth from the Lord, O God. If help is what I need, then send it, Lord, right now in the name of Jesus." Margie spoke a few words in tongues. "In Jesus' name, amen."

She washed her hands, dried them, and then went to her office. As she approached the lobby she could see her secretary. She was talking to a man, a very tall man. He was a tall, dark man. Margie couldn't see his face, but she could tell from his hands and the side profile of his face that he had the same complexion of Blair Underwood.

"Oh, Pastor, there you are," the church secretary said upon noticing Margie. "This here is Lance. Lance, this is the pastor, the woman you've been waiting to meet."

Lance turned with an extended hand to the pastor. He was tall. He was dark. And now, from what Margie could see, he was handsome. She shook his hand.

"Well, it was worth the wait," Lance said, shaking her hand firmly. "Because I can feel the anointing all over this woman just by the shake of her hand. Glory," Lance said in reference to Margie but talking to the secretary.

Anointing, Margie thought to herself. Yeah, maybe that's what it was, anointing. Because she could swear that when she shook Lance's hand, she felt something too. Shaking off any thoughts, Margie asked, "So, Lance, you've been waiting to meet me? Did I have an appointment with you for something?"

"Oh, no," the secretary interrupted. "Lance here is my cousin. He's here to take me to lunch. It's just that I talk about you all the time in trying to get him to come visit our church."

"So, you don't attend church?" Was that disappointment Margie heard in her own voice?

"Yes, I do," Lance informed her. "I attend a Baptist church over in Blacklick. But my cousin here is always going on and on about how great a word you deliver and how great you deliver it; and about how I should come visit sometime."

"Oh, okay," Margie nodded. Was that relief she heard in her own voice? "Well, I am a fisher of men, but I don't go fishing in other pastors' ponds. I'm sure you're getting just as good a word over there at your church. Perhaps it is me who might have to come visit there one day." Had Margie *really* said that? She had to ask herself that same question.

"We'd love to have you. There is a women's conference coming up in a few months. I'd love to drop your name in the hat as one of the guest speakers, if you don't mind."

"I, uh, don't mind at all," Margie replied.

After just a few seconds of silence, Lance spoke. "Well, I guess we better get going, cuz," he said to the church secretary. He then turned back to Margie. "Pastor, if you're not too busy, how about you join us? That way, I could run down the theme of the women's conference to you so you can pray on it just in case you're called on as one of the speakers."

"Oh, yes, Pastor, that's a lovely idea," the secretary cosigned. "Besides, you don't have anything on your calendar. And in addition to that, you're always eating in that office of yours. Come on and see how the rest of us do lunch."

"Well . . ." Margie sounded indecisive. With all that had just gone on in the board meeting—Mother Doreen practically threatening to leave the church—she didn't know if she needed to be out having a good ol' time at lunch instead of praying or seeking God for direction and help. But then that's when Margie's thoughts stopped . . . on the word *help*.

Not five minutes ago, had she just said a prayer for herself? Not five minutes ago had she just asked God to send her help? Could—Maybe . . . Was Lance somehow part of God's answer to her prayer? After all, Margie had encountered many men in her lifetime. In her capacity as a pastor, she'd prayed with them and laid hands on them. She couldn't very well recall the last time she'd simply shaken one of their hands and it caused feelings to rise up in her.

"Well, what do you say?" Lance asked Margie.

Without even giving it another moment's thought, Margie replied, "Yes. I don't mind if I do join you two for lunch." To her surprise, though, it would be a lunch for two. After all, three's a crowd anyway.

Chapter Twenty-eight

"I've been worried sick about you," Tamarra said as soon as she opened the front door and saw Paige standing there. "I had to end up having to go and see your pastor at the church. She's the one who told me that you were staying with Sister Nita. I . . . I don't understand, Paige. What's going on? Were you afraid Blake would find you here at my place? Is that why you left without saying anything? You didn't want him to interrogate me regarding your whereabouts so you just didn't want me to know? I mean, what? What is it? Say something." Tamarra had tons of nervous energy.

It wasn't as if Tamarra had even given Paige an opportunity to speak. And eventually she realized just that. "Oh, look at me going on and on. Come on in here." She let Paige in, and then started right back in on her. "I just left Sister Nita's place. I saw your car, but you didn't answer."

"I was in the bath when you knocked. I saw you driving away." Paige wasn't completely lying. She'd just omitted a few things is all.

"Well, sit down." Tamarra pointed to her couch.

"That's okay. I'll stand."

Tamarra detected a hint of coldness in Paige's tone. Not really just a hint, but instead, enough to put a chill on Tamarra's arms.

"But you, on the other hand, might want to sit down," Paige shot.

Tamarra snapped her neck back to take a look at her best friend. She had this cold diva thing going on in her voice, and Tamarra had no idea why. "No, thank you. I think I'll stand too. What's going on?" Tamarra shot right back, with a little diva in her tone as well.

"Blake came up to the church the other day."

"Ewww, I knew this had something to do with that man," Tamarra spat. "Did you call the police? Make sure you tell the judge about it. Isn't the court date coming up here soon?"

"Stop it!" A thunderous boom came blaring out of Paige's voice. She quickly regained her composure and took a deep breath and then exhaled. "Will you just stop it with all the talking and listen? There is something I have to say. Something I have to ask you, and I don't want to lose my nerve."

"Ask me . . . about what?"

"That's what I'm trying to get to if you'd just let me finish." Paige's words were sprinkled about with frustration and agitation.

"Paige, why the attitude? I'm just trying to help. You know I'm here for you. You know I'll always be here for you. That's all I ever tried to be as your friend."

"Really?" Paige said doubtfully.

Tamarra was taken aback; it showed by the expression on her face. "Are you saying that I haven't been trying to be there for you when you've needed me? I mean, you're the one who decided to keep what all you were going through from me. I would have been there for you sooner had I known sooner."

"So, Tamarra, just answer this one question for me. All this time were you really, I mean truly, trying to be there for me? Or were you trying to *be* me?" Paige asked.

Tamarra put her hand on her chest, surprised at Paige's words. Surprised at how Paige was coming at her.

"Blake came by the church, and he said some things," Paige started again. "He alluded to something. Something about him . . . something about you."

Just then, Tamarra looked as if every drop of blood had been drained from her body. Her complexion turned ghastly pale. She even looked as though something were caught in her throat, like she couldn't breathe.

Tamarra's expression alone, and her lack of defending herself against the words Paige had just spoken about her, caused Paige's eyes to water. Her breathing intensified as she filled with hurt and anger. Could it be? Could it be true? Had her best friend slept with her husband?

Paige knew in her spirit it was true. She began shaking her head as tears dripped from her eyes. "No no no no!" she began to weep. "Oh my God. Oh my God." She sounded as if she was beginning to hyperventilate.

"Paige, please, just let me explain. It's not what—"

"Don't you dare!" Paige shouted, putting a flat hand up at Tamarra, who had taken a couple steps toward her. It looked as though she was going to make an attempt to comfort her. "Don't you dare come near me." Paige let out a scream, a wail, a cry so loud that anyone within earshot could feel her pain. Her heart thundered in her chest. Tamarra could feel her pain as tears began to pour from her eyes too.

"Paige, neither of the times were the two of you even married yet," Tamarra tried to explain.

"Neither of the times?" Paige screamed. "How many times were there?"

"Twice," Tamarra mumbled.

So consumed with anger, Paige looked for the nearest thing to pick up and bash Tamarra upside the head with. That first thing was a crystal vase from off of one of Tamarra's side tables.

When Tamarra saw Paige pick it up, she just protected her head with her arms and braced herself.

With the vase gripped in her hand over her shoulder in a position to be thrown, Paige fought off the desire. She lowered her arm with the vase still resting in her hand.

Once Tamarra didn't feel an impact, she peeked between her bended arms to see that Paige was no longer in position to throw the vase. Tamarra slowly lowered her arms to her side. "I'm sorry, Paige. I . . . I didn't know how to tell you. I mean, I tried." Tamarra swallowed tears. "I tried to tell you that day at my house when you told me that Blake had asked you to marry him and you'd said yes."

Paige began laughing and crying, and crying and laughing . . . all at the same time. "So that's it. That's why you reacted the way you did when you found out I was going to marry Blake. It was more than just the fact that you'd set me up to meet him outside of my job. And here I was thinking it had been some powerful, divine setup by God. Oh no, it was much more than that. You not only knew him prior to me meeting him, but you'd slept with him." Paige smacked herself upside the forehead. "Oh my God. I'm so stupid. Why couldn't I have seen this before? I mean, I never really could get why you were making such a big deal out of the fact that you and Blake already knew each other and had mastered this plan to hook him up with me. I mean, it might have been kind of cute—made good for a fairy-tale romance; that is, if you hadn't spread your legs for him, you . . ." Every curse word under the sun was on the tip of Paige's tongue, but she remained in control. "Ugh!" she screamed as loud as she could.

"I'm sorry, Paige. So sorry." Although Tamarra's apology was sincere, it fell upon deaf ears.

"You said you slept with Blake twice. When was the second time?"

"You two still weren't married yet," Tamarra confessed.

"When?" Paige demanded to know.

"It was when I went to him. It had been bothering me that he and I had slept together in the past. I knew it shouldn't have mattered because it was long before you two had ever gotten together."

"Tah, it couldn't have been that long. You hadn't been too long divorced yourself," Paige said, staring at Tamarra in the eyes; that was, until Tamarra's eyes zoomed down to a piece of nonexistent lint on the rug.

"You didn't . . ." Paige said. "You slept with Blake while you were married to Edward?" Paige shook as if she'd just eaten something disgusting.

"It was toward the end of Edward's and my marriage. I was feeling . . . and . . . I did an event for Blake . . . He'd stayed late to help me clean up . . . He was just so slick, so smooth . . . and he knew I was a married woman. He knew it. He was the kind of man who he felt could get any woman he wanted. I could tell that from the start. The way he talked to them and treated them at the function earlier that night. I should have known. And yet, me in my vulnerable state fell right into his trap." Now it was as if Tamarra was talking to herself. "Then when I ran into him a little while later, he still had that same attitude, like he could get any woman he wanted. I wanted him to just meet his match. Meet that woman who would shoot him down after only the first date."

"And that woman was me," Paige figured. "You'd watch me date man after man, none of them ever being good enough and me sending them on their merry way. And that's exactly what you thought I'd do when it came to Blake. You thought I'd destroy his ego once and for all and send him off like a wounded puppy."

"But instead you married him." Tamarra almost said it as if she was angry Paige had ruined her plan. "Talk about a plan backfiring. I mean, he ended up winning over the one woman I thought was for sure going to be Superman's kryptonite."

"So if that's how you felt about him, then why did you sleep with him again?"

"Stupid. Because I was stupid," Tamarra sniffed. "When I went to his place to discuss with him one last time my concerns about not telling you the entire truth, we just ended up . . ."

"It sounds like I'm the one who's stupid," Paige said. "Stupid, stupid girl. I've been running around here all this time—" Paige cut her own self off. "Does anyone else know?"

Tamarra hesitated. "Your pastor does, but I just told her today when I went up to the church. I was afraid this is why you'd left. I just got this sickening feeling in my stomach, the same feeling I always got when I figured there was a chance of you finding out."

Paige held her arm over her eyes and just began to cry hard. In between cries she managed to ask, "When? When was the second time you and Blake . . ."

Now it was Tamarra who covered her eyes with her arms and began to bawl like a baby.

Unmoved by the obvious hurt and regret Tamarra was experiencing, Paige stared at her coldly and yelled, "When?"

"It was right before I came to the church to help you get dressed," Tamarra cried.

"Get dressed for wh . . . in my wedding gown . . . *for my wedding?*" Paige spoke between tears. "You slept with him the day of my wedding?"

"I'm so sorry," Tamarra continued apologizing.

"Ahhhh!" Paige screamed as she charged toward Tamarra with the vase raised over her head. Once again, Tamarra assumed the position. She shielded her head with her arms. Once again, the expected blow never came.

Paige's flesh and the Holy Ghost fought like cats and dogs to control the hand that held the vase. It trembled back and forth in the air until finally her fingers released it, and it crashed to the floor, spraying sparkling shrapnel. Paige just stood there taking in deep breaths, and then exhaling them. Finally she had stopped crying, wiped her eyes with the heels of her hands, and regained complete composure of herself.

She walked over to Tamarra's front door, opened it, and prepared to leave. As she exited Tamarra's house, she told her, "Let me know how much I owe you for the vase," and was on her way.

Chapter Twenty-nine

Lorain hadn't even noticed Eleanor's car parked close to hers. She'd even been looking down, fiddling with her keys as Eleanor got out of the car.

"We need to talk," were the words that made their way through Eleanor's mouth and into Lorain's ears.

"Mom?" Shocked, surprised, elated; those were just some of the words that could describe how Lorain felt. "What . . . what are you doing sitting out here?"

"Waiting for you. Well, not really waiting for you . . . just . . ."

"Have you been out here long? Why didn't you come in and have the receptionist call me to the lobby? You didn't have to wait out here. I mean, what if I'd decided to eat lunch at my desk or something? You could have even called me, and I could have come down and met you."

"I know, dear," Eleanor finally spoke. "I guess I just didn't know what I was going to say to you is all."

Lorain allowed her mother to gather her thoughts in the silence that separated them.

"I'm sorry I had you hauled off to jail."

"You had every right to. The way I was acting, not to mention the fact that I . . ." Lorain cringed every time the thought crossed her mind, let alone having to speak on it. ". . . that I hit you." She ran her hands down her short, edgy haircut.

"It's not like I didn't deserve it. I mean, with all those god-awful things I said to you."

"They said worse and did worse to Jesus, and yet, He never said a mumbling word. I had no right . . . no right at all . . . to lift a hand to you. No right to do that to a stranger on the street, let alone my mother. So, will you forgive me, Mother?" Lorain asked.

"I forgive you. But I need you to forgive me too."

"Of course," Lorain replied. "That goes without saying."

"Yeah, but I still needed to hear it." There was silence again before Eleanor spoke. "It's been a long time since I've cooked a big dinner. I was thinking about making your favorites, maybe tomorrow for dinner or something."

"That sounds nice, although I don't think I need to be rewarded with my favorite dishes."

"Oh, it's not for you."

"Huh?" Lorain felt that in the gut.

"I, mean, it's not *just* for you anyway. See, I was kind of thinking that maybe you could invite my gran . . . granddaughter . . . my granddaughter and great-grandkids," Eleanor managed to get out.

Lorain's jaws dropped. "Mom, are you serious?"

"Yeah. Why wouldn't I be? I mean, they're blood. They're my blood. I don't care how they got here. They're here now, and they're mine. They're ours."

Lorain was speechless.

"So will you call her and ask her?" Eleanor asked. "Do you think she'll agree?"

"I . . . I don't see why not." Lorain could barely speak through the smile on her face. All of a sudden the smile faded though. "Then again . . ."

"What? What is it?" Eleanor asked.

"Well, Unique and I haven't told her kids about me yet, let alone you. Maybe she can just come to dinner."

"Oh, no. If we're gonna do this thing, we're gonna do it right. I'm not about to go through all of this mess twice; once for her, and then again for her kids. You and her might have thought it was a good idea to keep all of this on the down low, but look how that turned out. I won't be a part of it." With eyes closed and arms folded, Eleanor stood in the parking lot shaking her head.

"Perhaps you're right. Besides, I'm sure the kids at church are going to start talking. All it's going to take is for one of them to overhear their parents talking on the phone or something and go run and tell it to the boys in children's church."

"And trust me, through the grapevine is no way for them youngins to find out. Take it from me," Eleanor declared.

"I have to agree with you there. I'll give Unique a call. Maybe she can go ahead and have the talk with the boys. That way, it will all pretty much be out in the open by the time they arrive for dinner." Lorain just looked up at the big blue sky. "Hallelujah!" she shouted, not caring who heard her. "Thank you, Jesus!" She had a praise that she had to get out. "Oh, thank you, God." Her praise was turning into joyful tears.

"Stop that now before you have me over here crying," Eleanor demanded of her daughter, fluttering her tears away before they could drop.

"Mom, I'm just so happy. God is so faithful. He has His hand in everything. I mean, just when things look crazy and you feel like you're going to go out of your mind, when everything feels so out of order that you can hardly focus, God shows up and shows out. He reminds us that it doesn't matter how bananas things look like in our eyes, He is God, and He is a God of order. Our madness is part of His method, and we have to learn to just stop trying to figure this thing out and allow Him to be God. That's all I'm saying." Lorain sniffed and wiped away her tears.

"And you've said it all, right there," Eleanor said, this time unable to keep her tears from falling.

"Oh, Mom." Lorain raced over to her mother, and the two embraced for what seemed like forever.

Finally, Eleanor pulled away. "Go on and get now. I gotta run so I can go to the store and start getting the things I'm going to need for tomorrow's dinner. Besides, you wouldn't want to get arrested, would you?"

"What?" Lorain replied.

"Remember, there's a restraining order out on you. You're not supposed to be all up on me like this."

"Oh, Mom," Lorain chuckled.

"I'm just teasing. I had it lifted before I came here to see you. I didn't want to jeopardize you getting arrested and all once again."

"I appreciate that, Ma," Lorain told her. "Well, I'm going to go inside and call Unique. I'll call you later, okay?" Lorain kissed her mother on the cheek.

"All right. Bye, dear," Eleanor said before getting in her car and leaving.

As Lorain galloped back into her office building, the smile on her face was plastered there so hard, she'd probably need a doctor to remove it. Speaking of a doctor, Lorain was so excited about her breakthrough with her mother and that she wanted to share the news with Unique that she didn't give her lunch date with Doctor Nicholas Wright a second thought.

Chapter Thirty

After her lunch with Lance, Margie felt compelled to go see about Mother Doreen. It wasn't until she arrived back at the church that she even remembered the episode in the conference room that had taken place prior to her lunch with Lance. It was a lunch that initially was supposed to be with both Lance and her secretary. As they were getting ready to leave, though, the secretary suddenly remembered a doctor's appointment that she had and couldn't reschedule.

"I've rescheduled the appointment once before. I can't do it again," the secretary had told her cousin and Pastor. "You two just go ahead and enjoy lunch without me."

And that's exactly what Lance and Margie did; enjoy lunch. As a matter of fact, Margie couldn't remember the last time she'd enjoyed herself so much. And there had not been one moment of talk about the church, church members, issues of the church, or the church's ministries. Arriving back at church, she almost felt guilty when she sat back down in her office to tend to church business.

Was this normal? Was it normal for a pastor to not feel like a pastor for just one hour of the day? Because for the first time since Margie could remember, she hadn't felt like a pastor. She'd felt like a . . . a . . . What was the word her mind searched for?

"A woman," she said out loud.

"Excuse me? What did you say, Pastor?" The church secretary suddenly appeared in the doorway.

"Oh, my goodness, you scared me," Margie chuckled. "Oh, don't mind me." Margie shooed her hand. "I was just talking to myself."

"Well, you must have really been enjoying the conversation, because you had a starry look in your eyes that shined so bright that it could have reached Lake Michigan."

"Oh." Margie quickly straightened up and allowed a more serious pastorlike look to cover her face.

"No need to put on a mask for me. Go on and let it out." The secretary invited herself into Margie's office, where she closed the door behind her and took a seat across from Margie.

"Let what out?" Margie played dumb.

"Come on, Pastor, I've been your secretary for years, and I've never seen that look in your eyes before. Now, don't get me wrong. I've seen the look before, just never on you. So spill it. It was lunch with Lance, wasn't it?"

Margie sat in her chair looking just as serious as she could for as long as she could. Just when she thought she was about to bust, she let it fall from her lips. "I enjoyed lunch with your cousin so much I feel ashamed," Margie admitted. "His conversation was just so exciting, so engaging. The fact that he travels all over the country on his job sounds so exotic. That also explains why I've never met him before in all the years you've been my secretary."

"Ashamed? What in the world do you have to feel ashamed of? It wasn't anything but lunch."

"I know," Margie downplayed it.

"Besides, you deserve to have a fine man like Lance taking you out."

"Whoa, hold up." Margie put her hands up. "He didn't 'take me out.' It just happened to end up being the two of us, remember? You were supposed to be there. It was never just supposed to be him and me."

The secretary's eyes wandered off to an old water spot on the ceiling as guilt plastered her face.

"Wait a minute." Margie's eyes squinted in as she examined the look on her secretary's face. "There was no doctor's appointment, was there?"

The secretary nearly sank down in her chair.

"You set me up, Vegas. How could you?"

It was clear that Margie was upset. The only other time she'd ever called her secretary by her first name was when she failed to put a speaking engagement on her calendar. She'd been so embarrassed when she received a call from the event coordinator questioning her about being a no-show.

"Pastor, I'm sorry," Vegas apologized as she stood. "But had I just had him outright ask you out, there's no way you would have agreed to go. So we didn't have a choice."

"We? Do you mean Lance knew he was going to end up having lunch with me alone all along?"

Vegas nodded.

"Wow, talking about tampering with fate. When will folks, especially *Christian* folks, just sit back for once and let God have His way? For real. He's God all by Himself. He doesn't need your help, or anyone else's, for that matter."

"I'm . . . I'm sorry, Pastor. I had no idea you'd get this upset. It was just lunch."

"Sure, it was just lunch, but it was lunch with a man. You could have at least asked me first."

"Ohhhh, I get it." Vegas tapped herself upside the head. "You're right, Pastor. I should have asked you first. I should have never taken it upon myself to just assume that you'd want to date somebody like Lance. I mean, even people who aren't prejudiced still might have an issue dating outside of their race," Vegas concluded.

Margie turned quickly and shot her secretary a sharp stare. "Do you think I have a problem being out with Lance because he's black and I'm white?" Margie questioned. "Because that would be the furthest thing from the truth. His race has nothing to do with this." Margie raised her arms. "Look around. I'm surrounded by people outside of my race. Eighty-five percent of the New Day members are African American. They look just like Lance."

"Yeah, but preaching to black folks is one thing; dating them just might be another," Vegas reasoned.

Okay, this was the last time Margie was going to be offended, and that was that. Flinging back her blond hair, Margie allowed her eyelids to cover her blue eyes. She said a silent prayer to God before opening her eyes and facing the woman who had been her secretary since she began pastoring at New Day. "I hope you don't think that just because I'm a white woman that I'd have a problem dating a black man."

That's exactly what Vegas had thought. She knew that Margie was pastor to a flock that was predominantly black. She'd seen Margie pray with them, pray for them, lay hands on them, whatever. Heck, she'd even allowed one to move in with her. But when it came to relationships, actually dating someone outside of one's own race, even Vegas knew that might be where some people drew the line. But that wasn't the issue in Margie's case.

"Did you *not* hear what I said earlier?" Margie asked her secretary. "I had a wonderful time at lunch with

Lance. I don't care if he were green. What I have a problem with is being tricked and manipulated."

"Well, I'm sorry you feel that way, Pastor. Honestly, I didn't see it as tricking or manipulating you." With a long face, Vegas stood and walked toward the doorway.

"Wait a minute, I'm sorry," Margie apologized. "I didn't mean to be so harsh. It's just that this entire thing about me being a single pastor, a single *female* pastor, has me a little spent. Forgive me."

"Sure, Pastor," Vegas said. "I forgive you."

"Good. Please just forget about everything I've said."

"Not a problem, Pastor," Vegas said, then pushing the issue continued. "So does that mean you'll go out with Lance again?"

"Oh, no," Margie went and sat back down in her chair.

"Why, Pastor? Lance is a good man. I wouldn't have set you up with just any old body. Don't punish him for my mistake."

"Vegas, you just don't understand . . . that man . . . that man could finish my sentences. It was like he *knew* me," Margie said about Lance.

"And what's so wrong with that?"

"Nobody should know me that well; nobody but God. It was scary. Scary enough to make me forget that I was a pastor."

"Humph."

"What was that for?"

"Oh, nothing," answered Vegas. "It sounds to me like this is a dead issue, so I'm just going to return to my office. And again, Pastor, I apologize for interfering in your private life. It won't happen again." Although Vegas hated throwing in the towel, she didn't want to jeopardize her relationship with her pastor by pressing the issue. If it was meant to be for Margie to eventually become her cousin-in-law, it would have to be through the grace of God.

"Thank you, I appreciate that. But please do tell your cousin that I had a wonderful time and thanks again for lunch, but that will be our last lunch together. If I'm gonna get set up, I want a divine setup." Pastor winked at Vegas. She opened her Bible to Psalm 37:23 as Vegas exited.

"The steps of a good man are ordered by the Lord . . ."

Margie looked up and smiled after reading that scripture. "I hear you, Lord, and that's just what I told my secretary."

Margie continued to read the Bible, but after awhile she couldn't seem to focus on the words. That lunch with Lance had stirred something in her that she didn't know what to do with. She now knew firsthand why a Singles' Ministry was so important to have in the church. "I know, I still hear you, God," Margie said, getting up from her desk and leaving to go see about Mother Doreen.

Chapter Thirty-one

Paige felt like an infant, curled up in Norman's arms in her office, crying like she'd just lost her best friend. Funny thing was, she had just lost her best friend. She'd lost trust as well.

"I hurt, Norman," Paige cried. "My heart hurts. It really, physically hurts."

"I know. I know." This was all new to Norman, this comforting women thing. His experience with women had mostly been sexual—intimate. But here lately, when it came to Paige, he'd had to take on roles he'd never played before. First, he was defending her from her husband, and now he was playing the comforter. He didn't know he had it in him.

"No, you don't know." Paige lifted her head from Norman and pulled herself away from him. "And I hope you never find out."

"It's going to be okay. I know it hurts right now, but it's only going to get better. It always does. It has too. You have to get it together. It's not even an option. It's a matter of life and death—mine."

Paige looked at her coworker strangely. "What do you mean?"

"I mean, if you break, then I'm pretty much broken. You're the one I look to for strength . . . you know, like Pastor says . . . to walk this thing out."

Paige shook her head. "So those three times a year you come to church, you really are listening?"

"Hey, I told you once before that I'm listening. And enough of the wisecracks here. I'm serious."

"I'm sorry, it's just that you always appear to be so together."

"It's not an appearance, I actually am together. And I'm together because of you. I watch you, Paige. I see how you handle things; situations and people. I've seen you go through a great deal of things, and each and every time you've held strong in your faith. You've never let anything break you. I know there were times you might have felt a little bit bent out of shape, but broken . . ." Norman shook his head. ". . . uh, un . . . never. And because of that, Paige, I know there is a God. Yeah, I know I used to give you a hard time at first when you got all," Norman used his fingers to make quotation marks, "saved, sanctified, and Holy Ghost-filled."

Paige chuckled.

"But that's because I was jealous."

"Jealous?" Paige questioned.

"Yes, jealous. I used to be your go-to guy. The one you talked to all the time. Then He took over." Norman nodded upward. "God stole my partner in crime from me. And try as I might to pull you back over here into the world with me, you just wouldn't take my bait."

"You little . . ." Paige play punched Norman in the arm. "All this time you had me thinking that I wasn't acting Christian enough or something; like I wasn't doing this Christian thing right. I would try to figure out what I was doing so wrong that you couldn't see the God in me and see that I had changed. Then Blake came along looking, talking, and acting like he could see all of that and then some in me." Paige shook her head.

"I hate to think that my actions are partly to blame for you hooking up with that—"

"Hey, watch it. That—whatever you were going to call him—is still my husband . . . for now anyway."

"So you're really thinking about throwing in the towel on your marriage?"

"I don't want to, but I can't hang around thinking I can save someone that only God can save. And not even God can save Blake if he doesn't want to be."

"That's true. So what are you going to do?"

"Just keep praying that God will lead me, give me a sign, show me the way . . . something," Paige replied. "The court date for the charges the state filed against him is tomorrow morning at nine o'clock." She looked at the clock on her desk. "Think God can give me my answer within the next fourteen hours or so?"

"You never know," Norman replied. "After all, He is God."

"You got that right," Paige agreed. "Well, you better get back out to the ticket booth. What's her name is probably having a fit relieving you."

"So what. Let her. My best friend needs a shoulder to cry on right now, and I have to be here for her."

"Oh, that's sweet, Norman, but you don't have to pretend that I'm your best friend just because I just lost mine."

A sad look swept across Norman's face. "Pretend? Paige, you really *are* my best friend. I mean, have you ever heard me talk about anybody else being just a friend, let alone a best friend? The things I've shared with you over the years, I've never shared with anyone else. All these years I've truly looked at you like a best friend; a real true friend. I guess I kind of thought you felt the same about me."

"Really, Norman?" Paige was surprised. "That's really how you've seen me over the years?" Paige was truly touched. She'd honestly had no idea what a pertinent role she'd played in Norman's life, both on a personal and spiritual level. A tear formed in her eye.

"Yes, really." Norman noticed Paige tearing up and walked over to her. "Don't cry. You've shed enough tears for the day already."

"It's just that the people who I knew to be—who I thought to be my best friends—hurt me so badly. And all along, God's had you right here the entire time. I'm so sorry for not seeing that, Norman."

"You have nothing to be sorry about. Like I said, you've been the best friend any person could ever have. If Tamarra and Blake want to mess that up, then that's too bad for them. That just leaves more of you for me to love."

The word *love* seemed to have caught both Paige and Norman off guard. It became sort of awkward at that moment.

"Well, uh, I'm gonna . . . go . . . back out to the ticket booth." Norman walked backward toward the office door. "What's her name is probably, you know, uh . . ."

"Yeah, uh, I know." Paige was amused by Norman's nervous reaction to letting the word *love* slip out. Love in any form or fashion was not his MO.

"Okay, then, I'll see you—" Norman turned and ran smack into the door. He instantly grabbed his nose. "Ow, shhh—" He caught himself from letting a curse word slip.

"Careful," Paige flinched. Norman had hit the door pretty hard. She knew that had to hurt.

"Yeah, I'm gonna go to the concession stand and grab some ice first."

"Yeah, you do that," Paige agreed. "Oh, yeah, and Norman," Paige called out as he opened the door and walked out.

"Yes?" He turned around, still holding his nose in pain.

"I love you too . . . friend."

The painful expression that had just been on Norman's face quickly faded. It was as if Paige's words wiped all the pain away. He simply smiled and left her office.

Paige smiled too as she flopped down in her chair. Unfortunately, that smile wouldn't be long-lived. In less than fourteen hours, in Courtroom B on the tenth floor of the courthouse, there would be absolutely nothing to smile about.

Chapter Thirty-two

"I don't know. What if this is all just some kind of setup?" Unique asked through the phone.

"Setup?" Lorain replied. "How in the world do you suppose my mama could be setting us up?" Lorain had gone back to her desk and immediately shared with Unique her mother's invitation for dinner the next night. Lorain was still ecstatic and overjoyed. Unique, on the other hand, was suspicious.

"I don't know. I just can't see her turning over a new leaf and accepting me and my kids just like that." Lorain could hear the snapping of Unique's fingers through the phone.

"*Just like that?* Are you serious?" Lorain begged to differ. "The woman has been slapped, I've been locked up, and you talking about 'just like that'? We've been through the fire in just the little bit of time she's known the truth about you. Besides, I've been praying, and prayer works, obviously."

"Why are you so amped about a dinner?"

"And why are you so scared?" There was silence on the line. "Huh, Unique? Tell me, why are you so scared?"

"Who said anything about me being scared?"

"What else could it be? I mean, can you honestly say this is something that you haven't dreamed about just once? You being with your biological family?"

"Yeah, sitting around like one big happy family one minute, and then the next thing you know, someone is fighting and going to jail. I'm not sure if I want to involve my boys in all of that. They've been doing just fine not knowing, so who's to say that knowing will make things better?"

"Who's to say it won't?" Lorain countered. "Come on, Unique, where is all of this coming from? I thought this is what you wanted."

"No, this is what *you* wanted. You're the one who is probably still running around feeling guilty and just want to make things all better over spaghetti and garlic bread."

"That's not true. Well, I mean, yes, I want things to be right between us, but I know it's going to take more than a dinner. But this is a start, Unique. Can't you see that? My mother is putting forth an effort. The least we can do is meet her halfway."

"Why tomorrow? Why so soon?"

"Why not tomorrow?"

"Let me pray about it and see what—"

"Will you stop it already?" Lorain snapped. Unique had brought her down off of her high. "Stop stalling. Stop making excuses. Stop being afraid."

"I'm not afraid!" Unique yelled back.

"You are, and that's what I don't get. There's nothing to be afraid of."

"There's plenty to be afraid of," Unique begged to differ.

"Like what?"

"Like this not being real. Like us getting together to have some fancy dinner, pretending to be a family; then the next thing I know, you take these two babies, and then you throw me away again just like before. Only this time, it will be worse, because this time, you'll be tossing my boys right alongside of me."

Lorain could hear Unique's voice crack and could tell that she was crying. At that moment she felt so selfish. She hadn't looked at things from Unique's perspective. "I'm sorry, Unique. I'm sorry that you feel that way. Maybe you do need some time to pray on it. But before you do, please hear me when I say this. I love you. I love you and the boys so much." Now it was Lorain's voice that was starting to crack. "I'd stop breathing first before I ever let you out of my life again. And if in the back of your mind you think I'm trying to use your babies to make up for what I did to you, you're wrong. Dead wrong. Babies or no babies, Unique, you are my baby. You are my firstborn. Nothing and no one will ever be able to replace you. Ever. And I mean that from the bottom of my heart."

Waiting for some type of reply from Unique, all Lorain heard on the other line was some sniffling. "Look, I'm going to let you go," Lorain said. "Try to get some rest. Just call me tomorrow and let me know what you decided. Bye, Unique." Lorain ended the call wondering how one minute she could be on cloud nine and the next minute she felt as if she were at ground zero.

"I need some air," Lorain said to herself. She stood up from her desk and walked back outside. As she made her way through the reception area and out of the door, that's when she crashed right into the gentleman coming inside. "Oh, goodness, I'm so . . . Nicholas?" Lorain was stunned to see Nicholas standing there with a take-out bag in his hand.

"It's Chinese," Nicholas stated. "I hope you like Chinese. I figured that maybe a hospital cafeteria wasn't the best place to take a lady on a first date. I figured that's why you didn't show up."

Instantly realizing she'd forgotten all about her lunch date with him, Lorain's hand flew over her mouth. "Oh my goodness. I'm so sorry. I didn't mean to stand you up. It's just that when I got to my car my mother was out there, and she forgave me and I forgave her, and then she wanted to have dinner, and then . . ." Before Lorain knew it, she was standing there in tears trying to explain to Nicholas all that had gone on in the last forty-five minutes.

People walked by and looked strangely at the couple as Lorain whined on and on. An entire five minutes must have gone by before she stopped talking and just buried her face in Nicholas's white hospital coat. She cried hysterically as he held the take-out bag, not knowing how to react. Finally, he spoke. "I guess you really don't like Chinese, do you? I knew I should have gone with Italian."

Chapter Thirty-three

By the time Margie arrived at the hotel where Mother Doreen had been staying, went inside, and requested the clerk inform Mother Doreen she had a visitor, she was surprised to hear the clerk say, "You just missed her. Miss Tucker checked out already."

She'd missed her indeed. Mother Doreen was now driving down the highway with less than thirty minutes to go before crossing the Kentucky state line.

That entire scene in the church conference room had really gotten to Mother Doreen. She couldn't believe herself that she'd even threatened to leave New Day. "But that's exactly what the devil wants me to do," she'd spoken to herself out loud. She wasn't about to leave the only church home she's ever really known in Ohio. Not because of man and not because of the devil.

Never let man keep you from the church. Never let man keep you from growing closer to God, Mother Doreen recalled her pastor preaching.

That's exactly what Mother Doreen had almost let happen. Those board members had made her so angry. She couldn't have cared less if she ever stepped foot in that church again. She had prayed all the way back to her hotel. Come to think of it, it hadn't really been much of a prayer; just a bunch of complaining about a few of God's saints; namely the ones who served on the New Day Temple of Faith board.

By the time she got back to her hotel room, God had brought something back to her remembrance. It was that day she stood in Deborah's living room where she witnessed her get delivered from old demons. Deborah had been the co-leader of the Singles' Ministry up under Mother Doreen. The two women had gotten pretty close as a result of working together on the ministry. So close that Mother Doreen learned that Deborah had been haunted by a late-term abortion she'd gotten.

Mother Doreen recalled the words she'd spoken to Sister Deborah. *"God says you ain't finished yet. . . . Whatever this thing is inside of you that you are holding back, give it to Him, child."* Mother Doreen placed her hand on Deborah's stomach. *"You've got to birth it out of you. God said He's been trying to push it out of you Himself. He's been using people and situations to get you to push it out, but you won't let go. What you have inside of you is taking up space. See, God wants to birth something new in you, but you won't make room for it because you're protecting that thing that's stillborn inside of you. God says what you have in there is dead. Push that dead thing out so He can birth new life in you."*

Mother Doreen began to cry a river as she recalled those very words. She cried tears of joy, for the message God was using her to give had been for the messenger first. It was Mother Doreen who needed to take heed to those very words.

"The accuser has been standing up there telling God all about it. Now it's your time to shut the accuser up. Send him to hell where he belongs. . . . Send the accuser to hell with nothing more to say to God about you that you haven't already told Him yourself."

"Oh, God, I thank you, Lord," Mother Doreen had begun to shout in her hotel room. "I thank you for opening my eyes at this very moment so that I may see what you've been trying to get me to do in my life. You've been trying to get me to share my story . . . my whole story. But I wouldn't tell it, so the devil did. But I'm shutting Satan up today, Lord. Yes, I am," Mother Doreen declared.

Mother Doreen closed her eyes and thought back to how Deborah had confessed that she had killed someone. Ironically, that was Mother Doreen's confession too. Deborah had aborted her baby in the last trimester of her pregnancy. Mother Doreen had killed another woman's baby who was in the last trimester of her pregnancy. She'd never told a soul until confessing it to Pastor. She hadn't even told her own family. She didn't want anybody to know. Everyone she knew looked up to her; her sister, her brother-in-law, her niece, and her nephew. Heck, she was even looked at as one of the church mothers at New Day. How would anyone have possibly looked up to her had they known she killed someone? A baby, no less? It had been the baby of one of her late husband Willie's mistresses.

"But that's my past!" Mother Doreen had shouted in the hotel room. "I will not be bound by my past. I will not be robbed of my future because of my past. And dang on it, I will not be robbed of the husband you let find me, Lord." And with that being declared, Mother Doreen packed up her things, hit the highway, and drove to Kentucky.

It wasn't long before she pulled up in front of her destination. She turned off the car and tried to release some of the nervous energy she had all balled up inside of her. At first, she was going to say a little prayer about what she was about to do. She closed her eyes and folded her hands.

"I've done enough praying about it. Now it's time to move." Mother Doreen had heard God speak to her concerning this situation. She didn't need Him to keep repeating Himself.

She opened her eyes and went to open the car door. That's when she saw something that disturbed her. It was the man she'd claimed as her husband the entire ride there escorting another woman out of his house. She took note of Pastor Frey's hand on the woman's back and the way the woman smiled, seeming to like his touch.

All of that fire Mother Doreen had just had only moments ago seemed to fizzle out just like that. With her hand still on the handle of the slightly opened car door, Mother Doreen watched Pastor Frey converse with this woman. They looked into each other's eyes like they knew each other . . . knew things about each other that no one else in the world knew.

Once Mother Doreen saw Pastor Frey grab the woman's hands, she couldn't stand to sit there and torture herself any longer. She closed the car door, started it up, and pulled off. Pastor Frey had been so into speaking to his lady friend that he never even noticed her car in the first place. He never even noticed her.

By the time Mother Doreen hit the stop sign at the corner, a tear had fallen from her eye. "Instant obedience," Mother Doreen said to herself, figuring she'd waited too long to do what she needed to do.

Although God had initially given her the vision for the Singles' Ministry, Mother Doreen knew that it was only to prepare her for the other vision she'd suppressed; that one day she would marry again. That God would send her a husband.

"Looks like I blew the latter, Lord," she spoke out loud.

Mother Doreen was so bummed and down and out that she wasn't even going to go see her family who were only fifteen minutes from Pastor Frey's place. Then she'd have to explain why she'd come there in the first place and go through the embarrassment of telling them the outcome. Figuring she'd have to crawl back to her pastor, apologize, and repent for her fleshly threats of possibly leaving the church—knowing darn well God hadn't told her to consider any such a thing—she was going to suffer enough humiliation.

Turning left at the stop sign, Mother Doreen drove toward the highway that would take her back to Malvonia, Ohio. Just as she was about to turn on the entrance ramp, she heard the words, *"You ain't finished."* And like a puppet under a puppeteer's control, she turned her car around.

"Oh, it's about to be finished, God," she declared with a passion, "once and for all."

Chapter Thirty-four

Paige arrived at the courthouse with Nita by her side. She honestly didn't know if she'd make it through this. It was like the closer she got to the courtroom, the more the spirit of fear rose up in her.

What am I afraid of? she kept asking herself. Blake hadn't come around and tried to harm her since the day at the church. So why was her stomach aching? Why were her palms sweating? Why were her hands shaking?

The unknown; it was the fear of the unknown that had Paige on edge. She knew that whatever happened in this courtroom today was going to play a part in her future as Mrs. Blake Dickenson. Even up to this very moment, to this very second, she still believed that God could heal her marriage. She knew God could heal her marriage. He could do all things. But did Blake want to be healed? A great deal of the marriage being repaired required some healing and deliverance, and that included Paige too. She knew she wasn't perfect by any means, but she served a perfect God who could do a perfect work in both her and her husband. God knew her heart. God knew her desires, but none of that mattered to Paige.

"God, do your perfect will," was all she asked as she and Nita got on the elevator that would take her to the courtroom.

As the elevator doors closed, Nita and Paige stood side by side. Nita reached down and took Paige's hand and began to pray. "Father God, we come to you asking that you prepare that courtroom right now in the name of Jesus. Touch the atmosphere up in that place, O God, so that it is conducive to the work you are going to do in there."

Both Nita and Paige stood with their eyes closed, so neither cared that the elevator was jammed-packed with folks probably looking at them like they were crazy. Nita continued. "Father God, we know that Satan is always so ever ready to do his evil works in man's life and through man, but Father God, we know he is defeated. Yes, Satan has been defeated, but we must always be mindful to know that he is not destroyed. So we won't let down our guard, Lord. We will keep on your full armor, O Lord, as you bring Paige out of this situation. As you allow her to come through with the victory, no matter what it looks like. In your precious Son's name we pray, Jesus Christ, amen."

The array of "Amens" that Paige heard around her nearly brought her to her knees. Almost everyone on that elevator, without her even knowing, had touched and agreed in the prayer Nita had just recited. And there were at least seven other people on the elevator. Paige tried counting in her head how many demons had just been put to flight to the pits of hell. The elevator stopped on her floor before she could do the math.

"O devil, all I know is that you gon' get it now," Paige declared as she stepped off the elevator and walked boldly to the appointed courtroom. It was as if with each and every step she took, that spirit of fear was shedding off her as she began to walk in the authority given to the heiress of a throne. "Yes, Lord. Hallelujah. I thank you, Lord. Glory," she said softly, but loud enough for Nita to hear, who was having a time keeping up with her.

"That's right, praise Him," Nita mumbled beside her. "Praise Him like Paul and Silas praised Him," Nita encouraged. "Paul and Silas praised God with their hands in chains. Paul and Silas praised God with their feet chained up. They had blood pouring from their backs, but they praised Him." Nita reminded Paige of the Bible story where, despite the pain Paul and Silas were going through, they still had praise for God.

"Hallelujah," Paige said.

"That's right, give Him the highest praise," Nita continued to cheer her on. "Remember, as Paul and Silas praised God, the Lord Almighty shook the prison they were being held captive in. The walls of that prison came tumbling down, and they were set free. Your walls are all falling down right now, Sister Paige. You're being set free in the name of Jesus," Nita boldly declared.

And that's exactly what Paige felt like, as if she were being set free, and right there in the courthouse. "Praise God," was all she could mumble. "Praise God."

Paige was on such a high that she didn't even realize she'd passed up some members of New Day. She didn't realize that she'd passed up the courtroom too, that was, until Nita informed her. Getting herself together, Paige backtracked and entered the courtroom. Her knees, for the second time in the past five minutes, nearly gave way again when she entered the courtroom to see her pastor, her choir director, and a couple other members of her church family there for support. But her heart really smiled when she saw her mother and father sitting there. She'd made it a point to not share everything that was going on in her and Blake's marriage with them. She didn't want them to know what she was going through. But, "a mother knows," her mother had told her over the phone one day.

"Thank you, Jesus." Paige began to weep tears of joy. "Thank you, Jesus." She then spoke to her supporters. "Thank you all for being here. Thank you so much." Paige was feeling way too much love and joy right now to be consumed with even an ounce of fear. Too bad, though, as her eyes scanned the row behind where the New Day members were sitting, anger decided to rear its ugly head. "Get out of here. How dare you. The nerve." Paige couldn't help that those words had escaped through her lips so quickly.

Everyone immediately looked behind them to see who Paige was directing her angry words toward.

"I just wanted to be here to show you some support," Tamarra spoke up, feeling two feet tall instead of the five feet nine inches that she was. It was written all over her face that perhaps she should have reconsidered showing up in court today, but it was too late. She was already there. But not for long. Not if Paige had anything to do with it.

"You've done enough, now leave!" Paige spat. That's when the bailiff began eyeballing the situation.

Figuring she'd witnessed enough people be escorted in handcuffs, Margie turned and said, "Please, Sister Tamarra . . ." her eyes urged Tamarra to just go for now. Tamarra had come to Margie's office the day before looking for Paige. She was worried sick and concerned about her whereabouts. Paige hadn't been taking Tamarra's calls. Margie knew how close the two women were, so just to keep Tamarra from worrying herself into an anxiety attack, she informed her that Paige was safe and sound at Nita's. That didn't seem to remove the worry from Tamarra. Just knowing where Paige was hadn't been enough. She needed to know why she'd just up and left without saying anything. Next thing Margie knew, Tamarra was confessing her reasons as to why Paige might have pulled a disappearing act. Obviously, Tamarra had been correct in her assumptions.

The church sanctuary was not the time or the place for Eleanor to confront Lorain about Unique, nor was the courtroom the time and the place for Paige and Tamarra to have it out. So without another word having to be said, Tamarra stood and exited the courtroom.

Paige spotted the detective that had been handling her case sitting behind the prosecution. Nita confirmed Paige's concerns by saying, "Yes, you should go check in with them."

Just as Paige had taken a step away she heard a New Day member mumble, "The nerve of Sister Tamarra to show up after she done slept with that poor woman's husband. Heck, she was probably here to support him and not her so-called best friend."

One could hear Paige's heels scratch the floor as she turned and faced her pastor, who seemed to have a look of shock on her face just as Paige did. And as Paige's expression turned to hurt, so did Margie's. All Margie could do was lift her hands, shrug her shoulders, and shake her head. That was her way of noting that she had no idea how anyone could have possibly learned about those details.

Right now, though, Paige wasn't about to concern herself with that. The same way God was about to make her victorious in the courtroom, even if it meant Blake would have to suffer, He would make her victorious in other matters as well. He would make her victorious even if it meant Tamarra would have a price to pay. Even if it meant her pastor would have a price to pay. God don't like ugly, and things were definitely not pretty.

Chapter Thirty-five

"Will you stop fussing over my table?" Eleanor spat, giving Lorain a smack on the hand. "Everything is set and in order. Now all we have to do is wait for her to get here." Eleanor looked at her watch. "What time did she say she and the kids would be here anyway?"

After ruining Nicholas's white doctor coat yesterday afternoon with her makeup and running mascara, Lorain had finally been able to get herself together enough to talk to him in a way where everything would make sense.

Nicholas had led Lorain back to his SUV, where the two talked over beef fried rice. The good doctor listened to Lorain nonstop for over a half hour before he had to report back to the hospital. She'd given him an earful, and she knew it. In return, he'd told her to do exactly what he did every day in the emergency and operating room: to trust God. She found out that Nicholas wasn't a churchgoer or a practicing Christian. For the most part, he was a simple believer.

"I know that in order to make it out of this world, and even to make it into eternal life in heaven, one probably has to be more than just a believer," he had told Lorain. "After all, I know that just believing in God isn't enough to even get you by most days. But I see miracles happen every day that I know don't have a thing to do with me. When people who I've pronounced dead breathe, rise up off that bed, walk out of that hospital to live dozens of more years . . ." He shook his head in disbelief. "I know there is a God. Strange thing is, I believe more so that God is performing these miracles than some of the folks I see praying at their loved one's bedside for days in and days out. It's like here they are asking God to do something; to give them a miracle. Then when He does it, me, the only one in the room who doesn't even have a relationship with God, is the only one who believes that He did it."

"I hear you," Lorain had to agree. She had been one of those doubting Thomases at one point or another in her life.

"I guess that's why I can't really do the church thing." Nicholas scratched his head. "Church folks be playing with God. I can't get with that. Not with what I've seen Him do."

"Wow, sounds to me like you're a little bit more than a believer," Lorain observed.

"Nahhh, not me. But my mom, my sisters, my brother, even my dad, on the other hand, don't miss a Sunday. And I know they love the Lord. They don't play church because I've shared with them the miracles God has done and they've rejoiced and cried as if it'd been their own kin. But not everybody is like them. God is real, Lorain. And the same way He performs miracles in my life, He's going to perform them in yours. Heck, wasn't your mom coming up here a miracle in itself? Let alone inviting Unique and the boys over to dinner. And I think He'll touch Unique's heart to accept the invitation."

Nicholas couldn't have been more right. God had performed a miracle. Before Lorain's workday was even over, she'd gotten a call from Unique, who'd let her know that she and her three boys would be at the dinner at Eleanor's. Right after Lorain let out a squeal of excitement and right before she was about to ask Unique if she'd told the boys what was going on, she heard them yell into the phone, "Hi, Granny Lorain!"

The phone slipped from Lorain's hands. It was just like Nicholas had told her; a miracle; something that only God Himself could have had a hand in. And to God be the glory as Lorain sat mumbling her thanks and praises to God as softly as she could without her coworkers thinking she was a Jesus freak. It took several minutes before she remembered that Unique was on the phone. She quickly picked up the phone and put it to her ear. For some reason she wasn't surprised at all to hear faint whispers of praise coming out of Unique's mouth.

"My God, my God," Lorain said as Unique's words faded out. "I better get myself together here and do what they're paying me to do."

"All right. I better go too. The kids want to make you and their great-grandmama something. You know they have to Christen Eleanor's shine board."

"Oh, yes, indeed," Lorain smiled.

"Okay, then. Well, my sister is going to let me use her car to drive to the dinner. She's off work tomorrow."

"Good. Dinner will be at my mother's." Lorain proceeded to give her the address. "I'm going to skip my lunch break tomorrow to make up for today's lost time. That way, I might be able to slip out a little early as well. How about we have dinner at around five o'clock? How's that sound?"

"I can hardly wait."

"Neither can I," Lorain replied, and then ended the call.

For Lorain, it felt like it had taken forever for five o'clock to finally arrive, but it had finally gotten here. And at five o'clock on the nose, Eleanor's doorbell rang.

Both Eleanor and Lorain stopped everything they were doing and looked at each other.

"Who's going to get it?" Eleanor asked.

"It's your house. You get it," Lorain suggested.

"Yeah, but they know you better."

The doorbell rang again. Still, both Eleanor and Lorain just stood there staring at each other.

"Well, go ahead, get it," Eleanor ordered her daughter.

"No, you," a nervous Lorain insisted.

This time there was a knock.

"Oh, shoot, girl, move out of my way." Eleanor brushed past Lorain. "Somebody better get it before they turn around and leave."

Lorain followed on Eleanor's heels. Just as Eleanor was about to open the door, she turned to see Lorain breathing right over her shoulder. "Now, if you were going to do all that, why didn't you just get the dern door in the first place?"

"Oh, Ma, answer it already . . . would ya?"

Eleanor turned and opened the door. Standing on the other side of the screen was a picture-perfect family. Dressed in a yellow dress with her seven-month pregnant belly protruding was Unique. And instead of the long weave she normally wore in her hair, today, she wore only her natural hair. It was short and tapered to her neck. Eleanor swore the girl was a younger version of Lorain. And it was obvious Unique had been brushing up on her makeup application skills, because she had just enough Mary Kay cosmetics on to make her look corporate. She had coordinated the colors to perfection to complement the sunshine-yellow dress she wore.

Standing next to her were her three boys, lined up like stair steps, just like they were in age. They each wore matching jeans with brown loafers. They had on white shirts with lightweight yellow sweater vests over them.

"You Ma 'Lenor?" the youngest asked.

"Are you *Great*-Grandmama Eleanor?" the oldest son corrected.

Speechless, all Eleanor could do was nod.

"Then these are for you," the middle boy said as they each held up a sunflower they'd made out of craft material and paper.

Eleanor just stood there frozen, staring at them through the door. Then her hand flew to her mouth as she took off running to her bedroom. The door slammed behind her seconds later.

"Guess she don't like sunflowers," the middle boy said.

"*Doesn't* like sunflowers," the older boy corrected. "She *doesn't* like sunflowers." He lowered his hand sadly, his younger brothers following suit.

"Here, guys, come on in." Lorain opened up the screen door and allowed them to enter. "Grandmama Eleanor does too like sunflowers. As a matter of fact, she likes them very much. That's why she just ran off like that. She's overjoyed with happiness. But I'm going to go get her. You guys sit down and make yourselves comfortable."

Lorain looked up to see the worried expression on Unique's face. It was exactly this type of thing that she'd wanted to avoid. This had been her initial fear. She hoped she hadn't made a mistake in coming and bringing her children along with her.

"I'll be right back. Everything is going to be okay," Lorain assured Unique as she walked quickly to Eleanor's bedroom. "Ma, it's me," Lorain said, knocking on the door as she simultaneously pushed it open. She saw

Eleanor sitting at the chair in front of her vanity bawling her eyes out. "Mom, what's wrong?"

"They're so beautiful! They're just so beautiful," Eleanor cried. "And they're mine. I don't deserve them." She looked at Lorain in her eyes. "I don't deserve you. Nothing I have ever done in this entire world gives God a reason to give me such a wonderful and beautiful gift." Eleanor cried harder.

"Oh, Ma, don't cry," Lorain insisted. "I can't think of another woman in the world more deserving than you. And what I don't understand is how come you can't see it. Up until our episode a couple of weeks ago, you and I have never had any issues. I couldn't have asked for a more perfect mother-daughter relationship. You've always been there for me."

Eleanor started shaking her head. "Uh-uh. No, I haven't. If I had, then all of them wouldn't be standing out there like that. I would have long had a relationship with them." Eleanor started crying hard again.

"Ma, as bad as some of the things that happened to me in my life were, I promise to God I'd go through it all over again if it meant being able to experience this very moment right now; being able to share this day with my mother, my daughter, my grandsons, and Unique's unborn daughters."

"Daughters?" Eleanor looked up, sniffling.

"Yes, Unique is having twins."

"Oh my Jesus," Eleanor declared. "Two more grandbabies." She buried her face in her hands and sobbed again.

"Mom, come on. I need you. I need you now more than ever. I can't do this alone. I know God is going to see this thing through, but I need you right there with me. Please, Ma. Will you be there for me? Will you be there for Unique, the boys, the babies?"

Wiping away her tears and wiping her runny nose, Eleanor straightened up and replied, "Yes, I'll be there for you . . . for all of you."

Both Eleanor and Lorain embraced before returning to the living room for Eleanor to be properly introduced to her grandchildren. Being the loving, kind-hearted boys that they were, they took to Eleanor like bees to a sunflower. And Eleanor and Unique ended up hitting it off better than expected as well.

"I'm sorry for all those times I called you ghetto, hoodrat, and a project chick," Eleanor told Unique. "I really don't think those things about you. I was just jealous that you were taking up all of my little girl's time." Eleanor squeezed Lorain tightly. "Time that she used to just spend with me." Eleanor smiled. "But I guess now I see why."

"Yeah, and I'm sorry for all those times I called you an old fresh-mouth battle-ax," Unique apologized.

"Oh, that's okay. I probably was acting kind of . . ." Eleanor's words trailed off. "Hey, I don't remember you calling me those names."

"Oh, but I did," Unique assured her. "Oh, but I did."

All three women laughed. Then they sat down and enjoyed a delicious dinner, followed up by a scrumptious dessert and a wonderful talk. Finally, they were about to call it a night and Unique had gathered the boys to go home.

"Dinner was great," Unique said, rubbing her belly as she made her way out of the door with her little ones in tow. "Tell Grandmama Eleanor thank you," she ordered her children.

The boys had been ecstatic to learn that Lorain, who they had grown tremendously fond of, was their grandmother, and that they had another grandmother too. They immediately took a poll on how they address the women. Both Eleanor and Lorain loved the names they'd been given.

"Thank you, Great-grandmama," the boys said in unison.

"You are welcome, boys," Eleanor replied.

"I'll see you boys later," Lorain called out. "I have to go with Mommy to the doctor's next week. What do you all say that afterward we hit up McDonald's?"

"Yipee," they screamed and hollered.

"You have a good mommy," the youngest son said to Unique, causing the adult women to laugh.

"Yes, you do, but . . . but . . ." the older boy started. Actually, he wasn't starting anything at all. He was finishing up what Eleanor had started that day in the church sanctuary. But so much had taken place afterward that the subject was never spoken about again. However, now it looked as though this time it would have to be.

The oldest boy walked right up to Lorain and said, "So if you're our mommy's mommy, then who is her daddy?"

Chapter Thirty-six

Mother Doreen felt bad about not being there for Sister Paige's court hearing yesterday. The pastor had asked everybody to pray for her. The pastor had also asked any members of Paige's church family who could be there to support her to show up. She'd wanted to be there, but by the time she finished what she'd needed to do in Kentucky, it was too late to get back on the road. She stayed at her sister Bethany's for the evening, and that's where she was now.

Her sister's house had been her second stop after turning the car around. Pastor Frey's house had been her first. By the time she pulled back around to Pastor Frey's house, he and that woman were still chatting it up on the front lawn. With every ounce of power and authority God had ever given to Mother Doreen, she got out of her car and marched right up to Pastor Frey.

"So, Wallace," Mother Doreen said, calling Pastor Frey by his first name, "you and I need to talk, but first . . ." Mother Doreen turned to the woman. "I don't know who you are, ma'am, but you seem like a nice enough lady. Nice enough to keep your hands off my man." Mother Doreen shooed the woman with her hand. "Because this right here is the man God said is my husband." She looked at Pastor Frey. "*I* am the woman God told him was his wife." Mother Doreen turned back to the woman. "That means *you're* pretty much committing adultery, because what God has said is already done in my eyes. You know what I mean?"

The woman nodded, and the silly grin on her face made Mother Doreen feel like the woman wasn't taking her seriously.

"So what I'm going to need you to do right now is to say your final good-byes and keep it moving." Mother Doreen cleared her throat. "In Jesus' name, of course."

With that grin still plastered on her face, the woman looked at Pastor Frey. "I guess this must be Doreen."

"So you *do* know who I am," Mother Doreen said to the woman. "Sorry, I don't know who you are."

"I'm—" The woman started to introduce herself and extend her hand to shake Mother Doreen's before Mother Doreen cut her off.

"I'm sure you've got a pretty little name to go with that pretty little face of yours. Since I don't plan on seeing you around anymore, no need in you even wasting either of our time introducing yourself."

The woman chuckled, right there in Mother Doreen's face. This was starting to really get up under Mother Doreen's skin.

"I've tried to be as Christlike as possible, but I see that's not working," Mother Doreen said. "So listen up, toots. This here man, he's mine. And I'm willing to fight for mine. I done already took my earrings off, and I have a tube of Vaseline in my glove box in the car. And last but not least, I ain't afraid to catch a case . . . in Jesus' name, of course."

"Oh, Wall-Wall, she's adorable," the woman smiled at Pastor Frey. "I love her already."

"*Wall-Wall?*" Mother Doreen questioned. This woman had a pet name for Pastor Frey and everything. Had Mother Doreen waited *that* long to claim what God had for her?

"Yes, uh, Mother Doreen," Pastor Frey started to introduce. "This is—"

"Oh, allow me." The woman inched closer to Mother Doreen, still smiling that great big Kool-Aid smile. "Doreen, I'm Jessica, Wallace's cousin."

All the life nearly flushed out of Mother Doreen's face. "Cou . . . cou . . . cousin?"

"Yes," both Pastor Frey and Jessica said at the same time.

"Jessica was just leaving. She lives in Oregon with her husband Monty," Pastor Frey explained.

"Yes, that's right. I made a surprise visit to Wall-Wall here," she paused and smiled. "That's what the family calls him," then she continued. "Anyway, I came to visit a couple weeks ago. I'd planned on just driving through. But he was so bummed out that I ended up staying longer to get his mind off things." Jessica cleared her throat as if Mother Doreen was one of the things that had been on her cousin's mind. "Anyway, I've been here long enough. It's time for me to return to that husband of mine." Jessica grabbed Mother Doreen's hand and patted it. "I wish I could have gotten to know you better, but from the sound of things, I'm sure I will. Besides, sounds like we'll get the chance to spend some time together when I come back for the wedding." Jessica winked, then turned to Pastor Frey. "Good-bye, cousin . . . and nice meeting you, Doreen."

Mother Doreen had never felt so embarrassed in her entire life as she stood there and watched Pastor Frey's cousin, the woman she'd practically challenged to a fight, in Jesus' name, of course, drive away. Once Jessica's car was out of sight, she turned to Pastor Frey. "I'm sorry I just made a fool out of myself in front of your people like that. Will you forgive me?"

"Does this answer your question?" Pastor Frey asked as he walked over to Mother Doreen and planted a nice long kiss on her lips.

Initially, Mother Doreen was deep into the kiss, but then she pushed Pastor Frey away. "Wait, there's something I have to tell you." An expression of dread covered her face, and then contemplation took over.

"What is it, Doreen? You can tell me. You can tell me anything. A husband and wife are supposed to be able to share everything. I know I haven't officially gotten down on one knee and—"

"Hold up," Mother Doreen said, cutting him off. "After what I tell you, I'm not even sure you'll still want to have me as your wife."

"Sweetheart, there's nothing you could possibly ever do or say that would make me doubt the woman I want to marry," Pastor Frey told her. "That is, unless you told me you killed somebody or something." He chuckled. Mother Doreen didn't. "Oh God. Doreen, you didn't really kill somebody, did you?"

It was all like a scene out of a bootlegged *Madea* film, directed by the Wayans brothers. But Mother Doreen did what she had to do. She and Pastor Frey went inside, and she shared all the details about the incident that had landed her in prison for almost a year. And now here she was at her sister's house, about to share the same story with her.

"Did you get a good sleep last night?" Bethany asked her older sister as they sat at the kitchen table. It was almost noon. Mother Doreen had only been awake for the last hour. She'd gotten up, showered, and then dressed. Discovering that she and Bethany were the only two in the house, she decided to share with her what thus far she'd only shared with her pastor and Pastor Frey.

"I slept very well, thank you."

"So what is it that you wanted to talk to me about?"

Mother Doreen paused for a moment. "Beth, you know you are my baby sister and I love you. I've always tried to do right by you. I've always tried to be the perfect example of what a perfect Christian should be like. But I've failed you." Tears filled Mother Doreen's eyes.

"Reen, no. You've been the best sister I could have ever asked for. With both Mama and Daddy gone, and us losing two of our sisters to diabetes and high blood pressure, I don't know what I would have done without you. You've always been there for me."

"No, I haven't. Remember that one time I was out of touch with the family for over a year?" Mother Doreen reminded Bethany.

"Oh, girl. We all knew you were just chasing ol' Willie around. Nobody took that personal."

"I was in prison, Bethany. Locked up. In the slammer."

One could have heard a pin drop it was so dead silent.

"Prison? But for what?" Bethany was stunned.

"Murder. For the murder of a child."

Bethany gasped. It was as if a cloud of air were stuck in her throat. "That's not possible. You'd never hurt a fly, let alone a child—a baby." Bethany stood up in anger. "Is this some joke? Is this your way of making me feel better about all the mistakes I've made, because if it is—"

"It's not a joke, baby sis. I went to prison for the death of a baby."

Bethany dropped back into her seat, too weak to stand.

"It was an accident. It was all one big awful accident," Mother Doreen reasoned, and then went on to explain in detail. "You know how I was always chasing Willie around." She looked up. "God rest my Willie's soul." She drew an invisible cross across her heart with her index finger and then continued. "Well, one day I found him shacked up at this hotel with some woman. Willie had gotten the room under his name, so after proving that I was his wife, I managed to finagle a key to the room from the clerk at the desk. Lo and behold, I walk into the room and found him rustling around in the bed with some woman. Well, back then, I wasn't the fine Christian woman that I am today. I didn't ask no questions; I just jumped on that bed and got to beating that girl like she'd stole something."

Mother Doreen stared off with a faraway look in her eyes. "She had stolen something, in my eyes anyway. She'd stolen my man. Anyway, the girl just kept saying, 'My baby. My baby.' Heck, I thought she was calling Willie her baby, trying to be affectionate, and right in front of me. Something inside of me just snapped, and I just kept pounding on her. Not even Willie, try as he might, could pull me off of her. After I got a couple more good whacks in, Willie had practically dragged me off the bed. With the sheets gripped in my fist, when Willie pulled me off the bed, the sheets came with me. And that's when I saw it."

Standing to her feet, Mother Doreen walked over to the sink. She gripped it, trying to maintain her strength so that she could continue. "I saw that that girl was pregnant . . . and she was lying in a puddle of blood between her legs still crying out, 'My baby. My baby.' I was frozen in shock. Willie called the ambulance, and they came and got the poor girl. She lost her baby. Come to find it was Willie's baby too. It didn't take long for the police to come looking for me. They didn't have to look too far, because I turned myself in.

"From the day I turned myself in, I served eleven months and twenty-three days in prison and was on probation for five years after that. I later learned from Willie that the baby had been a little boy. It would be the only baby my Willie would ever have, because while I was in jail some women did some pretty bad things to me after they learned I was locked up for harming a child. Inmates really frown upon that kind of thing. After what those women did to me, I was in the infirmary almost a month. The result—I would never be able to have babies of my own.

"I thought that was God's punishment for what I'd done. And I gladly accepted anything the good Lord felt I was deserving. Only thing is, I was never able to give Willie a baby of his own, and I'd killed the one he'd had."

"Oh, Doreen, I'm so sorry."

"Don't be sorry for me, child. Be sorry for that woman who had to bury her baby. Be sorry for the baby and my Willie. Because even though he had no business knocking that girl up, it was still his baby. He didn't deserve that. None of them did." Mother Doreen looked up and smiled. "But Willie didn't turn his back on me. No, he visited me, wrote me, put money on my books, and was there to pick me up the day I got out of jail as if nothing had ever happened. Everything went right back to normal. Even his running around on me. But I felt indebted to him. So instead of beating both his behind and those women's, I prayed for 'em."

"Doreen, that's a miserable way to exist. You didn't deserve to have to deal with that. He was your husband regardless," Bethany reasoned. "He didn't deserve a green card to go sleep around with whomever."

"I know. That was some stinking thinking on my part. But hey, it's done now. It's in the past, and I gotta let it go, Beth. I gotta let it go." Mother Doreen sniffled. "That's one of the reasons why I ran from here quick, fast, and in a hurry once I saw where things between Wallace and I were headed. I couldn't ruin his future with my past. I didn't want to have to tell him about it, and I sure didn't want him having to hear it from someone else. But surely with all that Internet business going on, someone would have found out. I didn't want to chance that." Mother Doreen, for the first time in a while, smiled at her sister.

"He came to Malvonia looking for me. He said he wanted to marry me, Beth. God actually wants to give me another chance, even as old and as gray as I am," Mother Doreen laughed.

"So are you going to tell him?" Bethany asked. "Are you going to allow God to give you that second chance?"

"I did. Last night. I actually went to Pastor Frey's place before coming here."

"And what did he say after you told him about your past? Does he still want to marry you?"

"I don't know. He didn't say one way or the other, and I didn't want to put any pressure on him by asking. I know I at least need to give the man some time to think about it, you know?"

"But if God told him that you are to be his wife, then what's to think about?"

"Child, you know like I know that just because God tells us to do something doesn't mean we always do it. God's children are just like any other child; hardheaded as all get out. Anyway, just releasing that information has removed some chains from my life. And I'm not going to sit around worrying about whether other folks operate in obedience. All I know is that I want to be his wife. I just hope he still wants to be my husband. Right now, I'm going to hop on the road and return to

Malvonia. I got some things I need to take care of there as well."

"You know you're welcome to stay," Bethany told her.

"Yes, I know, but—"

The ring of the doorbell interrupted Mother Doreen midsentence.

"I'll get it," Bethany said, walking to the living room. Mother Doreen followed behind her. Approaching the door, Bethany looked out to see who it was. She then looked over her shoulder at Mother Doreen while opening the door. "Pastor Frey, it's good to see you," Bethany said, letting him in.

Immediately spotting Mother Doreen, he rushed over to her. "I'm so glad you're still here. I was hoping I didn't have to drive all the way back to Malvonia." He sounded out of breath.

"Pastor Frey, are you okay? Can I get you some water?" Bethany asked.

"Sure, that would be nice," he accepted her offer, and then continued speaking to Mother Doreen. "Doreen, back when I came to Malvonia, I meant what I said, that I was there to claim my wife."

"Then why did you leave?" Mother Doreen had been wanting to know the answer to that question.

"I could see that I was causing confusion between you and your pastor, so I figured the timing wasn't right. Not that my being there, coming to tell you what was on my heart, wasn't right, but just the timing. Besides, you didn't even want to spend dinner time with me, let alone the rest of your life. Then when I got back here, my cousin made a surprise visit and . . . well . . . but I was coming back for you. But before I could, you ended up on my doorstep." He paused, then spoke. "I wasn't prepared for yesterday, Doreen."

"I know," Mother Doreen told him. "Nothing could have prepared you or any other man for what I shared with you yesterday. And I don't blame you if you have a change of heart."

"Woman, I don't have no change of heart. You sharing that with me made me want to be with you even more. Do you know what it made me feel like to know that the woman I'm in love with don't mind sharing every bit of her soul with me? That she trusts me enough to tell me the things she doesn't even want to. Please, woman. When I said I wasn't ready, it was because I didn't have this yet." Pastor Frey pulled out a small white velvet jewelry box. "But now I do." Getting down on one knee, Pastor Frey said, "Doreen Nelly Mae Tucker, would you do me the honor of becoming Mrs. Doreen Nelly Mae Frey?"

"Wallace, my love, nothing would honor me more. Yes, I will," Mother Doreen smiled.

Pastor Frey removed the diamond ring from the box and slipped it on Mother Doreen's finger.

Just then Bethany walked in. "Pastor Frey, would you like some . . ." Her words trailed off when she saw Pastor Frey down on one knee slipping a ring on her sister's finger. "I was gonna ask you if you'd like some ice, but I already see there's plenty of ice up in here," she said, referring to the bling-bling Mother Doreen was now wearing. "What's going on in here? Did what I think just happens really happens?"

Staring into Pastor Frey's eyes, Mother Doreen replied, "Yes, yes, it did." She looked at her sister. "I'm getting married. I'm going to be Mrs. Wallace Frey." Next, Mother Doreen looked up and whispered to God, "Now is it finished?" And before she kissed her husband-to-be on the lips, she could have sworn she heard a small still voice whisper, *"Not yet."*

Chapter Thirty-seven

Paige lay across her bed as if she were making snow angels in her mattress. It was like a dream. Lying across her bed in her house naked. Naked, both physically and spiritually. She felt like a newborn. She felt reborn. This was a new life. A fresh life.

She sat up in the bed and looked at herself in the mirror. Ordinarily, she might have thought she was only a shell of who she used to be, she'd lost so much weight. She didn't know how much she was going to like being a size borderline twelve-fourteen. When she was bigger, she was tight and toned. Now she felt flabby. But that was because she hadn't been doing any of her walking. All she needed to do was tone up. She knew she was having to use the holes further back on her belt in order to keep her pants up, but she had no idea she hadn't been taking care of herself to the point that she'd lost that much weight.

"Thank you for keeping my health, Lord. Thank you," she said out loud. She stared at herself in the mirror a few more moments, and then fell back on the bed.

"Ahhhhhhhhhhh," she squealed, still beside herself. "Lord have mercy; should I feel this good?" she asked.

Should she? After all, her husband just got locked up. Prosecution assured her that this time he wouldn't be getting out on bail either. As a matter of fact, she was told that more than likely, he wouldn't be a free man again for a couple of years at least. Ironically enough, it wasn't Paige's testimony or anything that sealed the deal. She didn't have to testify at all.

There's a saying that actions speak louder than words. Well, this time, just like the time that landed Blake in court anyway, his actions landed him behind bars for good.

Paige too was shocked when Norman showed up in the courtroom to support her. Shocked wasn't the word for how Blake felt, especially since the prosecutor had just mentioned the scene that took place at Paige's job. That, and the fact that Blake was still under the impression that Norman and Paige had been having an affair really set Blake off.

Dressed in the suit Blake had worn to take a picture on that *National* magazine cover, he looked like the perfect gentleman. He spoke like the eloquent, well educated man that he was.

"Your Honor, this . . ." and "Your Honor that . . ." Blake had been explaining as he stood before the judge to enter his plea. In doing so, he turned to gesture at Paige to tell the judge how much he loved his wife, how he would never hurt her, how this all had just been a simple misunderstanding. That's when he saw Norman squeezing beside her. The next words out of his mouth weren't quite so eloquent.

Before even the bailiff saw it coming, Blake had leaped from where he stood to reach Norman and Paige. "You whore!" he screamed as he clawed at Paige, who was desperately trying to get out of his reach. "How are you going to bring the man you've been sleeping with in here? You deserve everything I've done to you, and when I get out of here, you're *really* going to get it. I'm going to kill both you and him."

By now, the bailiff and everyone else was trying to either rescue Paige and Norman or pull Blake off of them. All Blake felt was people tugging on him, and, in turn, he started swinging. One of his punches nearly took the bailiff out, so, of course, the bailiff was forced to pull out his gun. Just as Blake raised his fist to land a blow on Paige that probably would have knocked her lights out, there was cold steel at his temple and a clicking sound. Being the smart, college-educated man that he was, Blake assumed the correct position by raising his hands.

"I'm sorry," he immediately began apologizing.

Just who he was apologizing to, no one was sure, but it didn't matter. His words automatically fell on deaf ears. Blake had just pounded the nail in his own coffin. He'd just sealed his own fate. So any guilt Paige might have had had Blake been sent to prison on her testimony and what he'd done to her alone was no longer an issue. It should have never been an issue. Just as what he'd done in that courtroom yesterday was not her fault, the things he'd done to her during their marriage were not her fault.

As Paige lay there in bed, there were still some issues she had to deal with. Although he wouldn't be a part of her life for the next couple of years, unless Paige officially and legally did something about it, Blake would still be her husband. Is that what she wanted? Is that what God wanted for her? Should she stay with Blake just in case he actually did get rehabilitated in prison? Just in case he did get healed and delivered?

She'd heard that no rehabilitation ever really took place in a prison, so could Blake get the help he needed while there? Could he come out a different man? A changed man? A better man? Sure, he could. But would he? Did he want to?

God performed miracles every day. He healed the sick. He put life in barren wombs. He made the paralyzed walk. He delivered men and women from homosexuality. He restored relationships. There was no reason why, with all the counseling and praying, God could not restore Blake.

Paige sat up and leaned over toward her nightstand. She pulled out a book that Nita had given her. It was titled *Abuse and Religion: When Praying Isn't Enough*, by Ann L. Horton and Judith A. Williamson, eds. She opened up the book with the intent of just flipping through it to get the gist of it. Before she knew it, she was halfway through with it.

Feeling a little weak and tired, Paige decided to slip on some clothes and go put something in her stomach. She went to the kitchen and opened the refrigerator. It was filled with all of her favorite foods that she and Blake had been eating since she'd changed her diet.

"Wow," she mumbled under her breath. "He really thought I was going to come back to him." That's the only reason Paige could figure out why he'd made sure that everything she needed was there. He'd been convinced that he could kiss it and make it better, just like old times.

Paige made herself a turkey sandwich and got some light potato chips. Biting into the sandwich, she found it to be pretty tasty. She hadn't eaten a good full meal in so long, though, that what she really wanted to do was to drive over to the Golden Corral Buffet and eat everything in sight. Just the thought of that place brought back memories; memories of her and Tamarra. Instantly, she lost her appetite and pushed her plate away.

She sat at the table staring down at it before, out of nowhere, she just began to weep. "God, I'm so mad right now I don't know what to do. I mean, yes, I'm happy, I'm grateful for how you brought me out of my abusive situation with Blake. I'm thankful for how you showed up, protected, and fought for me in the court-room. But I'm mad as you know what that I can't go talk to my best friend right now. Because I don't have one anymore. I'm mad that I'm mad; that somebody else's actions have me feeling this way. Stealing my joy."

Paige began to bang her fist on the table. "I want my joy back. All of it, God. I don't want to be spoon-fed lit-tle bits and pieces. I want it all back!" she proclaimed.

"Then go take it back." That came out of Paige's mouth. A voice she had no control over rose up out of her throat and spoke the words again. "Go take it back." And again. "Go get your joy back." And again. "Man did not give it, man can not take it. Go get it back!"

Paige didn't have to tell herself twice. Well, actually she had to tell herself four times, but who's counting? She grabbed her purse and her car keys, then left the house. She was going to get back her joy.

Chapter Thirty-eight

When Mother Doreen arrived back at Malvonia that afternoon, she was on a high like never before. "Ohh, I wish I had a convertible," she said as she drove into the small city. Instead, she just had to opt for having every window in her car rolled down while the wind put on a wrestling match in her car.

At first she was going to go check back into the hotel. Tomorrow was her scheduled walk-through because her tenant would be moving out and she would be moving back into her home. She and Pastor Frey hadn't yet talked about what their living arrangements would be, but most likely, she'd be moving back to Kentucky. She would have to move wherever his ministry took them. She figured she had chased Willie around most of her life while he served the devil, so she would have no complaints going wherever her future husband's ministry would lead them.

Instead of going to the hotel, however, she decided to stop by the church first to see if the pastor was there. When Mother Doreen pulled up, she saw a couple of familiar cars; Pastor's was one of them, so she knew she'd be inside. For a second, Mother Doreen thought that perhaps Pastor was in the middle of a counseling session, but there were way too many cars for that. And most meetings at the church took place in the evening. It was only two o'clock in the afternoon, so something else had to be up. As Mother Doreen parked her car and went inside, she immediately sensed that whatever was up was no good.

She followed the loud, angry voices to her pastor's office. When she entered the office, she saw her pastor, Paige, and a couple of members from the board. She was disturbed to see the pastor sitting in her chair with her hands on her forehead, massaging a migraine, and the others talking over each other.

"Peace, be still," Mother Doreen's voice boomed. "In the name of Jesus, peace, be still." Every eye in the room turned to her. "I could hear you all out there in the parking lot. What in God's name is going on?" Everyone remained silent. "Oh, so now nobody wants to talk?"

"I will," Paige offered. "Something that happened yesterday at court bothered me. I mean, besides the fact that my husband tried to kill me."

"By the way," Mother Doreen interrupted, "I'm sorry I couldn't be there, but I hope everything turned out in your favor."

"It did, Mother Doreen, and thank you," Paige said. "But something was said by one of the church members. It was something that hadn't been shared with anyone besides Pastor . . . at least to my knowledge." Paige figured that when Tamarra went to visit her pastor to find out where she was staying, she'd shared the details about her and Blake. But Paige knew beyond a doubt that Tamarra would not have shared that information with anyone else at New Day. Yet, others seemed to know. Others seemed to know a lot of information that was supposedly only being shared with the New Day pastor.

"And that's been happening a lot lately," one of the board members said. "We even lost a member last week—their entire family. They felt as if they couldn't worship in a church where things weren't sacred."

"Basically, what they are saying is that," Margie stood up, "they can't serve under a pastor who runs her mouth." Margie looked at everybody in the room. "But I promise by the God I serve," she lifted her right hand, "anything a member has shared with me in counseling, in prayer, or just because, has never left my lips except for when I lift it up in prayer for God's ears only."

"I hear you, Pastor, we all hear you," Sister Perrin said, "but that can't be the truth."

"You're calling our pastor a liar?" someone said, and then all the voices started talking over each other again.

"Jesus!" Mother Doreen shouted, which brought silence back to the room. "I can't even believe what I'm hearing in this room, let alone what I'm seeing. Now I know that for a minute there, I too was a little upset when I felt as if something I'd confided to the pastor was shared. Most of you all were there." Mother Doreen pointed to the board members. "I practically threatened to leave the church. But I know my pastor. I've known her for years. I've also been at this church many years, and it ain't nothing new for someone to walk into the ladies' room and hear a little bit of gossiping and backbiting going on. So instead of pointing our finger at Pastor, we should be pointing it at ourselves. If we weren't the ones doing the talking, we've certainly been the ones doing the listening a time or two."

Everyone fell silent, guilty as charged on either end.

"But still, how do the things get out in the first place?" one of the board members asked, set on shifting blame back to Margie.

"Well, I don't know," Mother Doreen said sarcastically, walking over to her pastor's desk. "I guess just as soon as y'all leave, Pastor picks up the phone over here and . . ." Mother Doreen had her hand on Margie's phone, preparing to demonstrate, but a little red light that was lit up on the phone caught her attention. Without saying a word, she turned and walked back to the door and marched out of the office.

Curiosity from the peculiar look on Mother Doreen's face had everyone else following her. Mother Doreen recalled seeing a car out in the parking lot, only the owner of that car wasn't in Pastor's office, which meant she must have been in her own office.

Without even knocking, she opened the church secretary's closed door. And there, they saw the church secretary hunched over her phone. Her unannounced visitors startled her. All she could do was sit there looking like a deer caught in headlights; actually, a deer after it had been caught in headlights and was lying helpless on the side of the road.

"Do me a favor, Pastor," Mother Doreen said. "Go back into your office and talk. Just say anything."

Margie quickly walked back into her office and began to speak. Everyone in the church secretary's office could hear her loud and clear . . . over the secretary's intercom.

Mother Doreen walked over to the secretary's phone, pushed a button, and said, "Okay, Pastor, you can come back in here. We've got this thing figured out now."

A few seconds later, Pastor returned to the secretary's office. "So what's going on?"

Pointing to the church secretary, Mother Doreen explained. "What's going on is that she's been going into your office, turning on your intercom, and listening to everything that's being said in private."

Margie didn't want to believe what she was hearing. She looked at her secretary. "Is that . . . is that true? Have you been listening in on the conversations that take place in my office?" Before allowing her to answer she continued. "And then you're repeating what you've heard? That's how folks are finding out things they have no business knowing?" Margie's shoulders sank with disappointment. "Vegas, how could you?"

"Pa . . . Pastor, it's not what you think," Vegas said in her own defense. "I wasn't doing it to be spiteful or anything. I just wanted to, uh, you know, be able to touch and agree. Yeah, that's right; be able to touch and agree with you in prayer. I wanted to know what was going on with my brothers and sisters in Christ so that I could pray for them; so that I'd know exactly what to pray for."

"In all my years of pastoring or just being a prayer warrior in general even before I became a pastor," Margie said, "I never had to know a person's business in order to pray for them. Even as a pastor now, I have to cut folks off when they start telling me too much. Whenever anyone, especially a pastor, feels as if they need to know every single grimy detail in order to pray for someone's situation, then they need to reevaluate their intentions or what God has called them to do."

"Amen," Mother Doreen stated, a prayer warrior herself.

"So, although you are the only secretary I've ever had serving under me," Margie said, "I'm going to have to ask you to step down from that position."

"Pastor!" Vegas responded, surprised that that would be her pastor's reaction. "You can't mean that. I've been your secretary for years; since you started pastoring at New Day."

"I understand that," Margie said. "But see, as a pastor, any relationship I'm in is like a marriage. I have to be very careful and protective. And as you know, one of the ingredients to the glue that holds a marriage together is trust. And if I can't trust you, I can't be married to you," Margie explained. "Now, I'm not saying that you have to leave the church. By all means, I think you need the church now more than ever, and we'll be here for you. But I can't have you functioning in any capacity in the church, though, until you seek deliverance and walk in it."

"I love this church, Pastor." Vegas was nearly in tears. "You can't expect me to keep coming here and not be the church secretary. Folks will start asking questions. Folks will start talking."

"Oh, dear Sister Vegas," Margie said in a compassionate tone. "Perhaps you really do need the church far more than I thought. Didn't you pay attention to Church Lesson 101? We reap what we sow."

Vegas looked downward.

"Sure, people are going to talk. You're going to get back what you gave out," Pastor warned her. "But that's the law of the land; God's and man's. So just pray on it. But you can pray while you are boxing up your personal things." Pastor looked at Sister Perrin and one of the other board members. "Can you two stay in here and help Sister Vegas get her personal things together, please?" After they agreed to do so, Pastor turned to exit the office. "Oh, and Sister Vegas, if you do decide to remain a member of New Day, I think you owe this church an apology. Now, I'm not telling you that's something you have to do, nor am I making it a condition that you do so in order to remain a member. I'm just saying that I feel it would be the right thing to do."

Margie walked out of the secretary's office with Mother Doreen and Paige following behind her.

"Pastor, I have to go," Paige burst out. "I have to do something really important." She gave Margie a Holy Ghost hug. "What you said about trust in there, that was good, Pastor. And I'm sorry that I doubted your trust for even one minute. But right now, I gotta go." And just like that, Paige was out of the door.

"Lord have mercy," Mother Doreen exhaled. "What a day." She rested her right hand on her chest.

"Lord have mercy is right," Margie exclaimed, grabbing Mother Doreen's hand. "What in the world is *that?*" She pointed to the bling-bling that rested on her friend's ring finger.

"It's just what it looks like," Mother Doreen said proudly. "I said yes. I said yes to both the Lord and to Pastor Frey when he asked me to marry him."

Both women screamed and embraced like girlfriends. But the excitement would be short-lived.

"Mother Doreen!" a frantic voice called out. Everyone turned to see Sister Nita entering the lobby area. She was holding her sliding touch phone in her hand and was practically out of breath. "Wasn't that Culiver basketball playing fella the one Sister Deborah ran off to marry?" Nita looked at her cell phone screen and read. "Elton Culiver?"

"Yes, Elton," Mother Doreen confirmed. Margie cosigned with a nod.

"I was taking a break from cleaning and just happened to come across this headline on an online paper that reports foreign news," Nita exclaimed. She handed Mother Doreen the phone.

Mother Doreen looked at it with agitation. "I don't know nothing about these minicomputers. Just tell me what it says."

"I think you better sit down," Nita suggested.

"Child, if you don't read me the dern thing . . ." Mother Doreen could sense she was about to receive some not-so-good news.

With trembling hands, Nita tried to hold the phone at a steady distance as she looked down at the screen. "Elton Culiver . . . he lived in Chile, right?"

"Child, I'm telling you . . ." Mother Doreen warned. Now she herself was trembling, so much so that Margie held one of her arms in order to keep her balanced.

"That earthquake in Chile. It says that Elton Culiver and his wife were killed."

"Oh, Lord Jesus!" Mother Doreen cried out. "No, no, it can't be."

"Yes, it says so right here." Nita pointed to the phone. "And this news is old. It says that they had a burial and memorial over in Chile. The couple have already been laid to rest."

That's when Mother Doreen's body laid out to rest as well; to rest in the spirit. She just lay right there on the church-lobby floor. She didn't move. She didn't say a word as her eyes remained closed, and she rested in the spirit of the Lord.

Chapter Thirty-nine

The words Pastor spoke in her office just moments ago were like magic to Paige's ears. With those very words she'd had an epiphany. *". . . any relationship I'm in is like a marriage. I have to be very careful and protective. And as you know, one of the ingredients to the glue that holds a marriage together is trust. And if I can't trust you, I can't be married to you."*

Who was it that Paige could and couldn't trust in her life now? Was it trust, or lack thereof, in people that was stealing her joy? Well, Paige had definitely gotten a piece of her joy back by going to see her pastor. Learning that she could trust her pastor 100 percent after all had lifted some weight off of Paige. It had given her some of her joy back. But that wasn't enough. She wanted all of her joy back.

Pulling up in front of the downtown office building, Paige went inside. She signed in at the desk and then waited. She waited and waited, and then waited some more. She started to feel like her efforts would be a lost cause. She couldn't spend the rest of her life in there waiting for someone to help her. Finally, God showed Paige favor by touching someone's heart to help her get the ball rolling on some things she needed to do.

After leaving the office building with yet more of her joy restored, Paige drove to the place she needed to go in order to get the rest of it. Parking her car, she walked up the walkway, onto the porch, and rang the doorbell.

She could hear some rustling on the other side of the door and was glad when Tamarra opened the door. She was glad that she'd been home. Had she not been, Paige probably would have sat on her doorstep and waited for her to return. But it would have been worth the wait. She wanted her joy back . . . all of it . . . right now.

"Paige! I'm so happy to see you. Come in." Tamarra greeted her maybe-still-best friend, and then moved out of the way so that Paige could enter.

"No, it won't be necessary for me to come inside," Paige informed her. "What I have to do, what I have to say, it won't take long." Paige took a deep breath. "I forgive you, Tamarra, I really do. I'm not forgiving you just because the Bible says that's what I should do. I'm forgiving you because I love you and I want to set you free. I'm forgiving you because I want to be free. Walking around with unforgiveness in my heart will not only keep me bound, but it will block my blessings."

"Thank you, Paige. Thank you for forgiving me," Tamarra said, relieved. She went to hug Paige.

Paige held up her hands, keeping Tamarra at a distance. "Hold on. Just because I've forgiven you doesn't mean I still have to be your friend. So with that being said . . ." Paige reached down in her purse, pulled out an envelope, and handed it to Tamara.

"What's this?" Tamarra asked, confused as she opened the envelope and pulled out some papers. As she read them, a puzzled expression covered her face. "These are divorce papers . . . for you and Blake."

"Oh, my mistake." Paige had given Tamarra the wrong envelope. That envelope held copies of the divorce papers Blake would be served with. The clerk down at legal aid, the office she had sat at half the day, had assisted Paige in drafting up the documents.

Initially when Paige showed up at the downtown office building, she was told that it would probably be months before anyone could assist her with filing for divorce. There were just too many requests in that area and not enough volunteers. Paige filled out some paperwork. The completed paperwork was placed on top of a stack of about a million other people's paperwork.

"We work from the bottom up," the clerk told her, making it clear that the other million clients would be served before her.

As Paige was about to leave the building, a man came and carried away the stack. With Paige's paperwork being on top, he scanned it a little, then looked up to see if the person who'd completed the paperwork was still in the office. "Paige Dickenson," he called out. "Is that you?" He looked at Paige.

After informing the man that she was, in fact, Paige Dickenson, the man asked her if she could come to his cubicle. He then informed her that he'd recognized the name of both her and her husband from the little bit of publicity Blake had received after appearing on the magazine cover, Paige's arrest, and then the arrest of Blake.

"So you're going to divorce him?" the man had asked her.

"Yes," Paige informed him. "They said it would be months, though, before they could assist me here. I'll probably just go find me another attorney or something. I honestly don't know what led me here in the first place."

"You can't wait. You have to do it now. I'll help you. Between now and a few months, or even between now and you finding another attorney, you could change your mind. Something could happen. Anything could happen." The gentleman had a sense of urgency in his tone; like it was a matter of life and death. Turns out it was.

He went on to tell Paige how he'd watched his stepfather abuse his mother for years. One day she finally got the courage to divorce him, but during the process, he beat her so badly, that to this day, she has to eat all of her meals through a straw. From that moment on, he dedicated the next two hours in helping Paige do whatever she needed to do in order to get the ball rolling on her divorce from Blake. And he didn't think Paige's next request of him was strange either; not after she briefed him on the circumstances surrounding it.

Paige reached down in her purse and pulled out the envelope she'd intended Tamarra to have. The enveloped contained the second request she'd made from the man down at legal aid. "Here, this one is for you."

Once again, Tamarra began to read the letter, and once again a puzzled look covered her face. "But these are still divorce papers. I don't get . . ." And just like that, Tamarra got it. "You're divorcing *me?* You're divorcing me as a best friend?"

"That's right," Paige said with confidence, then repeated the very words about trust she'd heard her pastor say to the former New Day church secretary. After that she said, "I love you, Tamarra, and I thank God for putting you in my life. When you were a friend, you were a good friend. But I just can't forget the fact that, more than likely, the reason my husband couldn't touch me on our honeymoon was because he'd slept with my best friend the day of the wedding. It wasn't me. It wasn't my size, it wasn't something I did, something I didn't do. None of what you, Blake, or anybody else has done has had anything to do with me. God gave us freewill. What we do with that freewill we can't blame anyone else for. So, on that note, it's been real, Tamarra." Paige smiled, hit her ex-best friend with a nod of the head, and was on her way.

"Paige, no, you can't do this. You're already divorcing Blake. You can't stop being friends with me too." Paige kept on walking. "Who will be there for you during the divorce? You need somebody, Paige. I know because I needed somebody when I was going through my divorce." Tamarra exited her house and followed Paige. "You were there for me. Let me be there for you. We can work this out. Don't go through this by yourself. It will be better if you have someone there for you." Tamarra did not want to lose her best friend. She'd made a mistake; she knew that. And she knew it would take some time for Paige to get over it. But she never imagined in a million years Paige would stop being her friend altogether.

Paige stopped in her tracks and turned to face Tamarra. "You know, there was a time when I felt that I did always need somebody there for me, somebody to make it all better. But through all of this, you know what I've learned?" With a huge, confident smile on her face and before getting into her car and driving off Paige said, "I've learned that I can do better all by myself."

Chapter Forty

"So if you're our mommy's mommy, then who is her daddy?"

As Lorain sat down alone in the chair, those words kept going through her mind. She couldn't answer that question right then and there when it had been posed; not in front of the boys. It was too grown-up of a matter for them. But Unique had answered for her.

"He's dead," Unique had told her sons. "Your grand-pa, Mommy's daddy, is dead." She looked up at Lorain, "Isn't that right?"

All Lorain could do was nod as Unique hustled the boys off the porch and into the car. When Lorain closed the door, she turned around to see Eleanor studying her knowingly.

"She's Broady's girl, isn't she?"

Once again, all Lorain could do was nod. She was expecting Eleanor to fall out, lose control, or something. But she didn't. "Are you going to tell her?" she asked her daughter. "Are you going to tell the girl who her daddy really is?" Lorain didn't reply because she didn't know. "Well, if you ask me, I'm beginning to think that some things really are best left untold." Eleanor walked away, and the two didn't speak about it anymore. And it was kind of like a nonverbal agreement that they wouldn't, especially not to Unique. Why? After all, he was dead. What good could possibly come out of Unique knowing the truth about who her biological father was?

"Hey, sorry, I'm late," Nicholas's voice interrupted Lorain's thoughts. She'd forgotten where she was, that she was in the hospital cafeteria waiting on him to join her for lunch.

"Oh, it's okay," Lorain smiled and stood.

The two walked over to the line and picked out the choices of food they liked, and then returned to their table.

"When I got here, your mind looked as though it was a million miles away," Nicholas said to Lorain.

"It was," she replied. "Just thinking about things with my daughter, my mother . . . just everything."

"Yeah, I must say that listening to you tell it to me in my truck that day, keeping in mind that I'm sure that was the condensed version, you've dealt with quite a bit." Nicholas ate a spoonful of the vegetable soup he'd ordered. "But don't worry. You've got me now. I'll be your sounding board, so don't ever hesitate to share anything with me."

Lorain sat there quiet and stunned. It showed by the expression on her face, so Nicholas decided to call her on it. "What? Why are you looking like that?"

"I don't know, it's just that I've only known you a minute and already you're talking as if you're going to be in my life forever."

Nicholas looked at Lorain momentarily, then put down his spoon. "Listen, perhaps I should have made this clear. But then again, I guess this really is the first time we've had time to talk-talk. I don't make it my business to introduce myself to women and give out my number. Especially women I meet at the hospital. You were . . . I don't know . . . I just liked your smile, I think. And I know that may sound corny, but believe it or not, I'm a plain and corny guy. But what I'm not is a player.

I don't play around; I don't play games; I don't juggle women—none of that."

Lorain nodded, letting him know that he had her attention; that she was listening.

"I'm not in this to take you out once or twice a week, talk on the phone here and there, and make an occasional bedroom appearance. I'm a doctor. I'm thirty-nine years old. I don't have any kids, and I don't have a wife or a girlfriend on the side. I don't like side dishes. I don't like appetizers. I'm looking for the main course. You dig?"

Lorain snapped her neck back. "Check you out, hip doctor."

"Seriously, I'm not saying that I'm trying to propose to you or marry you by the end of the year, but I am sitting here with you, hoping that the outcome can be that one day you could be my wife. I don't know everything about you. You don't know everything about me. We may end up having absolutely nothing in common and get on each other's nerves. That's fine. But just so you know, when I extend myself to a woman, I don't just want it to be any and every woman. I'm in this to find a wife, point-blank. If that's not what you're looking for when you go out with a man, then just say that. We can finish our soup, salad, and sandwich and go about our merry way." He went back to eating his soup.

Lorain just sat there staring at the good doctor. "You finished?" she asked, folding her arms.

"No, you have mayo in the corner of your mouth." Nicholas took his napkin and gently wiped Lorain's mouth.

"Thank you." She put her head down in embarrassment. Without saying anything, she ate a spoonful of her soup. After chewing it and swallowing it, she said, "But you're not saved."

"Who told you that?" he asked.

"You did. You said it yourself that you don't go to church."

"But I didn't say that I wasn't saved." He began counting on his fingers. "My pops is an elder, and my mother is president of the usher's board. One of my sisters sings in praise and worship whenever she's in town; the other is on the dance ministry; and my brother is a youth leader. Do you actually think with all those witnesses at Christmas dinner that I ain't get saved?"

Lorain chuckled. "I guess you have a point there."

"See how you Christian folk are? Just because somebody ain't all up in the church seven days a week, y'all think they ain't saved."

Lorain laughed again. "Okay, okay. You got me. I guess with that being said, I can give you a chance." Realizing what she'd just said, Lorain fell silent.

"Does that mean you want to pursue a relationship with me? Not just any relationship, but the ultimate relationship?"

Lorain looked at Nicholas, and then chuckled. "Is this guy serious?" she said to the air. "I mean, like how many women have you run off with that spiel?"

"Look, sister," Nicholas leaned in, "if you didn't scare me away with everything you shared with me on our first date, then I know I can't possibly have scared you off with what I said on our second date."

"Oh, so we're dating?" Lorain blushed.

"Oh, mama, I'm gonna date you all right. Like I said, I'm not trying to get married tomorrow, I'm just giving you a heads-up on the direction I'm going in. But I'm going to date you for sure. I'm going to take you out to eat, other than having Chinese in the front seat of a car and soup and salad in my job's cafeteria." They both chuckled. "I'm going to take you on trips. I'm going to send you on trips with your girls when I can't make it. I'm going to wash your car for you. And get this," he leaned in close to Lorain again, "I'm going to buy you flowers just because it's Monday."

Before Lorain knew it, she was sitting there with tears falling out of her eyes. Snot was running out of her nose and everything. She closed her eyes and said a prayer. *God, if this man is not real, if none of this is real, when I open my eyes please let him be gone.* When Lorain opened her eyes, to her sheer amazement, Nicholas was no longer sitting in front of her. All of a sudden she gasped when she felt a touch behind her.

"Come on. Let's get out of here." Nicholas had gotten up from where he sat and walked behind Lorain to comfort her.

"I can't," Lorain told him. "I'm too embarrassed to get up and walk across this room right now. Can you please just come put your arm around me and pretend you're the doctor who just gave the patient bad news?"

"Are you serious?"

"Please just do it," Lorain pleaded.

Nicholas sat down in the seat next to her. He hesitated, and then put his arm around her like he was comforting her. "Is that better?" he asked her.

She nodded as she picked up a napkin and wiped her tears. "Oh my God, you must think I'm a nutcase."

"No, I know how it is. Women go through so much. As a doctor, I learn things from women that they have never even shared with their husbands. Now that's sad. I don't ever want my wife to feel as though there isn't anything she can't tell me because she's afraid or worried how I might react. Do you know that other than finances, lack of communication is one of the top reasons for divorce?"

"Really?"

"Yes, really."

"Then I guess you won't have to worry about divorcing me." She'd done it again; said something that forced both of them into silence.

"I guess I won't," Nicholas replied. Removing his arm from around Lorain, he felt the need to clear some things up. "Look, I know about the Lifetime Channel and those Brenda Jackson romance novels you women cling to. A lot of those books and movies have boy meet girl, girl falls madly in love with boy, they get married after knowing each other a brief spell, and then live happily ever after. I know that's not always the case. But I do know that it happens. I do know that every woman deserves the fairy tale."

"I guess every woman does want her Prince Charming."

"Well, don't get it twisted because I'm not him," Nicholas was quick to say. "I drink milk out of the carton; I leave my underwear on the floor sometimes; and I still forget to put the toilet seat down."

"Okay, that's it then. I'm out of here." Lorain pretended to get up and start to walk away.

Nicholas playfully pulled her back down by her arm. "Sit back down, woman," he ordered. "But anyway, I get that we haven't even known each other long enough to know what each other's favorite color and food is. All I'm saying is let's strive to get there. You dig?"

"I dig," Lorain said, and as soon as she said it, Nicholas's pager went off.

"Ah, see why I have to stay close to the job?" He pulled out his pager and looked at it. "I gotta go. They need me in ER." He looked down at their pretty-much untouched meals. "Shoot, and we didn't even get to finish eating." He thought for a second. "What do you say on my off day next week we have dinner? I'll cook for you."

A bland look covered Lorain's face. She'd learned as part of the Singles' Ministry that it wasn't a good idea to have a date in a person's home.

"What's up with the jacked-up face, woman? I can cook," he assured her. "My buddy owns a little restaurant. It's nothing fancy. He's just getting started. I'm sure he'll let me burn a special dish in his kitchen for you. I'm not going to poison you or anything. I at least want to wait and do that after I marry you and get a life insurance policy out on you or something . . . You know what I'm sayin'?" He did his best *Fresh Prince of Bel-Air* expression, and that's when Lorain realized who he reminded her of. A brown-skinned Will Smith . . . right down to the laugh.

"Yeah, I know what you're sayin'," she smiled, not able to believe just how quickly God had turned her concerns about the dinner date around.

"Okay, then, woman, let me go save a life." He began walking away. "Oh, let me take that back. I got church folk in my presence," he teased. "Let me go let God use me to save a life." He winked, and then he walked away.

Lorain sat there and smiled. Then she yelled out without even caring if it would embarrass her or not, "Purple and pizza."

"What?" Nicholas said, stopping in his tracks and looking confused.

Lorain cupped her hands around her mouth and yelled once again, "Purple and pizza. My favorite color is purple, and my favorite food is pizza."

Nicholas gave her a head nod and a smile, then exited the cafeteria with a light jog.

Lorain looked down at her food. She was too beside herself to even eat. And as if she hadn't embarrassed herself enough already, she let out one big loud, "Who-hoooo!" She then looked around the room at all the people she had startled. "I'm sorry, y'all, but he had me at 'Hey.'"

Chapter Forty-one

"Have you been able to get in touch with Deborah's mother?" Margie asked Mother Doreen as she helped her get settled back into her house. The tenant had taken great care of Mother Doreen's house during her stay there.

"No. I thought I had her information in my address book, but I don't."

"I'll have to check the church records again to see if I can come up with anything. I think she might have visited a couple of years ago and filled out a visitor's card. I'll double-check real good."

"My soul is fit to be tied. I just can't believe she's gone. Sister Deborah was like the daughter I never had."

"Yeah, I know you two were growing pretty close while serving on the Singles' Ministry. Speaking of which, I still intend on reinstating it. I guess I'm just going to have to see who God will put in the leadership position. I don't want to get you involved considering all the changes that are about to take place in your life. And I just can't go putting anybody in the position. It has to be someone with integrity that the members can trust."

"In the meantime, then, I think you should serve as leader."

"You are just bound and determined to have me serve on that ministry, aren't you?"

"It's just that you're single and, well, people follow your lead. You are the shepherd."

"True, but Jesus is the Ultimate Shepherd," Margie confirmed. "Yes, God uses me to lead His flock, but I think every saint should ultimately follow the direction of the Lord. I'm flesh and blood. I can surely fall and falter. God can not and will not." Margie picked up a box, carried it over to the couch, and sat down to rest. "That's what gets people in trouble most of the time; they get so focused on man and what he or she is and isn't doing that they lose sight of God."

"You're right about that, Pastor," Mother Doreen agreed as she unpacked a box of photo albums and placed them under the coffee table. "My Wallace got wrapped up in following his former pastor, Pastor Davidson. That just goes to show that there are some bad shepherds that can only take you so far because they sometimes lose sight of Jesus."

"Amen," Margie agreed. "For a minute there I thought my congregation was starting to think I was a bad shepherd; I mean, up until Sister Vegas was found out."

"Yeah, and no one might have ever known what she was up to had she just kept her mouth closed."

"I guess what goes on in Vegas doesn't necessarily stay in Vegas after all." Both women laughed. "Even a fish wouldn't get caught if it kept its mouth shut." The women shared another laugh.

"Ohhhh, I think I'm going to call it a day, Pastor." Mother Doreen flopped down in a chair. "I'm worn out."

"I don't even know why you bothered doing all this. You know eventually you're going to have to move back to Kentucky."

"I know, but I couldn't continue to stay with you."

"Nonsense. I loved having you."

"And I appreciate it, Pastor." Mother Doreen let out a long, deep breath. She sat there with a faraway look in her eyes.

"Thinking about Sister Deborah?"

"Yes," Mother Doreen answered. "A part of me feels like I let her down some. I was like her spiritual counselor. God would send her to me, and I'd lead her. I'd guide her, but not to the fullest. I feel like there is so much more I could have shared with her that might have made her make different decisions; decisions that might have her alive today."

"You know that's not true, Mother Doreen. You can't blame yourself for an earthquake."

"I know, it's just that God keeps telling me I'm not finished. For some reason, now, I feel like Sister Deborah had something to do with it. Like I just needed to be real with her and tell her my story. Once upon a time she told me, 'Mother Doreen . . . sometimes it helps to be able to look around and know that the person you think has got it all together really doesn't. Then you don't always feel like such a mess.' That was my opportunity right there to really minister to her. And I missed it." Mother Doreen broke down and cried. "Dear God, I wanted to finish. I'm sorry I failed you. If there was any way you could bring Sister Deborah back, I promise you I'd finish. I promise you I'd tell her my story . . . all of it."

Margie went over and began laying hands on and praying for Mother Doreen. She knew deep in her heart that if God said Mother Doreen wasn't finished, then He'd see to it that she did finish.

Chapter Forty-two

"If you suspect someone may be in a verbally abusive relationship, don't expect them to tell you. I didn't tell anyone." Paige looked at Nita, who was sitting in the front row of the sanctuary. "Not at first anyway." Nita winked, and then Paige continued on with her testimony.

It was Saturday afternoon and New Day was holding its first open SWATC Ministry meeting. It was both an informative meeting as well as tutorial. Both Nita and the pastor thought it would be a good idea to end the meeting with a testimony from Paige.

"Even if you suspect abuse is going on, over ninety-nine percent of the time, the person being abused will lie and tell you that everything is fine. Even if they are a Christian, yes, they will lie." There were a couple of light chuckles. "So what you need to do is watch for some signs."

A hand went up in the audience.

"Yes, do you have a question?" Paige asked the man with his hand up.

"Yes, Sister Paige." Paige's choir director stood up. "First off, I want to thank you for sharing your moving testimony. But I'd like to know just exactly what some of the signs are. I mean, we saw you in church every Sunday. I worked up close and personal with you in the choir, and I had no idea."

"I'm glad you asked that question, because I have some handouts that list the signs." Paige nodded toward the stack of papers on the table next to where she had been sitting before getting up to give her testimony. Nita handed her the papers. "Thank you, Sister Nita." Paige then passed out a pamphlet to each person in the sanctuary as she spoke. "One of the signs is withdrawal. The victim may begin to withdraw from people or things they used to do."

"Like all those choir rehearsals you missed," the director joked. Again, there were some chuckles.

"Yes, kind of like that," Paige smiled. "Another is a change in the person being abused, their personality, appearance—"

"Like why you're a size three now?" the choir director joked again. Paige laughed and appreciated him using specific examples in her own life.

"Yes, kind of like that," Paige said, and then saw to it that each and every person received a handout. "Before I go, if anyone in the room now is a victim of abuse or is an abuser, I want you to know that there *is* a way out. The first thing you need to do is realize that you are being abused or that you are being an abuser. If you are being abused, you have to know that nothing you did or nothing you said is the cause of that abuse. It's not your fault. Everyone say, 'It's not your fault.'"

"It's not your fault," the people repeated.

"And if you are the abuser, you have to realize that in order for things to change, in order for you to get better and stop the abuse cycle, you have to recognize that what you are doing is wrong. Back to those being abused, if the abuser is unwilling to get help or even recognize that they are being abusive, then you need to remove yourself from the situation. I know it's easier said than done. Trust me; but with the help of some loving, kind, and caring people to support me . . ." Paige looked up, ". . . and with the strength of Jesus Christ Himself, I got out. I got out. He brought me out."

The congregation stood and began applauding.

"Thank you. Thank you so much, New Day," Paige said. "But before I sit down, I'd like to know if there is anyone here in this room who needs prayer about an abusive situation or relationship. It doesn't have to be with you. It can be with you, your sister, your mother, or even that neighbor you hear getting beaten and you feel helpless lying in your bed listening."

"Say that," a member shouted out.

"Now is not the time to be ashamed or prideful. So please come." Just as expected, no one came forward. "Then I just ask you all to stand and pray where you are. To intercede on the behalf of those—"

Before Paige could finish, a gentleman walked to the altar.

"Yes, brother in Christ," Paige said to him.

At first he just stood there with his head down.

"What is it you need prayer for?" Paige asked him.

Again, he just stood there unable to speak. Then tears filled his eyes and fell. Next he began to tremble. Before Paige could speak again, a woman came and stood next to him and began to comfort him. "It's okay, baby," she began to cry. "It's okay." She wrapped her arms around him, and the two stood at the sanctuary and began to cry out.

Without even having to give the congregation instructions, they all lifted their hands and began to pray for the couple that stood at the altar. After about five minutes, they got themselves together, then stood hand in hand looking at Paige.

"Sister Paige, I'd like you to touch and agree that God is going to help me get better. That God is going to help me keep my hands to myself. I love my helpmate, and I want to be better. I don't want to hit my helpmate anymore. I don't want to hurt my helpmate anymore. That's not why God gave me a helpmate."

The congregation began to pray harder as the woman continued confessing.

"I love my husband, and he loves me. He loves me despite the fact that I've been abusing him for the last three years of our five-year marriage. But today, I'm seeking help. Whatever it takes," the woman cried out. "I'm willing to do it, counseling, whatever. I know what I'm doing is wrong, and I need to stop it. But I know I can't do it on my own because I've tried." She looked at her husband. "He's tried. He's tried to love me through it. But I need more than his love. I need the blood of Jesus," she wailed.

"Amen," some shouted.

"Hallelujah," others called out.

After Paige touched and agreed with the couple, they returned to their seats and so did Paige. Sister Nita then thanked everyone for coming out and passed on one last nugget of information. "October is not only National Domestic Violence Awareness Month. It's also the month of the anniversary of the Violence Against Women Act in the U.S. This act has made significant statutory changes and provided a funding stream to support efforts to end violence against women. Money was made available to programs at the state and local levels. Faith Trust Institute, along with other national programs, was funded to provide technical assistance to those programs."

Once Sister Nita was finished, lastly, Pastor stood and informed the congregation as to what New Day would do and what other churches could do to address the issues of domestic violence. "We can educate the community through sermons, speeches, and prayers about the subject of domestic violence, healthy marriages, and relationships. For our youth, we can develop curriculum on bullying prevention, healthy dating relationships, and domestic abuse for children's classes and youth groups. We can develop a resource list, and other churches can hang up posters and even create a SWATC Ministry like we did here at New Day and create a fund to help displaced domestic violence victims in the community."

After closing in prayer, everyone was dismissed to go. Margie had pulled the couple from the altar aside and offered information on counseling. Then she, Mother Doreen, Nita, Lorain, and Paige were the last in the sanctuary.

"You did a wonderful job giving your testimony," Mother Doreen praised Paige.

"Thank you so much, Mother Doreen." Paige kissed her on the cheek. "And thank you so much for coming out and showing your support."

"Don't even mention it." Mother Doreen shooed her hand.

"I won't," Paige said, grabbing hold of the hand Mother Doreen had just flung in the air. "But I *will* mention this ring," Paige examined the ring, "which looks a lot like an engagement ring to me."

"If it looks like a duck, and it walks like a duck . . ." Mother Doreen confirmed.

"I'm so happy for you, Mother Doreen," Paige told her. "But I heard the Singles' Ministry was about to start up again and that you were going to be in charge of it."

"Really?" Mother Doreen was surprised that Paige knew this information. "How did you find that out?" And then as if a light bulb had gone off in Mother Doreen's head, she said, "Ohhhhhhh. The same way everyone was finding out about everything else around here."

"Now, now," Margie interrupted. "Sister Vegas did come down to the altar this past Sunday and apologized to anyone she may have wounded in the church by her actions. That's a start. Let's give her some credit and support her issue just as much as we'd support any other issue."

"Amen, Pastor, amen," Paige and Mother Doreen agreed.

Even Nita and Lorain, who were making sure the sanctuary was back in order, agreed with a hardy "Amen."

"But back to what I was saying," Paige continued. "If you're about to be married off, Mother Doreen, then who in the world is equipped to be in charge of the Singles' Ministry?"

"How about me?" a voice rang out through the sanctuary doors.

Mother Doreen turned around to see the woman dressed in all-white standing in the church doorway. Every ounce of color drained from Mother Doreen's complexion; from Paige's, Margie's, Lorain's, and Nita's, for that matter too.

The woman in the doorway ran her fingers through her short Afro. "What? I know I look different now that I have my sister locks cut off, but dang, you all act like you've seen a ghost."

All Mother Doreen could fix her lips to say was, "Sister Deborah, is that really you?"

"Why, of course it is," Deborah smiled. "In the flesh."

Chapter Forty-three

"Sounds like some strange stuff happens in that church of yours. I'm going to have to visit it one day," Nicholas said to Lorain as the two talked on the phone. She'd shared with him what had happened earlier at church, with Deborah showing up and all.

"Yeah, fact is much stranger than fiction," Lorain agreed.

"So let me get this straight," Nicholas decided to recap what Lorain had just told him. "This Deborah woman left and went off to Chile with this Elton cat? Y'all thought Deborah had married him, come to find, he already had a wife in Chile when she got on the plane and left with him."

"Uh-huh. That's what she told us," Lorain confirmed.

"So unfortunately, dude and his wife did end up dying in that earthquake, but it was his real wife; not Sister Deborah, who you all just assumed had married him and was his wife?"

"That about sums it up."

"And you see why I don't fool with church folks?" Nicholas laughed, and even Lorain let out a chuckle on that one.

"Hey, church folks, Christians, whatever; we're just like regular folks."

"I'm glad to hear that, because I'm regular."

Lorain smiled, "Sure, you are," she said, *but not for long,* she thought. Lorain ended the call with Nicholas shortly after and thought about the words her pastor had shared with her. Lorain had been concerned about the fact that she was a practicing Christian and Nicholas wasn't. She had asked her pastor's thoughts on it.

"Let me tell you something," Margie had told Lorain. "You don't know how God is going to use you to witness to that man. You never know; he may have a calling on his life that is bigger than anything you could ever imagine, and you, Sister Lorain, could be a part of that calling. Now when I say you are going to be a witness to him, I'm not talking about deliberately Bible and Jesus bashing the man."

Lorain had laughed.

"If the man asks you how you're doing, don't reply with all that 'blessed and highly favored' stuff. Just say you're doing fine, for crying out loud."

Again, Lorain laughed.

"And don't invite him to church every Sunday. You can extend an invitation, let him know the doors of our church are open, and we would love to have him visit anytime he gets good and ready. That's it. And, honey, please, don't give him scripture for everything under the sun. The Bible has sixty-six books, but you are book number sixty-seven. He's going to read you every day. So let your actions say it all. Amen, Sister Lorain?"

"Amen, Pastor," Lorain had said, giving her pastor a great big Holy Ghost hug.

"Oh, yeah, and don't worry about what other people think either. Do you think I'd be pastoring today if I worried about what folks thought? Some folks think I shouldn't be doing this. Some folks think I shouldn't be doing that. Some folks think I should be married. Some folks think I should be single. Some folks even think I'm single because I'm gay."

"Stop it, Pastor," Lorain had said in disbelief.

"It's true. But all I do is turn to the Father and say, 'Lord, do not charge them with this sin.' Just like in Acts 7:60." Margie looked at Lorain dead in her eyes. "When God first spoke to me that I had a calling as a pastor on my life, do you know the first thing I did?"

Lorain shook her head.

"I had the nerve to run to man for confirmation. 'What do you think about this?' and 'What do you think about that?' I asked folks. She looked up and with a smile on her face recited Galatians 1:15–17 from the New King James Version. 'But when it pleased God, who separated me from my mother's womb and called me through His grace, to reveal His Son in me, that I might preach Him among the Gentiles, I did not immediately confer with flesh and blood, nor did I go up to Jerusalem to those who were apostles before me; but I went to Arabia, and returned again to Damascus.' I had to remind myself of that scripture. I had to remind myself that when God spoke to Paul, not even he ran to seek counsel on what God had said to him."

Margie took Lorain's hands into hers. "When it comes to you and this new man in your life, you have to trust God to guide you, and not man."

And that's exactly what Lorain intended to do. "A doctor's wife," Lorain said to herself as she sat there with stars in her eyes. "Someday, maybe. Someday."

Chapter Forty-four

Mother Doreen was in the living room of her completely unpacked house. Deborah sat next to her nursing her little bundle of joy.

"I can't believe you ran out of the country and was knocked up."

"Mother Doreen," Deborah stated. "I guess for a lack of a better term, that is about right, though."

"And he's just the cutest little thing."

"Yes, he's Mommy's little angel," Deborah smiled, looking down at her bright-eyed son who was the spittin' image of his now-deceased father. "Because of him, I want to keep on keeping on, Mother Doreen. Because of him, I don't want to make the same old stupid mistakes anymore. You know?" Deborah looked up from her baby at Mother Doreen.

"Yes, I know," Mother Doreen assured her. "Lordy, do I know."

"Uh-huh, and what do you know about making mistakes over and over again? You've got it all together. You're even about to get married and become a first lady. Praise God," Deborah cheered, celebrating Mother Doreen's engagement. Mother Doreen, though, wasn't joining in on the celebration. "What's wrong?"

Mother Doreen sat up straight. "There's something I need to tell you, Sister Deborah. It's something about me. It's something that I should have told you a long time ago, but I just thank God that He has afforded me the opportunity to tell you now."

"What is it, Mother Doreen?"

"Remember when I told you how I used to catch Willie in hotel rooms and whatnot with other women?"

Deborah nodded, recalling such conversations between her and Mother Doreen. "Yes, and you said you used to pray for them. I'll never forget it. You're such a better Christian than I'll ever be."

"Well, I didn't always used to pray for those women," Mother Doreen told her. "You see, one time . . ." Mother Doreen proceeded to tell Deborah about the incident that landed her in prison. Deborah listened intently, astounded that Mother Doreen had carried such a past with her. "I wish I had shared my testimony with you long before. Perhaps it would have saved you from some heartbreak."

"Maybe," Deborah agreed. "But I thank you for that word now. God restored your life, Mother Doreen. I got delivered from a lot of demons from my past, but after hearing your testimony, I'm not going backward. I'm going to walk in my deliverance . . . for real this time," Sister Deborah winked. "Because see, Junior, here, he's going to be protected from all of that mess. Not to say that he won't have trials and tribulations, because he will." Deborah kissed her son on his forehead. "But he's going to have a mother," she looked at Mother Doreen, "and a godmother who's going to be real and honest with him. Who's going to raise him up in the way in which he should go. And you know what? If we can do that for just this one little boy, he can change the entire course of the world. And I mean that," Deborah said with conviction.

"And I believe it," Mother Doreen affirmed, standing up, then walking over to Deborah and her godson, "and I receive it, in Jesus' name."

Deborah held her hand out for Mother Doreen. Mother Doreen reached out and grabbed it as they both stared down at the sleeping baby. And with a tear strolling down her cheek, Mother Doreen looked up and whispered, "It is finished," knowing that this time, it really was.

Reader's Group Guide Questions

1) In books one through four of the series, the pastor of New Day Temple of Faith was not described. Were you surprised to discover the race and the sex of the pastor?

2) Why do you think God chose Nita to stand in the gap for Paige and not her best friend, Tamarra?

3) Considering how Paige was set up with Blake, do you feel Margie was correct in choosing not to go out again with Lance?

4) Do you feel that the way Paige dealt with Tamarra after confirming what had gone on between her and Blake was believable? Or, do you feel that for the sake of "keepin' it real," she should have acted a fool, called Tamarra out of her name, and went upside her head?

5) "God hates divorce" is what most Christians learn in church. So do you believe Paige should or should not divorce Blake? Why?

6) Paige claims that she has forgiven Tamarra, yet she does not want to be her friend anymore. Do you feel she's being a hypocrite? Why or why not?

7)   Mother Doreen drove back to Kentucky to "get her man." Do you believe she should have waited to see if he would have come back to her?

8)   If you've read the other four books in the series, do you feel book five wraps up the lives of all characters involved? Are there any characters you'd still like to continue to read about?

9) Lorain and Unique decided to go along with their plan concerning the twins. Do you think they are making the right decision, or are they still somewhat living a lie? Explain.

10) Do you think that there is a chance that Blake could ever get delivered from the spirit of domestic abuse? If he does, do you believe there is a chance that he and Paige could work things out?

11)   What do you think about Deborah's return?

12)   Of all the New Day Divas, which character did you find to be most intriguing?

13) Nicholas admitted to Lorain that he did not attend church and was not a practicing Christian. Should she or should she not consider forming a relationship with him? Explain.

14) Deborah had made the same mistakes over and over when it came to men. Do you think someone like her is a good candidate as a leader for the Singles' Ministry? Why or why not?

15) The New Day Divas series has been nick-
    named the "Soap Opera" in print. Did you
    enjoy the soap operalike writing style (an ar-
    ray of characters and multiple scene changes),
    or was it confusing, making you feel as though
    the story lines and characters were all over the
    place?

About the Author

E.N. Joy is the author of *Me, Myself and Him*, which was her debut work into the Christian Fiction genre. Formerly a secular author writing under the names Joylynn M. Jossel and JOY, when she decided to fully dedicate her life to Christ, that meant she had to fully dedicate her work as well. She made a conscious decision that whatever she penned from that point on had to glorify God and His Kingdom.

The "New Day Divas" series was inspired by her publisher, Carl Weber, but birthed by the Holy Spirit. God used Mr. Weber to pitch the idea to E.N. Joy. He planted the seed in her spirit, and she prayed about it. Eventually the seed was watered and grew into a phenomenal five-book series that she is sure will touch readers across the world for ages to come.

"My goal and prayer with the 'New Day Divas' series is to put an end to the Church Fiction versus Christian Fiction dilemma," E.N. Joy states, "and find a divine medium that pleases both God and the readers."

E.N. Joy currently resides in Reynoldsburg, Ohio, where she is continuing work on her next series, "Still Divas," as well as finishing up her "Street Preacher" series.

About The Author

You can visit the author at:

www.enjoywrites.com

or e-mail her to share with her any feedback at:

enjoywrites@aol.com

You may also visit www.swatcministry.com to learn more about the ministry.

The "Still Divas" Series

Coming 2012

Readers, you spoke, and I listened to you. More importantly, I listened to God as I wrote the final book of the "New Day Divas" series, and He kept saying, "You're not finished." Well, guess what? I'm sure not, and neither are these divas! Some of your most loved (and not so well liked) characters from the "New Day Divas" series will have their own book. Yes, that's right, and Unique starts off the show in book one of the "Still Divas" series titled *And You Call Yourself A Christian* (March 2012). Then, after that, you'll get to read Mother Doreen's story in *The Perfect Christian* (July 2012). Wrapping up the three-book series is Deborah in *The Sunday-Only Christian* (November 2012).

So, if you thought the lives of these New Day Temple of Faith divas couldn't get any more interesting, have I got news for you. Just wait until you discover that in spite of all that these women have been through in their lives, when the dust finally settles, they are Still Divas!

UC HIS GLORY BOOK CLUB!

www.uchisglorybookclub.net

UC His Glory Book Club is the spirit-inspired brain-child of Joylynn Jossel, Author and Acquisitions Editor of Urban Christian, and Kendra Norman-Bellamy, Author for Urban Christian. This is an online book club that hosts authors of Urban Christian. We welcome as members all men and women who have a passion for reading Christian-based fiction.

UC HIS GLORY BOOK CLUB pledges our commitment to provide support, positive feedback, encouragement, and a forum whereby members can openly discuss and review the literary works of Urban Christian authors.

There is no membership fee associated with UC His Glory Book Club; however, we do ask that you support the authors through purchasing, encouraging, providing book reviews, and of course, your prayers. We also ask that you respect our beliefs and follow the guidelines of the book club. We hope to receive your valuable input, opinions, and reviews that build up, rather than tear down our authors.

WHAT WE BELIEVE:

—We believe that Jesus is the Christ, Son of the Living God.

—We believe the Bible is the true, living Word of God.

—We believe all Urban Christian authors should use their God-given writing abilities to honor God and share the message of the written word God has given to each of them uniquely.

—We believe in supporting Urban Christian authors in their literary endeavors by reading, purchasing and sharing their titles with our online community.

—We believe that in everything we do in our literary arena should be done in a manner that will lead to God being glorified and honored.

—We look forward to the online fellowship with you. Please visit us often at *www.uchisglorybookclub.net*.

Many Blessing to You!
Shelia E. Lipsey,
President, UC His Glory Book Club

Notes

Notes

Notes

Notes